MIRA

MIRA

by Daoma Winston

ARBOR HOUSE New York

For Murray

CHAPTER 1.

MIRA PRIEST turned thirty-five on the fourth of May in 1979, only two weeks before she got to know Shelley Davis.

When she awakened that Friday morning, she told herself it was a day like any other, and sighed, and knew it wasn't true. Thirty-five was the pits. The end. People said it was prime time. The best for a woman. Finally shed of childhood. Finally into freedom. She knew better. She felt displaced. Out of touch with herself. The last one left in a rapidly fading world. There seemed to have been no past she wanted to remember. She saw no future ahead. She sensed that everything good that was going to happen to her had already happened.

On that bleak thought she opened her eyes. Sunlight glowed pink through the lace curtains at the windows and rose in the carpet's deep pile. It gleamed gold in the trim of the white furniture, and brought alive the burgundy carnations in the skirt of the dressing table.

The room was large, prettily decorated with prints of flowers, and wrought iron shelves of African violets, and stuffed velvet cushions. Mira had spent six months of the year before wandering through the big carpet warehouses on Rockville Pike, and picking over the prints in Georgetown art stores, and ambling through the florists' shops on Wisconsin Avenue. Somehow the place ended up looking as if a man had never lived there.

Her husband John had said that when he first saw what Mira had done with it. And she had answered, "I'm sorry it worked out that way. I guess it's because you're just not here that much."

It was a small dig, and she smiled when she said it. Maybe that was why he hadn't bothered to take the bait and pick up the old argument. He was away from home most of the time. He returned approximately once a month for three or four days. It had been like that for twelve years. She didn't like it, and never had, and never would. But they quarreled about it rarely now. Once they used to fight in hot whispers. She'd say, "It's a crazy way to live. I'm lonesome for you, John." And he'd say, "But you like living in Bethesda, don't you? And eating in the best restaurants in Washington? And going to the Kennedy Center?" Balancing the books. The C.P.A. in him taking over. And she'd say, "I'll move back to Silver Spring, if you stay home." But those long whispered arguments were long finished. When she wanted to, he didn't. When they both wanted to, her mother was around. It was hard to have a knock-down dragout husband and wife fight with a nervous elderly audience within hearing distance. It was even harder when the husband and wife didn't see each other very often.

Mira sighed again. Ignoring the leaden weight in her stomach, she flung back the pink sheet. She stretched and yawned. Flat belly and long slim legs flexed under the whipped cream froth of her gown. Her breasts rose up, small, sharply defined, the nipples hard and cherry red.

It was a good body still; firm, smooth, well-muscled. Nothing to show that she'd had two sons. Year-round tennis and swimming at the club had paid off. But it wasn't the fun it used to be when she had friends to go with, and steady partners.

Somehow they'd all gradually dropped away. Dora Weidemayer had gone back to school, passed the bar, and was now practicing law. Helene Hartley took some night courses to finish up for her A.B. and got so interested that she was doing her thesis for her Ph.D. now. It was the same with all the others. Mira hardly saw them, except when John was home, and they got together as foursomes. And that was always uncomfortable. She didn't have anything to talk about. No judge called her "dear," in court. No professor of literature pinched her behind. The other women had so much to say. And they were always at her to do something. As if what she did do, Donnie, and Seth, and her mother, and the house, wasn't anything. She had to admit it wasn't much. Her mother did the cooking mostly. The house was easy. Donnie and Seth were very nearly on their own. She had plenty of time to do something in. But she was scared, and didn't even know how to try.

So now, when she swam, it was among strangers. She played tennis with the club pro, a college senior, who yelled, "Great shot, Mrs. Priest," no matter what she did, and grinned, "I thank you, ma'am," when she gave him his tip.

As she got out of bed, there was a clang in the hall. It meant that Donnie had slapped the iron bannister on the way down. His shrill, "Bye, mom. Going," confirmed it. He'd have the railing off before he turned thirteen in October.

"Bye," she yelled. She didn't mention the bannister. They would discuss it later. Again.

She waited, knowing that Seth should be next. He was behind schedule. As usual. When he passed the door, it was on the run. "See you," he called, and slammed down the steps. In that one way unlike John, who always moved quietly. But already, at seventeen, too like him in most other ways. Turned in. Silent. Expressionless. Careful with his words. A hoarder of his feelings. Except on those rare occasions when, for an instant, a strange dark glint would shine from his eyes, and he would be a stranger.

Both boys had forgotten it was her birthday. She didn't care. She was willing to forget it, too.

She soaked for an hour in a scented bubble bath. She didn't let herself think of how old she was, or how she felt.

But as she dried with a thick towel, she decided she wouldn't go to the club that morning.

The kitchen was painted white, with maple furniture and cabinets, and avocado tile and appliances.

Ruth Baker smiled to herself as she loaded the dishwasher. She had warned Donnie and Seth to say absolutely nothing. They would all pretend to have forgotten. That way Mira would really be surprised.

But when Mira came into the kitchen, Ruth was startled to hear herself cry, "Happy birthday, darling!"

"Oh, mother." It was a groan, a plea.

"You're still my little girl," Ruth answered. "And always will be." Though sixty-eight, she was a pretty woman, with regular features, bright blue eyes and fair skin. She was small, very slender, and wore her white hair in an old-fashioned bob.

"Little girl," Mira repeated. She sank into a chair, tapped her pink fingernails on the polished wood.

"And what are you going to do today?"

The same question asked a hundred times before, a thousand times before. Mira answered, "I don't know yet. Haven't thought about it."

To Ruth, Mira remained a child, The small dependent being who was part of her flesh. It didn't matter that Mira was grown. She must be looked after, worried over. Until Ruth lay in her grave, she knew, she would always have Mira as child. She didn't want it different.

And to Mira, Ruth was always her mother, and she the daughter. Nothing could change that. Even her voice altered when she spoke to Ruth. Outwardly at least, the two women lived up to their shared vision of themselves and each other.

"It's a special day," Ruth said, serving both of them black coffee. "So you should do something special." Perching on the edge of the padded chair, she went on eagerly, "What if we have lunch together at the Magic Pan?"

"Next week maybe." Mira reached for the Washington *Post*, ignoring her mother's disappointed silence until the weight of it oppressed her beyond bearing. Then she raised her hazel eyes, smiled faintly. "I guess I'm in a mood. I'd better work it out myself."

Ruth hitched her chair closer. She enjoyed these early morning conversations with Mira. Woman to woman talk. It was good to have a daughter as well as a son. She said, "But you look so young. You haven't changed a bit, except for the better, since you were eighteen."

"And that was when I had a belly out to here with

Seth," Mira answered. She went on quickly, "Did you see in the paper? They're going to have a woman prime minister in Great Britain. Margaret Thatcher."

"That so?" Ruth murmured, knowing the woman talk was over, but still gazing hopefully at Mira's bent head.

Mira knew, but continued to read. The Department of Energy was being criticized for allowing massive fraud by oil resellers. There was trouble in Nicaragua. The Sandinistas were attacking. May 4th. She found herself wondering what had happened on the day she was born. 1944. She put the paper aside.

"What was it like, mother? The day I was born?"

"Beautiful. Like today. Sunny and warm and everything in bloom. And we were so excited. I'd been packed and ready to go for weeks. But the hospital was crowded. Garfield, you know. Closed down now . . . " Ruth's voice trailed off. It seemed as if it had just happened. The nervous twenty minute ride. The ten hour labor. And then tiny perfect Mira, with a head of black curly hair as shiny and dark as it was right now. Where had the time gone? She said, "And Washington's so changed, too."

But Mira got to her feet. "I'm going out for a while."

Ruth nodded. She had counted on that. It would make the surprise possible. She asked, "When will you be back?"

"I don't know. In the afternoon some time."

"Pot roast for dinner?"

"Whatever you feel like doing, Mother."

"Pot roast then," Ruth said, knowing that it wouldn't be. She had already made her plans. She listened to Mira's light footsteps on the stairs, and considered them. Steak. Spinach salad with bacon bits. Baked stuffed potatoes. A chocolate cake with a single white candle. It was a shame John couldn't be here. But the rest of the family would be. Donnie and Seth. Ruth's son, Alan, and his wife, Kit, would come, Kit bringing the gift she had picked up for Ruth. Ruth was lucky that she had a daughter-in-law like Kit, a son-in-law like John. She was lucky in her family, its closeness and love, and knew that.

When she heard Mira at the front door, she hurried out, smiling, "Have fun. And remember, you don't look a day over twenty-five, darling."

Mira got into her maroon Impala. It was dusty, needed a wash. That was what she would do, she decided, as she drove away from the house. It was the last of the convertibles made. She had been nursing it along for years, knowing she wouldn't be able to get another.

Waiting for the car to come through, she remembered her mother's words. Not a day over twenty-five. Mira was sure she had still had dreams then. But she couldn't remember what they were.

Soon the car was ready. She got in, put down the top, and pulled out, not knowing where she was going. But when she saw the Bethesda library on Arlington Road, she cut into its parking lot.

May 4th, 1944. The day she was born. She'd find out what had happened then.

The building was fieldstone and glass, carpeted and quiet. She asked a librarian for help, and soon had four thick books to go through. The U.S. 5th Army was fighting its way to Rome. World War II. And what about other years. She flipped pages. Audrey Hepburn and Roberta Peters had both been born on May 4th. No year mentioned. Mira grinned at that. She wasn't the only woman in the world who was sensitive to her age. Horace Mann was born on May 4, 1796, Thomas Huxley in 1825. In 1776 Rhode Island made its declaration of independence from Great Britain. In 1886 there was the Haymarket riot. In 1932 Al Capone entered the Atlanta, Georgia, federal penitentiary. None of which told Mira much of anything. She closed the books, and left them.

White Flint Mall. The newest shopping complex in the Washington suburbs. Bloomingdale's three floors. The House of Fabrics. Ann Taylor's. Idling from store to store.

She bought a shirt for Donnie. A yellow vest for Seth. She bought her mother a box of Elizabeth Arden bath powder. It was nearly time to stop for lunch, but none of the many places there appealed to Mira. The clustered women leaning close to murmur to each other looked like stuffed pigeons . . . the dim light made the checked table cloths seem gray . . .

She decided to go to the Red Fox Inn. A drink. Something to eat. In the past few months she'd gone there often, or to the Capricorn, or Whaley's. A way of getting out. Killing time. Hearing new voices. New words. Searching for a world in which she wouldn't be the last one left.

The Wisconsin Avenue traffic was heavy, funneled into narrow bumper to bumper lanes by miles of subway construction and compressed by high green barriers decorated with mild graffiti and the subway symbol, Metro, or simply a big white "M."

Impatient, tapping the steering wheel, she managed to jockey to the right. The car ahead blinked for a turn. She followed it onto a narrow paved road that swung west.

A few miles on she was surrounded by trees and fields. She didn't know where she was. As she slowed, looking ahead for an intersection, a road sign, the awful chill of a migraine headache crept up the back of her neck. It was a curse handed down by her mother, who had long since shaken it off, and forgotten the odor of alcohol and Ben-Gay in a darkened room. Forgotten the anxious silence that descended on the apartment. The unspoken guilt shared by Alan and Mira and their father. What had they done? What was the lack in them?

Mira told herself it wasn't fair. Not on her birthday. She shouldn't have to put up with it then. But now an iron band formed at her temples and began to squeeze. The onslaught of pain was sudden, intense. Her vision blurred with it. Through the veiling fog there were glimmers of pale lightning. She was familiar with the symptoms. Twice a month, some times more frequently, they were visited on her. She considered the migraine a disease, like measles. Contagious. Her mother's particular legacy to her. But Mira used neither alcohol nor Ben Gay for relief. There were new drugs. She had to stop, to find water so she could get the pills down.

But there was nowhere. Nothing. Broad empty fields and shaded groves. Then, just beyond, and on the right, she saw the Amoco station, the four one-storey shops huddled in a curve around a weed-filled parking lot. She saw the neon sign. Joe's Cafe.

She pulled in, parked. She tripped on the threshold of the place, hesitated. It was dark. Empty except for a few men. Pain-driven, she went to the bar, asked for water, gulped her pills, and rested. Embarrassed to stay without spending something, she ordered a drink and a sandwich.

For a little while she concentrated on fighting the pain. They were enemies. She and the amorphous tide that enwrapped her. If she were strong enough, she would survive. If she gave way, she would be drowned by it forever.

15

But in a little while she became faintly aware of the conversation around her, the deep relaxed voices crossing in easy banter, the chuckles and pauses and muted laughter. The pills, dissolving, wrapped her in a cocoon of unreality. Red-shaded lamps glowed dimly in the long dark room. The mirror behind the bar reflected only shadows. There was more talk. A few words came from someone five seats away.

The bartender said, "Hey, Shelley, I never knew you'd been in San Diego. I was there in the war. World War II, I mean."

Shelley.

Mira turned a carefully circumspect look at him, then couldn't turn away.

He was tall, judging by the length of his back, and the width of his shoulders. His hair was as dark as hers. When he swung his head sideways, she saw the flash of his eyes. They were a pale gray, almost silver, under thick dark lashes and brows. His face was square, big-jawed, but the hair brushed across his forehead gave him an artless look. His mouth was long and narrow, and fell naturally into a don't-give-a-damn smile.

He was saying, "I was only there a few months. Then I moved on."

"Anybody ever tell you a rolling stone don't gather no moss?" the bartender asked.

"I've heard it, I guess," Shelley answered. His don't-give-a-damn smile suddenly became sweet. A dimple appeared in his chin. For a moment he had the look of a lost child. He went on, "But I've still got a long way to go."

His voice was deep, soft. The words came slowly. And with pauses between. As if it were hard for him to talk, or he was holding something back.

He raised a glass of beer to his mouth, and Mira saw a

16

tattoo on his left forearm. A single word. She couldn't read it from that distance.

The bartender went to serve a man at the end of the counter.

Mira finished her drink, nibbled at the sandwich. Her headache was suddenly gone. She savored the relief, aware of the young man who sat five seats away. In a little while, she paid her bill and left, already knowing that she'd return soon in hopes of seeing him again.

"And it was a surprise, wasn't it?" Ruth asked, beaming.

"It was," Mira agreed, and smiled at her brother Alan, knowing he shared her amusement. How could the birthday gathering be a surprise when Ruth had done the same thing for years? It was becoming a ritual, like the two dozen American Beauty roses that John always sent her.

Alan smiled back at her. They were both old enough to be indulgent about their mother's foibles. He was six years younger than Mira, but now he was caught up. Once they had seemed of different generations. He had looked up to her. Everybody, including their parents had, too. She had been as pretty a girl as she was now a pretty woman. She had been bright, inquisitive, and expectant. Then she had fallen in love, married John.

She sat in a green high-backed chair, surrounded by colored tissue and ribbons and wrappings. Seth and Donnie had gone in together to buy her a Schiaparelli scarf, a shade of kelly green that she would never wear. Smiling, she had tied it around the neck of her black dress. Alan and Kit had given her a biography of Jenny Churchill by Ralph Martin. And Kit, for Ruth, had picked out a light blue shirt with a tucked yolk and tight-cuffed sleeves.

She said now, "I hope the shirt fits. You can return it if it doesn't."

"I'm sure it will," Mira told her.

"Lord and Taylor's," Kit said, crossing the room to pick up an ash tray. "Just in case."

Kit was twenty-three, but she moved with the grace of confidence and maturity. She knew who she was, what she wanted, and what she could do. Her face was heart-shaped, her blonde hair sleeked back to hang loosely on her shoulders. Her eyes were a clear cold green. She wore a sleeveless white shirt, a full white skirt, and no jewelry.

Mira never felt quite comfortable with Kit. Not that she had anything against her young sister-in-law. It was just that Mira was sure Alan could have done better. And should have done better, too. There had been a long ago time when he had said the same thing of Mira. He didn't say it any more.

The small silence seemed to go on for a beat too long. Mira and Alan started to speak at the same time. They stopped together, and laughed, and began again, once more together.

Seth broke the impasse. He was fed up. He'd had enough of the mother's birthday bit. Too much of the phony smiles on phony faces. He wished he were with his father. The two of them, shoulder to shoulder. Waiting in some quiet place. He saw it, the night, the shadows, as he got to his feet, yawned. "Party's over, I guess." Ignoring the silent plea in his grandmother's gaze he ambled out.

He was tall, with straight sandy hair and very dark brown eyes that seemed to look just past, rather than directly at, whatever they saw. Within moments he turned his stereo on full blast.

"Donnie," Mira said to her younger son. "Go tell Seth

we want that turned down. I can't hear myself think."
But she *was* thinking. Of a don't-give-a-damn grin that
became a sweet smile. Of a sudden dimple, and a tattoo
she couldn't read. A boy named Shelley. She wondered
how old he was, and what he'd been doing at Joe's Cafe,
and if he went there often.

Donnie pulled a sour face, rose from the floor. He
was slight. His hair was curly, a light brown shot
through with gold threads. His eyes were dark, nearly
black, wide open and deep-set and twinkling. He had a
broad grin. A charmer by anybody's standards. That
was the trouble. Or part of it. The rest was that he was
twelve years old. Growing time. Experiment time.
Boundary stretching time. He said, laughing, "Just wait
until I get my own stereo. Then there'll be two."

"And that'll be the day," Mira told him.

He bounded up the steps. The noise abated, but only
slightly.

"What did you do today?" Ruth asked.

Mira thought again of Joe's Cafe, of Shelley. There
was nothing left of the migraine now but a tenderness
at the back of her neck. It had gone as mysteriously as it
had come. She'd escaped one more time. And as always,
she was a little surprised that she had. She shrugged in
answer to her mother's question. "Nothing much." And
with a grin at Alan: "But I'll bet you don't know who,
aside from me, was born on May 4th."

"I give up."

"Roberta Peters. And Audrey Hepburn. For start-
ers."

"You're in good company then," Kit said, smiling.

"And did you know, Alan, that on that day the 5th
Army was fighting its way to Rome?"

He cut in, grinning, "Don't I get enough of that at
school?"

He taught American history in a Silver Spring junior high. The pay wasn't all that good, but he enjoyed his work. Most of the time. But there were moments, when he was visiting the family, when he felt uncomfortable. The house here was so big, so elegantly furnished. Close-in Bethesda. Trees where mockingbirds sang. More lawyers, doctors, Ph.D.s to the inch than anywhere else in the country. He ought to be able to give Kit what John gave Mira. It didn't seem to bother Kit that he didn't. But it did bother Alan. To go from here to their third floor walk-up . . .

He was getting to his feet when something fuzzy and gray shot through the air and fell to Mira's lap.

She jumped up, screaming. "My God! A mouse!"

Donnie gave a yelp of laughter. "You thought it was real."

Mira scooped up the rubber mouse, flung it at him. He ducked it, then slid down the door frame to collapse on the floor.

Alan said it was time for Kit and him to go.

"I thought I'd whip you at checkers," Donnie protested.

"Some other night," Alan told him. "Only I'm going to whip you."

Kit and Alan kissed Ruth good night, kissed Mira, and wished her 'happy birthday' once more, and went out.

As they got into the old green station wagon that Kit usually drove, she said, "You see? That wasn't so bad, was it?"

"No. It was okay. Only I wanted to go out to Annapolis to the Maryland Inn to hear Charlie Byrd."

"We can do it tomorrow night."

"I guess."

She snuggled against Alan. "And your mother was so pleased."

"Yes. She was."

"Your enthusiasm is overwhelming."

"Sorry, Kit."

"I feel as if it's my fault that you didn't have a good Friday night."

"Don't worry about it."

"I don't understand you," she said slowly. "You've always been such a close family. I can tell from how your mother talks. So how come you didn't want to go there tonight? And how come every time I suggest it, you come up with some kind of excuse or argument?"

"Charlie Byrd, Kit."

"Stop evading the issue. I want to talk about it."

"Okay," he sighed. "Maybe we've been too close. Maybe it's time to grow up. Be more separate."

"Oh, Alan."

He didn't answer her. He knew it was peculiar, the wrong way around entirely. He was the one who should be anxious to visit his mother, see Mira, his nephews. Kit should be the one who was trying to pull him away. But they had it in reverse. Kit liked his mother, sister, nephews. More than liked them even. He supposed it was because she had no family of her own.

"Well, *I'm* glad we went," she said tartly. "Especially since John didn't come home. And didn't even call."

"Maybe he couldn't."

"But it was important to Mira. A thirty-fifth birthday . . . that's something."

"In my family all birthdays are important."

"Then you should understand how Mira feels. Didn't you notice?"

"Notice what?"

Alan sped up to go through an amber light. Kit bit

her lip but said nothing. She was on the verge of losing her temper, and knew it. Alan was being obtuse. He rarely was. When he became that way it was deliberate. He didn't want to understand what she was talking about.

"Notice what?" he repeated.

"That Mira was different tonight."

"Different how?"

Kit wanted to let it go. She was tired of him passing questions back to her. But it was important. She said, "I don't know how to explain it. And maybe I'm wrong. But I think Mira's not happy. She's restless. She needs something."

"Why do you think so?"

"I told you. I don't know why. But I think she ought to have more interests. Hobbies. Something to occupy her. John's away such a lot. The boys are nearly grown up. Your mother's a sweetie, but she can't be full-time company for Mira."

Alan's voice was cool, but his mouth was tight around his words as he said, "You think every woman has to have outside interests. That's the trouble. You're stuck in the rut of believing that a housewife, and a mother, just isn't enough. Because that's how you feel."

"We're talking about Mira," Kit said quietly.

"No. We're not. We're talking about what you think Mira ought to feel."

"Okay," Kit said. "Okay. If that's what you want to think . . . "

"Mira's a very happy woman. She's got everything she wants. A home, a family . . . It's just your imagining."

Kit didn't answer. But she didn't think she'd been imagining. She thought it possible that she might have misunderstood. There was always this little something between Mira and her. Maybe that . . . that coolness, that sense that Mira wasn't quite there, was what Kit had felt. It could have been that Mira always remembered the six months that Kit and Alan had lived together before they were married two years ago. She hadn't wanted to get married right away, but Alan had. So, at his insistence, they'd lived together until she got her real estate broker's license.

It was different being married from just living together. Alan was different, and so was she. She couldn't quite put her finger on it, but she knew it was true. Everybody had known when she moved into Alan's apartment. It had never been a secret. But Alan's mother had acted the same as if they were married. And so had Mira. And when she and Alan did get married, finally, it was just the same. Except maybe that Mira remembered, and hadn't approved before and continued to disapprove.

"Don't fall asleep," Alan said. "We're almost home."

There was a faint question in his voice. He was asking if she were angry at him, if she was going to stay that way. She answered it by saying warmly, "I'm just thinking."

She oughtn't to have criticized Mira, Kit thought. People were what they were. It wasn't right to judge them.

"What are you thinking about?" Alan asked.

"Being thirty-five," Kit told him, snuggling close again.

CHAPTER 2.

ON A Saturday afternoon, when the sun was high and hot and black storm clouds hung over the willows in the north, Mira went into Joe's Cafe.

She didn't know it then, but she was ready for something to happen to her. She had been ready, waiting, since she first stumbled into the place two weeks before, and through all her visits since.

She swept the long bar with a glance as she took her usual stool. It was strategically centered, so that if there were conversation, it would cross and include her. At the same time the empty seats on each side of her suggested a certain remoteness that she felt necessary. They were barriers against intrusion. She wasn't interested in pickups. She didn't want anybody to offer to buy her a drink.

By this time the regulars in Joe's knew that. Richard . . . who owned the Amoco station and came in every day for a two hour lunch. Gus . . . the retired Navy man, a reed-thin alcoholic at forty, who stared glumly into his glass and spoke only to ask for a refill. Cable . . . the manager of the general store that was slowly going broke. They understood. But there were the occasional salesmen, truck drivers. Sometimes they would look at her assessingly. The empty seats set her apart, discouraged them before they got ideas. Which left available a place for Shelley.

He wasn't there yet, but he might still come. She had learned over the weeks that he had no fixed pattern. She hoped he would turn up. Only hope didn't express what she felt. It was a feverish hunger. A deep gnawing ache that hovered on the brink of pain.

She was faintly embarrassed by this. She could barely remember when she had last felt that way. Or didn't want to remember how long ago it had been. Shelley Davis was twenty-one. She knew that because she had heard him say so.

She pulled cigarettes from her purse, a lighter. She settled her slender hips to the curve of the stool, crossed her legs, and raised her eyes.

Jimmy, the bar's owner, was waiting, ham-like hands floating over rows of glasses. He was big, his weight collected in a full hump that rose just below his breastbone and sank into his groin. His face was round, dimpled. He was sixty-three and had a wife and one daughter. She was married, lived in New Mexico. Some crazy town he couldn't even pronounce. He had twin grandsons he didn't see often enough.

There was no Joe. He'd sold the place to Jimmy. Good terms, too. But the old name remained. And the old menu. Beer on tap. Wine by the bottle or glass. The usual hard liquors. Also Greek salad. Sandwiches. Spaghetti and meat balls. Plus the best goddamn pizza in Washington, D.C., and suburbs. Which is where Joe's

Cafe was. Bethesda. In Montgomery County, one of the richest in the nation.

Joe's had been a moneymaker once, but there were too many places now. And the so-called shopping center, its four shops and crumbling parking lot, was dead and close to being buried. Jimmy was filling in for a few years. Give him two maybe. And he'd be gone, too. A place in Florida. Fishing and family.

Mira had learned it all by asking discreet questions, and her interest had made the two of them something like friends. Along the way she had learned that Shelley's last name was Davis, that he'd been coming in regularly for the past couple of months, that he did odd jobs for a living, and that that was about what Jimmy knew about him.

Now Jimmy said, "Hey, there, honey. How are you?" It sounded as if he hadn't seen her for weeks. She'd been there two days before. Drawn there, instead of to the Red Fox Inn, or elsewhere, in hopes of seeing Shelley.

She shrugged. How was she? She didn't know. She felt as if she were teetering on the brink, but of what she wasn't sure. She smiled at Jimmy.

He knew what she wanted. The martini, dry, on the rocks, with a lemon twist. But double. And the tuna fish salad sandwich. One slice of bread only. No chips.

"Doing yourself any good lately?" he asked, putting the drink before her.

It was a line he always used. He had a few of them, went through each one, only slightly adjusted, for all the regulars.

"Not so much," she answered. "I guess I'm not trying."

"Hey, honey, come on. You've got to keep at it. Else you'll go stale. And life is short."

She didn't have to reply. He didn't expect it. Their conversations were predictable, undemanding, and meaningless, in spite of occasional innuendo. There was no need to pretend for him to be what she wasn't. He didn't care. So she was free to wonder about Shelley. Feeling his closeness, she supposed that it was hope that made her imagine he was somewhere near.

But her sense of him was true. He could see her as he walked down the shadowy corridor that angled to the restrooms off the end of the bar.

His step quickened. Mira. That was her name. In Spanish it meant "Look!" He wondered if she knew that. He moved toward her even faster. He'd already waited too long, had too many beers. He could hear faint echoes in his head. The murmur of faraway voices. He tried to ignore them, and concentrated on the woman at the bar.

She was small, narrow-waisted, with fragile wrists and slender ankles. Her body was smooth where it should be, with curves where curves belonged. It had a disciplined, well-honed look. He bet he could pick her up, carry her around as if she was a child. Her skin was tanned and cared for. Her hair was dark, curly, cut short to frame her face. She was older than he was. He knew that. But it didn't matter. Or maybe it did. Maybe that was it. Just that she was older. He didn't know what it was, nor care. But something about her, something he couldn't put a name to, drew him to her. It had been that way since he first saw her. Something drew him. Then the faraway voices in his head were suddenly louder, close.

He stopped. He rocked back as if he'd stumbled off balance into a stone barrier. His tall slim body sagged against the wall. Sweat broke out on his forehead, matted the black hair at the back of his neck.

"Goddamn you! Leave him alone . . . " The words, the shrill whisper. Familiar.

"Damn brat! I'll kill him. If you'd listened to me when I told you . . . " A deep bellow of hate. Familiar, too.

And sudden awful pain. Shoulder. Elbow. Fire. Singed flesh. Screams.

"No, no, no . . . "

Shelley took a deep shuddering breath, and broke through the dream that wasn't a dream. He turned, plunged away from the voices. The sweat dried. The fast pulses slowed. He washed his face, re-combed his hair, and returned to the bar, whispering silently, Mira.

She took a careful sip of her drink, and swallowing, she realized suddenly that he was sitting two stools away. Her heart gave a quick jump. She nodded at him.

Richard called, "Jimmy, I can have another, can't I?"

"Long as you can pay," Jimmy answered, and went to serve him.

Mira leaned toward Shelley, looked at the tattoo on his forearm. Mother. The letters blue. "I always wondered . . . does it hurt to get a tattoo?"

"Not enough to remember."

"I thought it would."

Jimmy came back to ask if everything was okay. They said it was and he went to stand in front of Cable, trading complaints about business.

Shelley said softly, "The trouble is that it's always the same old thing. Listen to them."

"It's what's on their minds."

"And what about you? Why don't you try something different for a change?"

"I like martinis. I like tuna salad sandwiches."

"I don't mean food."

"Like what then?"

"It's a free country. That would be up to you."

She laughed, didn't answer. Something different was already what she was doing. If he only knew.

But he did know. Or guessed. He said, "And I don't mean just sneaking away for a drink either."

"But I'm not!"

"That's not a drink I see in front of you?"

"Not sneaking away." And: "I don't have to."

He called for Jimmy, who came, bringing him a glass of beer.

"You just drinking? Or eating today, too?"

"Later I might want something to eat."

"I'll have another," Mira said. "And the sandwich."

"The sandwich!" Jimmy clunked his brow with thick knuckles. "Forgot it, for crying out loud!"

"No hurry." She smiled at Shelley, but he was watching Jimmy fold clumsily to duck out from behind the bar, then amble down the long narrow room toward the kitchen.

As he disappeared into the shadowed corridor, the front door opened.

The sun made a brief beam in the gloom, setting dust motes alight. Thunder growled faintly in the distance. When the door closed, dark and silence descended again.

Two men stood just inside. Both wore blue baseball caps pulled low over their faces, and faded jeans, and long-sleeved shirts under loose windbreakers.

They were motionless on the threshold, peering into the room, bony faces without expression.

It was their stillness that caught Mira's attention. She stared at their faint reflections in the mirror behind the bar, wondering if they were waiting for vision to clear after the brightness of out of doors.

"Be right there," Jimmy called. "Just have a seat."

They didn't answer, didn't move.

Within moments, Jimmy returned, ducked down behind the bar. "Sorry to keep you fellows waiting. And what'll you have?"

One of the men remained near the door. The other moved to the counter.

Mira was aware of Shelley's sudden small movement, but he didn't speak.

"The money." Quick quiet words. And: "You folks, you get your hands up on the bar and keep them there, and hold your mouths shut." A dull glint of gunmetal. A sigh that was a chill wind. "Quiet," the man at the bar ordered.

It wasn't real. It was like a dream. Maybe a scene from television. In a minute everybody would burst out laughing.

But Jimmy worked his lips and made no sound.

"Move, fat man."

"Yeah. Yeah, sure."

Richard, from the Amoco station, was frozen.

Gus, the ex-Navy man, mumbled into his drink.

"You shut up!"

"Drunk," Jimmy choked out. "He don't know what's going on."

"Get it!"

"Yeah. Yeah, sure."

All slow motion, muted. Like men moving under water, whispering under water.

Mira drew in a deep breath. It locked in her throat, building a scream. She'd never known such fear. She'd never thought to feel it. It came crowding up to explode out of her.

But in the same instant, she felt Shelley's touch. His long leg was stretching toward her. His ankle pressed firmly, warningly, against her calf. It was good. Good enough so she heeded the warning without thinking of it. His touch was what she needed. She felt the near-explosion subside. She let her breath out slowly.

Jimmy punched 'no sale' on the cash register, dug into the opened drawer with trembling fingers. He stretched his arm to full length, set the wad of bills out as far from himself as he could.

The man at the bar scooped it up with one hand. With the other he caught up a beer bottle. In a single smooth motion he pitched it hard and fast and straight into the mirror behind the bar.

It blew up in hundreds of flying pieces.

Light flashed as the door opened. Thunder drummed across the sky. The spray of glass subsided as the door closed.

The two men were gone.

It had taken only moments, had seemed to last for hours. Now it was over.

"Jesus," Jimmy said, shaking small glittery splinters out of the fringe of his hair. "Jesus! Everybody all right?"

The ex-Navy man thoughtfully smeared a trickle of blood from his wrist.

Cable coughed loudly.

Richard slid from the stool, reaching to open the door. "License number maybe."

"No," Shelley called. "Let it go, man."

"Get the cops," Richard said.

"Jesus," Jimmy muttered, his face shiny with sweat. Glass crunched underfoot as he went to the phone. He seized it, dialed, croaked out his address, the problem, then sagged against the counter. "They're coming."

Richard peered out, returned. He shook his head. "Nothing's moving out there." And: "I hope you didn't lose too much, Jimmy."

Mira heard, but it was all removed from her. The

words seemed to have no meaning. She couldn't move, speak. Shivers rode her from head to toe. She couldn't believe it had happened. But it had. She couldn't believe what she had just seen. The two men. The gun. The shattering mirror.

One minute they were just talking. She, Shelley. And the next . . .

"You okay?" Shelley asked.

Okay? She guessed she was. Nothing had happened to her. Except that she felt the world must be upside down.

When she didn't answer, he rose. He put a hand on her shoulder. "Come on. You need to get out into the air."

Jimmy said, "On the house, folks. I think we all deserve it," and got busy at setting up with a clinking of glasses, and gushes over their rims.

Richard accepted his drink, grinned. "Don't you have something useful back there, Jimmy?"

"Who, me? You think I'm crazy? Take it! Help yourself! Just leave me alone! Two more years, maybe . . . Just time to recoup what I put into this hole. Then I'm gone. So why would I try to get myself killed?"

"Let's go," Shelley said.

Mira put bills on the counter. "Skip the sandwich, Jimmy. I'll see you again soon."

"Sandwich?" Jimmy's brows drew down. "Yeah. I forgot again. Okay. I can see you lost your appetite. Only maybe you'd better wait. The cops . . . "

She fluttered her fingers at him, stepped outside.

The sun was gone now. The sky was black with clouds. The air was hot, heavy with the threat of rain.

"His place, his money. Let him answer the questions," Shelley was saying. He looked down at her. "And now?"

"Home, I guess." But that wasn't what she wanted.

She was excited still. The aftermath of fright left chill prickles in her flesh. It had been too fast. She wanted time to look back.

"Not home," he said. "What for?"

It was the same for him. She smiled. "Where else then?"

He didn't answer. He took her hand, and that was good, too. He led her to a battered tan VW.

She heard sirens rising in the distance as they drove away.

Down Wisconsin Avenue through the heavy afternoon traffic. Past the motel, the pancake shop. A right turn into Bradley Boulevard. Familiar territory. She often shopped on nearby Arlington Road. The Bethesda library was a few blocks on. Another right turn.

Excitement ripened in her. Her body became hot, suddenly afire. The drinks sang through her again. She said, laughing, "Who'd have thought . . . in that place . . . that neighborhood . . . "

"Neighborhoods are all the same these days. You never know."

"But they seemed so young, didn't they? And so . . . so . . . "

"So respectable-looking?"

"Yes. That's what I mean. I'd never have guessed, from looking at them . . . "

"You think they'd be wearing horns?"

But she said, "I was scared. I don't think I've ever been so scared in my life. And I couldn't believe it at the same time. For a minute I thought I'd pass out and fall off the bar stool. Or else that I'd start screaming."

"I thought you might. And it could have been a good way to get yourself hurt."

"And then you touched me."

"That was why."

"I knew that," she said. "And it worked. "But poor old Jimmy . . ."

"He can take care of himself."

She stiffened suddenly. "Shelley! I'm just not thinking. What about my car?"

"I'll drive you back later."

"But where are we going?"

"You'll see."

"I don't think we'd better." It was only because some small unwilling part of her demanded the protest. She didn't mean it.

"Please," he said. "I've been waiting a long time. You have, too."

"What are you talking about?" Again it was the small unwilling part of her who made the words.

"You know," he said.

She gave in then, nodding agreement. She couldn't do anything else. He was right. She'd been waiting since she'd first seen him in Joe's. On her birthday. Two long weeks ago. And what about all the time before?

She was glad when he parked before a big house. The yard was large well-tended. But the windows were dusty looking. The front porch had needed fresh paint for years. The roadway was empty and still.

"You live here, Shelley?"

He nodded.

"With your folks?"

A beat of silence. Then: "You must know I don't have folks. I was talking about it to Jimmy one day. You were there. You were listening." And with his don't-give-a-damn grin, "Or are you trying to catch me out?" For an instant he heard faraway voices, shouting. Then they were gone. It didn't mean anything, he thought. Everybody had memories. And they weren't real memories anyway.

"Sorry," Mira was saying. "I forgot what you told Jimmy."

"It doesn't matter. But actually I was telling you."

"I know."

His smile became sweet. A dimple appeared in his chin. He drew her with him to a side door. "Don't worry. There's nobody here but my landlady. She's an old woman, and won't bother us."

Mira winced inwardly. 'Old woman.' Was the landlady thirty-five, forty? To him, as to Seth and Donnie, anything over twenty-five would be old.

"Have you lived here long?"

"A while."

She knew better than to press him. He didn't like questions asked directly. When he was ready, he'd tell her how he came to be living in that house.

He was wondering if he'd imagined it, or if he'd really told Jimmy about it, and through Jimmy her. That his parents died, leaving him orphaned, when he was six. He'd survived five foster homes with no good memories. Had gone on his own at fifteen. Had drifted about the country ever since. Had settled in Bethesda by accident. Would stay until his reason for staying was gone. Then he'd move on. It was funny that he wasn't sure he'd said it. But he'd told it so many times, in so many places, he couldn't be sure any more. He told himself not to mind. It didn't matter. One thing he knew he hadn't said, never talked about, were those years before he was alone. The distant voices. Muddied images. He never talked about that because he wasn't sure of it himself. So it didn't matter. He pushed the door open.

It was dim inside. A long narrow room. The walls of

bare cinder block, stained with the leakage of countless rains. A furnace only partly covered by a torn Japanese screen that had once been beautiful. A ragged rug on the concrete floor. A sprung couch piled high with faded red pillows. Dirty windows at the top of the walls kept the room in perpetual twilight.

He stood very still, watching her face. It wasn't the kind of room she'd be used to. He might have made a mistake in bringing her here.

She saw his look and knew that whatever he read of her expression must have satisfied some doubt he'd had because he smiled. A smile so sweet that pain twisted through her.

"Welcome to my parlor," he said. "Even if it isn't much."

"Thanks for bringing me here, Shelley. I always wondered where you lived. How."

"I know. Now you've found out."

"So I've learned a little more about you."

"Not much though."

She agreed. "Places don't make all that much difference, do they?"

"Not to me. Just somewhere to bed down in. One more in a long line of them."

"Yes," she said.

"But not for you, Mira. That's not how it's been."

"You think not? You see me as another suburban woman. The big house, wall to wall with plush carpet. A dishwasher. Garbage disposal, back yard barbecue."

"Isn't that right?"

"Right as far as it goes. Only there's more."

"Maybe."

She heard thunder. The dirty windows were suddenly dark squares. She wondered what she was doing there. She said, "I guess I ought to go."

37

His silver eyes were pleading. When he spoke his voice was soft, pained, hesitant, "You're not going to make us play that hard to get stuff, are you?"

She wanted to say, "No." She wanted to say, "Yes."

But he opened his arms wide. She went into them.

She melted to him. All warm body. Savoring. Good. Good enough to make her want more and more. Her hands moved down his back, feeling ridged muscle under the tight shirt. Her fingertips drifted lightly through the hair at the back of his neck.

His mouth pressed hot and sweet on hers. She knew the fullness of his response, could feel it against her thighs. Big, thrusting. Pressing there, and pulsing. Twenty-one. Twenty-one was like that. Fast. Hungry. No time to waste. And no need to waste time. And she wasn't too old to evoke it, provoke it. She held him more tightly.

But he drew away. He was gone. Moving quietly around the screen and beyond it. A rustle. The rattle of a belt buckle. A rustle. The thud of a shoe.

Then a sudden thin stream of yellow light that bathed her from head to toe, and touched him, when he returned, touched his bare brown flesh with sun.

She was still, unmoving. His hands were deft. Her blue shirt slid off her shoulders, floated to the floor. Her white bra dropped away. Her panties and skirt slithered past the swell of her hips to become a pool at her feet. She kicked them away. Breathless. Waiting.

His eyes touched her. Here. There. Probing and stroking fingers. Even before she felt his hands, her flesh burned.

Her arms went around him again. As she stroked the curve of his back she felt a long ropy diagonal scar. At his shoulder, where her cheek rested, three small purple rings formed a triangle.

She forgot them as she and Shelley crumpled to the floor together, arms and legs entangled. Mouths glued until she broke the kiss to whisper, "Listen, this wasn't what I intended."

"You did. Always. Right from the first time you saw me. And I saw you."

"Two weeks ago. On my birthday. My birthday, Shelley."

"So . . .?"

"Shelley, I could almost be . . . " She had to say it. Punishment for herself. She had to be honest with him. He was so young. His judgment could be skewed. He mightn't know, realize. . . .

He didn't stop her. She stopped it herself. She would tell him later. She couldn't say it now. She didn't want to remember that she was nearly old enough to be his mother. That she *was* old enough, although she'd have to have started a few years earlier than she actually had. Later. Later she would think about that, too. But not now.

He buried his face in her breasts. For a long while she felt his tongue stroking. One nipple. The other. Then his lips, suckling. She felt his heart pounding just above hers. She felt his body tremble with hers. Then he was between her legs, fully on her. She began by acquiescing, letting it happen to her. Letting him touch and lick and give himself to her.

But there was a changing moment. She began to make it happen, too. And there was no stopping. Not until after a long long time. When he was thrusting slowly, slowly. Smiling down at her, the sweetness on his mouth again. The look of a lost child blended with the look of a man.

And thunder rolled across the sky, echoing through the dim basement room.

Some time as they still moved together there was a thump on the ceiling above them, and she moaned, "Oh, no. Not now."

Shelley said, "It's okay. Just the old woman up there."

And Mira giggled. Old woman. She'd think about that later, too.

The long slow excitement finally crested. It was over. She was chilled when he rolled away from her, lay silent beside her.

The floor was icy cold, grainy, hard. She ached in hips and thighs. Her insides were raw and wet and throbbing still. She heard his soft breath, and was suddenly overwhelmed by what had happened. By what she'd made to happen.

Guilt became nausea. Nausea became the anxious need for reassurance.

"My God," she whispered. "Do you think I've lost my mind?" Hot-eyed she stared at the exposed pipes on the ceiling.

He rolled, leaned on an elbow. His face hovered over hers, silver gaze intent. "I don't think so. Do you?"

"But this?"

"Is that what you're talking about?"

"Yes. Shelley . . . I never should . . . "

"Why not?"

"You know."

His eyes narrowed. "What's the matter? Not right for you?"

"Too right," she said unwillingly. "Too goddamn right." She looked past his face, stared blindly at the pipes overhead. "I'm old enough to be your mother."

"Only you're not."

"Just the same."

"And so?"

"It's wrong. I feel so . . . so . . . "

"You ought to feel good. I do. I'm glad we found each other. I'm glad we're here."

"But don't you see?"

"I see you. And that's enough."

"It's wrong, Shelley."

"Who says?"

"Anybody would."

"Fuck anybody. What do I care what anybody says?" He laughed. "Do you?"

"Of course," she said sharply. Her husband John. Seth and Donnie. Her mother. She tried to imagine them, and couldn't. She couldn't remember them. Shelley was right. She didn't care. This belonged to her. To her alone. She admitted it. "No. I guess I don't care either. I'm just used to thinking that I should and do."

"You're getting more smart all the time. More honest, too." He slid an arm under her shoulders, drew her close. "And I like smart honest women."

"Even old ones?"

"Stop it, Mira. It doesn't matter to me."

There was another thump from upstairs. Mira glanced at the ceiling. "What's going on?"

"She drops things. Mrs. Radman. My landlady. She's almost blind. So things fall down."

"We'll have to be careful," Mira said.

"Sure. Only the word's discreet."

She smiled at him. "Okay. Discreet."

"Don't worry. I'm not going to make trouble for you."

She took his face between her hands and kissed him gently. "I hate to do it, but I'm going to have to go."

"Not yet."

"Now," she protested.

But he lifted her easily, drew her over him. He settled her against him. "First this." And his hands on her hips guided her down. His body rose to meet her. Without knowing what to do, she knew. She did.

It was raining when they went outside. Thick hot drops. She turned to look at the house. A curtain moved at a first floor window. She didn't mention it. Mrs. Radman, the old half-blind landlady.

"You'll come again," he told Mira, helping her into the VW. "This is the beginning."

"I don't know." She was a little frightened now.

It had been crazy. She had Donnie and Seth, and John. She had her mother. She belonged to them, and they to her.

What was she doing with a twenty-one-year-old boy she had picked up in a bar? Why had she gone back to Joe's Cafe in the first place? Why had she kept going back?

"You'll come again," Shelley said quietly. "I know."

CHAPTER 3.

THE RAIN stopped before she reached Plumtree Road. It was a two mile long crescent that began and ended at the tree-lined and narrow main thoroughfare called Wilson Lane.

The houses on the crescent were set well above the road on a ridge forested with giant pines. They had been custom built in the mid-sixties, each one different from the others, and all having been designed for maximum privacy. In the more than fifteen years since, they had more than doubled in re-sale value.

As she turned into her steep driveway she saw a familiar green station wagon parked near the side steps.

Frowning, she jerked to a stop next to it.

She was still full of Shelley. His touch. His scent. She wanted to enjoy them. She considered slipping in through the basement entrance. But no. It wouldn't work. They'd hear her. The two of them. Kit. Her mother. They'd hear her, and nod over their coffee cups, and quickly change the subject. The subject being until then, Mira.

Scowling, she took the three boxes from the trunk of her Impala, and went inside.

As she dropped the packages on the green velour sofa, there was a hitch in the conversation. A brief pause. It picked up again . . . "should be cooler to-night." And : "I think so. We're getting too early a start on a real summer."

Mira stood in the kitchen doorway.

Kit smiled at her quickly, brightly. "I'm glad you made it before I had to leave."

"Been here long?" Mira asked.

"Just a little while. I was in the neighborhood, and stopped by to say 'hi.'" Kit didn't mention that she had come because Ruth had telephoned to the office. The older woman had sounded glum.

Now she said, "You missed John, Mira."

"He called so early? Where from?"

"I don't know."

"Oh, mother. Didn't you ask?"

"I didn't get a chance to. He was in a hurry."

"Will he call back?"

"Yes. I think so."

"Did he say when?" Mira asked the question, certain she already knew the answer. It was like John to be inde-finite about that. One of the few exceptions. Generally he was definite. But he would suppose that she'd be at home. Waiting. As she usually was.

Ruth was saying, "He didn't tell me that. He just didn't want to talk to me."

Kit laughed. "That seems natural. He's away so much. It must be hard on him."

"It's hard on me, too," Mira said.

She wished that Kit would go away. Disappear. Van-ish into thin air.

But Kit remained. She smiled sympathetically. "Of

course it's hard on you. We all know that. But at least you've got the kids, and us. And John's always on his own."

"If John doesn't want to work for Bull Baron he doesn't have to." Mira sank into a kitchen chair. She was suddenly tired. Just saying Bull Baron's name, thinking of him, could do that to her. John's boss, Viet Nam buddy. Alter ego. He'd taken John away from her.

"I guess it's not so easy to throw a good job away," Kit said.

"A C.P.A. doesn't have to worry."

"And there was another call," Ruth put in, as if there had been no intervening conversation. She allowed a significant pause. Then: "From the club."

"And?" Mira bent to unbuckle her sandals. She felt divided in two. One Mira moved through her body, listened, replied. The other stood watching. Uninvolved. Uncaring. Concerned only with the memory of Shelley. Already longing to see him again.

"They had a complaint. Against Donnie," Ruth told her. "And you'd better see about it."

But Mira ignored the portentous tone. She laughed, straightened, kicked off her shoes. "What's he done now?"

"It's not funny," Ruth grumbled. "I can't keep up with him. I'm too old. When you get to be seventy years old, you'll understand."

"Sixty-eight," Mira said.

"Seventy. I ought to know my own age. But either way, it's too hard on me. Donnie, much as I love him, and you know I do, is getting to be a holy terror."

"But what happened? What did he do?"

Kit answered. "It's a mountain out of a mole hill. I guess that's how they are at the club." She and Alan weren't members. They couldn't afford to be. She

45

didn't care, but it bothered Alan. She seemed to be defending Donnie, but she was expressing Alan's resentment for him. She went on, "Donnie got hold of a bottle of catsup some place, and spread it around the pool. Liberally."

Mira just looked at her.

Kit laughed. "I know it's not really funny, but I can't help it. Just try to imagine it yourself. You'll see what I mean. Catsup in the pool, around the sun chairs. And those stuffed shirts . . . "

"I don't think it's funny," Ruth told her. "I think it's disgusting. And if Donnie were my son . . . "

"A typical twelve-year-old prank," Kit went on. "That's all. A bored twelve-year-old prank. And they . . . "

"What's he got to be bored about?" Mira demanded. "We give him everything he can possibly want. There's the pool and tennis at the club. Money for going into town when he feels like it. A bike. Skates. Everything. Why, if I'd had . . . "

"You did," Ruth said quietly. "You never lacked for anything. Not anything you ever dreamed of. Or imagined. Or heard about. Your father saw to that. Even when we couldn't do it."

It was true, Mira knew. Her father had spoiled her. He thought the sun rose and set for her. A gold chain for her first "A" in high school. A gold ring for her second. A long velvet coat to wear to the senior prom.

But she answered, "And I wasn't bored." She wriggled her toes. "Where is Donnie anyway?"

"What are you going to do?" Ruth's voice quavered. She would complain about Donnie, but discipline frightened her.

"Talk to him," Mira shrugged. "What else?"

Kit had some ideas, but she didn't express them.

Maybe Mira ought to take him to the Science and Technology museum in town. Maybe they could go for a drive to Harper's Ferry. She said, "He was in and out. He's in the back yard now. We told him to hang around, and he said he would."

"And Seth?"

"I haven't seen him," Ruth answered. "I told you. I'm too old to try to keep up with the boys. Seth's got that jalopy of his now and goes where he pleases, and how am I supposed to manage him?"

"You don't have to. He can do that himself." But Mira was thinking of Shelley again. She imagined the triangle of puckered circles on his shoulders, the long ropy scar that zig-zagged across his back. An accident, he'd told her. He'd always imagined that they'd melt away with time. But they hadn't.

"Seth'll be home for dinner," Kit was saying.

"I made hamburgers and salad and baked potatoes," Ruth said. "I hope that's all right. I never got to check with you, Mira."

"Sure it's all right. Why not?" Mira went to the window. She noticed the small practice green. It needed a trimming. If John was coming home soon, she'd better remind Seth. She said, "Donnie's not there."

"He's around." Kit rose, stretched. "I guess it's time for me to think about dinner, too. I wish Alan would eat hamburgers."

"He used to," Mira told her. "We both always loved them."

"I suppose he outgrew that. Now he wants steak."

"The hamburgers I make," Ruth said, "you put in a touch of garlic, and plenty of onion."

"Mother," Mira cried. "Kit knows how to make hamburgers your style. The trouble is that Alan hates onion."

"He never hated my onion," Ruth snapped. "Alan's a good boy."

Kit smiled.

"He is okay, isn't he?" Mira asked.

"Yes. But busy. End of the term labors, you know."

"I guess that's why I haven't seen him."

"Time gets away from him. From everybody, I suppose."

"We were always so close." And Mira thought: Close until he married you, Kit. But the other Mira, the one who watched from the corner, listened without answering, felt only relief. She'd never be able to explain to Alan about Shelley.

"It's just the work." Kit tried not to sound as apologetic as she felt. Alan hadn't been to the Priests' in the two weeks since Mira's birthday. She'd mentioned it once. They'd nearly quarreled.

"And the day Mira and John married . . . " Ruth's voice was warm with fond memory, the words rehearsed through repetition. "Poor Alan. He was distraught. He was twelve then. Just Donnie's age. And he'd known about it for months. That's all we'd talked about for months. Mira's wedding. But I guess he never really believed it. You remember, Mira. How he put his head down and his face got red, and he doubled his fists and went at John?"

Kit made a forced smile. She didn't like to think of the young Alan, the boy before the man she had taken for husband. She wished she had known him forever, that he'd been hers forever.

Mira, sighing loudly, changed the subject. "And how's your business these days, Kit?"

"I've been showing a lot of houses. But the prices run high. And there's whispers that interest rates will go up again soon, so people are doing a lot of fast looking around."

"You like it, don't you?" But Mira wasn't really interested. She was just giving Kit something to talk about. And keeping herself from blurting out what had happened at Joe's. No need to mention the place, the robbery. No reason to give her mother one more thing to fear.

Kit said eagerly, "I do like it. And so would you. If you went ahead and got your license, you'd see for yourself. The hours being whatever you want just about . . . And then, the commissions when you do make a sale . . . " Kit wished she hadn't mentioned the money. Mira didn't need commissions. John did well, better than well. Not that it mattered to Kit. It was Alan who compared their one bedroom apartment in Silver Spring to John and Mira's hillside split level in Bethesda. It was Alan who hated her old green station wagon. "But meeting people," she said hurriedly. "Getting around. . . . "

A car roared in the driveway, and Kit let her words trail off. It was no use. She knew Mira ought to do something. Everybody did something these days. But Mira just wasn't interested. Not in real estate. Not in anything else that Kit could see. But Mira wasn't stupid, nor empty-headed. Kit knew from Ruth's many stories about Mira's accomplishments. How she'd won four essay contests. How she'd been elected to the National Honor Society in high school for getting good grades. How she'd been admitted to the University of Maryland. She'd gotten married instead. But now the kids were nearly grown. There was Ruth to take care of the house. Mira could do whatever she wanted. Only she seemed not to want anything.

"There's Seth," Mira was saying. "Now, if Donnie will show up . . . "

Kit smiled, said she'd better be on her way.

Ruth lifted her face, and Kit pressed her lips to her mother-in-law's cheek, and patted her back. Kit was fond of the older woman, enjoyed her, trusted her good sense as something precious.

Outside, Kit and Mira found Seth draped across the hood of his car, examining the grillwork below the windshield. He waggled a hand but didn't speak.

It was dark now. The storm was over, though an occasional raindrop fell from the trees overhead.

"Aren't you talking these days?" Mira asked Seth.

"Oh, hi, mom. Hi, Aunt Kit. I can't figure out what it was. Maybe an old acorn. Or maybe a pebble."

"What was what?" Kit asked. She always made a special effort with Seth. She felt she had to. There'd be nothing there if she didn't try. He was always pleasant to her, but she had the feeling that he was somewhere far away, just watching.

"Something fell here. There's a dent, see?"

Kit looked. "Lucky it didn't hit the glass."

He slid to his feet, grinned, "And how!"

Mira, silent through the exchange, burst out, "You should be more careful."

"It just came down, mom."

"From where?"

He shrugged. He knew how to handle his mother. The same way his father did. The less said the better. No matter about what. Don't talk about the thrill, the danger. That's how his father was, close-lipped, careful. That's how Seth himself was, too. No reason to say he'd been driving around with the boys. Thinking about his father. Imagining himself John Priest, alone, quiet, tough. When he drove into a dead end street in Wheaton full of nigger kids, he'd gunned the motor, gone straight at a group of them, yelling, "Back to Africa, blacks." And the laughter he'd heard in the jalopy had been his father cheering him on.

Kit said goodbye, drove away.

Mira and Seth went into the house. Since Donnie hadn't yet returned, they decided they'd wait dinner for a little while.

Mira fixed a drink for herself, carried it into the living room. She sat in a chair near the window, watching for Donnie. But she was thinking of Shelley. He was young enough to be her son. What would he want with her? What would she want with him? No. It was just crazy. Then why was she thinking of him?

She closed her eyes briefly. When she opened them, Donnie was making his way up the steep curve of the lawn. He disappeared for a moment. The front door closed with a loud bang.

"Donnie?"

"Yup. It's me. In the flesh. In the bone. Donnie Priest himself!"

Clowning. He felt guilty.

He grinned at her from the doorway. "You're waiting for me. The hangman. The man with the axe. Woman, I mean. Excuse it. I forgot for a minute. Hang person? That sounds funny."

She let him run down. When he did, she asked, "What's it about?"

"They called from the club."

"Somebody spoke to your grandmother."

"Then you know."

"I heard something very childish about catsup."

"Would you believe an irresistible impulse, mom?"

"I'd listen."

"It's the truth. Honest. I don't know what came over me."

"I'm going to be all over you in a minute."

He sighed deeply. "Okay. It's just that this morning, there was that pool, see. Empty. Sparkling in the sunlight. Not open for business yet. But ready. And there was that catsup bottle sitting there, left over from some boob's hamburger, I guess. And I just . . . well, I started some oldfashioned fingerpainting."

"You outgrew fingerpainting a long time ago." She added: "Or should have."

"This was different." He let himself collapse, slide down the door frame until he was a heap on the carpet. His shoulders shook. "If you'd seen their faces . . . The pool red as blood. And all that tile . . . "

"You think that's funny?"

"If you'd seen them . . . "

"Your irresistible impulse is going to cost you, Donnie. No pool for a month."

"Mom!"

"Sorry."

"But what'll I do? School's out next week."

"Think about acting like a grown-up."

She was almost to the kitchen when the house suddenly seemed to leap with sound. Seth's stereo. At full volume. She went to the steps, yelled, "Seth! Dinner's on. Shut that thing off."

No response.

She cocked a brow at Donnie. He sighed loudly and went up the stairs in two bounces, slamming the bannister on the way.

"Stop that. You'll break the railing," she said, and went into the kitchen.

"You didn't call the club," Ruth told her.

"I will. After we eat."

"What did Donnie say?"

"'Would you believe an irresistible impulse?'"

"Too much television."

"He's too smart for those impulses. And he doesn't need t.v. to give him ideas. He gets them all by himself. Only this time he's grounded as far as the club is concerned. No going there for a month. And don't you tell him different, Mother."

"If they ever let him back in."

"As long as we're members they will."

"They can take care of that, too," her mother said darkly.

"Oh, don't make so much out of nothing," Mira sighed.

When dinner was over, she called the club. Courtesy barely masked the manager's irritation until she offered to pay for the necessary clean up. Then the irritation was wiped out by laughter.

As soon as she put the phone down it rang.

John. She took a deep breath, answered. He asked if everything was all right. When she said it was, he said that her mother had sounded bothered. Something to do with Donnie.

Mira could see the frown between his brows, his dark eyes, narrowed. Donnie had his face. But the expression was so different, they didn't look anything alike. She explained about the catsup and the pool. He listened silently, didn't laugh. She heard static, and music, and a sudden chatter of Spanish over the wires. Finally he told her he didn't like that kind of thing. They'd be talking about the Priests at the club. She interrupted to thank him for her birthday flowers, then asked where he was.

"Caracas," he told her.

The chatter of Spanish. The music . . . It didn't matter where he was. He wasn't home.

"When will you be back?" she asked.

"The end of next week."

"Anything special going on?" She knew he would say no before he did. She also knew that he would tell her that Bull Baron sent his regards. She said good-bye to John, and put down the phone. She hated Bull Baron, had hated him for a long time.

"When is John coming home?" her mother asked.

"The end of next week."

"What day?"

"I forgot to ask him."

"It seems a long time until then," her mother complained.

"Yes," she agreed. But it didn't.

The triple mirror showed her body to be the same as it had been before Shelley touched her. Hard to believe that there was no sign of his mouth at her nipples. That his hands hadn't left blisters in the wake of their heat. Even harder to believe that now she felt nothing.

It had all been washed away when she came into the house. A switch pulled. With a click she had become Mira Priest again. Mother of two. Wife. And child.

She moved closer to the mirror. How old had she looked to Shelley? She saw no stretch marks. She didn't have a noticeable belly. Her waist was narrow. Her hips curved, but not too much. Her behind was flat enough. She saw no flaws in her shape. But that was her own vision. Maybe hope put blinders on her. Hope was ash in her mouth when she looked at her mother. Then she saw herself grown old. The fair skin wrinkled as crumpled tissue paper. The eyes faded. Once Ruth had been taller than Mira. Time had made her bones shrink. She ate meagerly now, and kept thin, boasting that she'd never had a weight problem, having forgotten that once she'd worn a ladies size fourteen and a half, and wept when she tried on clothes. To examine Ruth was to see Mira herself. With the tracks of the years burned into her own face.

She turned away from the mirror. It no longer flattered her. Hurrying to escape the thought, she filled the tub with hot water and liquid bubble bath. It was a ritual that always satisfied. She sank into pink froth, and allowed herself to think of Shelley.

Fourteen years between them. Enormous. Meaningful. Impossible to wipe away. She had told herself that he was a sweet boy, and only four years older than Seth, even though most of the time he seemed mature as a man. She told herself that the habit of having sons made her want to mother him. That's how mothers were. But with him she didn't feel like a mother. So she had kept going back to Joe's. And finally, she'd spoken to him; he'd spoken to her. The hold up. It seemed to have happened to someone else and in another time. And the lovemaking after.

What did Shelley think of her now?

She couldn't imagine it. He'd said he'd see her again.

She lay back, closed her eyes. Her hands cupped her breasts.

He would see her again. God yes. He would.

Seth's room was across the center hallway. By day it was in shade because of an enormous oak that grew just outside, spreading thick old limbs along the wall of the house. By night it was dark as pitch, untouched by moonlight or starshine.

He was at the window, easing it up, cursing the air conditioning, already turned on for the summer, that meant the window was normally kept closed and locked.

His door opened. He swung around as Donnie crept in.

"What do you want?"

"What are you doing, Seth?"

"Going out."

"That way?"

"No. I'm just taking the screen out for fun, and opening the window for fun, too."

"But why don't you use the door like anybody else?"

"And why don't you shut up?"

Donnie's voice came as an exaggerated whisper. "She's sleeping. And anyhow, what're you going out for?"

"I've got things to do, that's why. Now beat it."

The night. The dark. Shadows. The joy of danger. Seth Priest was his father's son, and had always been. As far back as he could remember he'd been fascinated by his imaginings of his father's life away from home. Now that Seth was grown he had his own life away from home. And that, too, was shadowed and dangerous and not to be talked about.

To Donnie he said finally, "Go back to bed."

Donnie shrugged. "Okay, okay. But if you let me go with you . . . "

"Beat it, I said."

Moments later, Seth's car drifted silently down the driveway to back into Plumtree Road.

CHAPTER 4.

WHEN KIT arrived home that evening, Alan was waiting. He dropped the wet lettuce leaves, shook water off his hands, and pulled her to him. "Have a big deal cooking?"

"I stopped to see your mother."

"She all right?"

"Yes. But when she called me at the office she sounded a little down so I thought she needed company."

"You're good to her, Kit."

"Why shouldn't I be? She's the only mother-in-law I've got."

The kitchen was small. There was hardly enough room for the two of them. The table was set in a corner of the living room, which wasn't very large either. Kit didn't care. She didn't spend much time in the kitchen, nor in the living room for that matter. She supposed she could fix the apartment up a little. But didn't feel like bothering. She and Alan were out most of the time anyway.

"Mira okay?" Alan was asking. "The boys?"

"Sure. But they've got their own interests."

"So have we all."

Kit ignored that. She grinned. "And Donnie pulled one of his stunts at the club. Catsup in the swimming pool."

"I guess John should spend more time at home."

"I guess so. But I don't see how he could." Kit rubbed her cheek along the curve of Alan's jaw, then drew away. "Since you've started the salad, I'd better get moving."

But he held her. "I'm not all that hungry, are you?"

She raised her brows. "It's dinner time."

"That so?" His arms tightened. He swung her toward the doorway. "My clock doesn't say that."

"Your clock?" She laughed. She broke away to dance ahead of him, hips swinging saucily, blonde hair swaying on her narrow shoulders.

He let her stay a step ahead, just beyond his reaching fingertips until she spun into the bedroom. By then her white shirt was unbuttoned to the waist. The narrow strip of her bra sharpened her breasts.

He caught up with her, wrestled her down to the bed.

Later he said, "We're lucky." It was always so good. He was surprised that it stayed that way. The six months before they were married. The two years since. He didn't get to take her for granted. She didn't seem to have gotten over the novelty of him. He'd known it would be like that. Had known it a week after he began seeing her. Had started to want to marry her then. Still, it surprised him how good it was.

"Knock wood three times," she was saying. "Let's not take any chances."

He rapped his knuckles firmly against his forehead. "Will that do it?"

"No. But it might help."

He got up on an elbow, looked down into her face. "Are you happy, Kit?"

"You know."

"I wonder some times." He did. He couldn't help it. Even knowing how good it was. But life was more than that. There were the other things.

She moved closer, spoke with her mouth against his arm. "Alan, no. How could you wonder?"

"The six years between us for one thing. You're still such a kid."

"You are, too."

"Twenty-nine's no kid. Besides, I'm a stick in the mud."

"Stick in the mud! You?" She laughed.

"It's true though. There I am, in the same old job I've had for the last five years. And not thinking about changing. I'll get my promotions, one after another, and one of these days, maybe we'll have enough saved up to get us a house here in Silver Spring."

"So? What's terrible about that?"

"All those purse-snatchings and muggings on Flower Avenue. A little bit of the ghetto developing and spreading out. The whole area's changing."

"I don't care. I like it here."

He went on, "And the other side of the county will always be too expensive for us. You know that as well as I do."

"I don't want to live in Bethesda. Or Potomac. I'm satisfied where we are."

"In this scrimy apartment? Don't pretend, Kit."

"You can only speak for yourself. I know what I prefer. And this is it." She sat up, wrapped her arms around her bare knees. "What's this all about?"

"My being a stick in the mud."

"No. It's not," she said. "It's because I didn't want to get married those first six months. That's right, isn't it?"

"I understood that. You just weren't sure."

"I was sure I loved you. I just wanted to get the broker's license." But it had been more than that. And he was partly right. She knew she loved him. She just had to be absolutely sure. She didn't want to take any chances. She already knew too much about divorce. Her own folks had broken up when she was fifteen. Her mother drank herself to death. Her father, already remarried and with a new young family, ended up doing the same thing when his new young wife walked out on him for somebody else. Kit had a thing about divorce.

But Alan was saying, "And maybe you should have hung on a little longer."

"It's got nothing to do with me," she snapped. And added accusingly, "You're thinking about John. And comparing yourself to him."

"Maybe I am. A little."

"Have you suddenly taken a dislike to teaching American history to seventh graders?"

He laughed, shook his head.

"You suddenly want to be a big-shot accountant rubbing shoulders with arms dealers all over the world?"

Again he shook his head.

"Then do yourself a favor. Stop comparing. You're you, thank God. He's him." She slid to the edge of the bed. "And I'll tell you one thing. I'd rather have you home with me, fixing the salad when I walk in the door, wanting me before I have time to shove an omelet onto the stove, than to have you traveling over half the

60

world, and not ever seeing you, and living in a fancy house that doesn't mean a damn thing."

"You're just trying to make me feel good," Alan told her. "And succeeding."

But, as he watched her pull on a shirt, step into faded blue jeans, he wondered. A girl like Kit, beautiful, intelligent, could have married money, or a moneymaker. He was unable to imagine what she'd seen in him. He gave her so little, it seemed to him. Nothing like what John gave to Mira. Yet Kit didn't seem to care.

Later, in the kitchen, he asked, "What about your day? How was it?"

She flipped the omelet, raised the flame under the pan. "Pretty much the same as usual. Except for the Treblings. I'm a little uneasy about them."

"The Treblings?"

She turned the omelet onto a large plate, carried it and a bowl of mixed vegetables to the table in the living room. Seated, beginning to serve him, she frowned slightly. "I have a funny feeling about them. As if, maybe, they're hiding something from me."

"You mean about their house?"

"Yes. They're so casual about selling, overly so. But too anxious at the same time. And they trot after me, step by step, whenever I'm there. Looking where I look. Waiting. Only I don't quite know what they're waiting for me to find."

"You're probably letting your imagination run away with you."

She said nothing. But she thought of Mira. There had been something odd about Mira, too. Something that made Kit uneasy. Everybody made jokes about women's intuition. But Kit thought there might be something to it. Maybe intuition was just another word for talking about what the mind took in, filed away, but never put together. What had it been about Mira? Just the sense that a part of her wasn't there that afternoon. That she'd been thinking of something else all the time. What did that mean? Maybe she was just tired. But Kit didn't think so. Mira had seemed to glow. To glow. Yet Kit knew if she mentioned it to Alan he would blame that, too, on her runaway imagination. Still, the feeling wouldn't go away.

He was saying, "After all, all you want to do is sell that house for them."

"Yes." She picked up her fork. "But if there's something wrong with it . . . that I don't know about . . . "

"Let the buyer beware," he laughed.

"That's what they say. Only I need to be able to sleep nights."

"Then ask the Treblings straight out. Tell them what you think. See what they say."

She nodded. "Maybe that's best." But she thought of Mira again. She wasn't sure she could ask the Treblings flat out what was bothering them. Not any more than she could say to Alan that she had a funny feeling about what his sister was up to. And even as she thought it, she realized that she didn't even *want* to say anything to Alan about it. She'd never been a tattletale nor a gossip. Whatever Mira was doing was her own business, and she had her own reasons for it. That ought to have settled it for Kit. But she remained uneasy.

CHAPTER 5.

T WAS Monday. Two o'clock.

Mira sat in Joe's. She had finished one drink, and was about to finish the second. Her sandwich was ragged where she had picked at it without appetite.

The regulars talked across her, but this time she didn't listen to them. They had to rehash the robbery . . . the men in the blue baseball caps . . . the arrival of the police . . . the questions and answers and who had said what.

Mira had nearly forgotten those brief frightening moments when she'd seen the glint of gunmetal. The plywood where the mirror had been was the only sign of what had happened here the Saturday before.

She glanced sideways at the door through the gloom. Shelley hadn't come. By now she knew he wouldn't. She ought to have known. No matter what he'd said, she should have realized she'd never see him again. She'd been his day's amusement. Now he'd have gone on to someone, or something, else. He'd never see her in the blue jeans and sleeveless white shirt she'd put on for him. He'd never smile that damn smile at her again.

She finished her drink, managed to say good-bye to Jimmy and the others. When she went out into hot sunlight, Shelley was leaning against her car.

Hurt exploded even as elation bloomed. "Why didn't you come in?" she demanded.

"First you're supposed to say 'hello.' Then maybe you say 'how are you?' Then maybe. . . ."

"But I was waiting inside. You knew I'd be."

He nodded.

"Then why?" She was so glad to see him she wanted to hurl herself into his arms. But she had to pay him back just a little for the hour of pain.

"I don't know why," he was saying.

Gray eyes silvered. Dark hair tousled. The don't-give-a-damn grin suddenly gone. A lost boy look. She had the feeling that there was a face behind this face that she wanted so desperately to kiss. A man she didn't know. "Oh, Shelley," she whispered.

"I guess I didn't feel like going in to Joe's today." And, with a light touch of his hand, "Let's go for a ride."

"Not to your place. If that's what you're thinking." Refusing what she herself wanted most of all. Punishment to her as well as him. He had to explain. What was the point? Why had he made her wait for nothing. Hope, then give up hope. Feel used, cheap, a one time stand. Feel *old*.

But he was laughing now. "You don't want to go back to my place? Okay."

"We'll ride in my car."

"Sure."

She slid behind the wheel, started the motor as he settled beside her. Her car. Her control. But she burst out, "I thought I'd never see you again."

"How come?"

"I expected you in Joe's. And when you weren't, I began to understand. You had me, didn't you? What else was there?"

"So you figured that was it?"

"Yes."

"It could have been like that." His voice softened. "Only it wasn't, was it?"

"You were teasing me, weren't you?"

"A little."

"But why?"

"Because."

Because. It reminded her of Donnie. Of Seth. She shook the thought away. "That's no answer." It was what she said to the boys, she realized.

Shelley shrugged. "It's the best I can do." Then he pulled something from his shirt pocket. "This is a present for you."

"A present? What for?"

"Because," he said, and laughed.

It was a gold chain hung with a pink enamel locket in the shape of a heart. Small, delicate.

"For you to remember me by," he told her.

Hurt forgotten. Anger forgotten. Suddenly she was afraid. "Are you going away?"

"No. Not now. But some time, I guess." Then: "Pull over. I'll put it on for you."

She parked at the side of the road. Ahead the traffic flashed by on Route 70S. Here it was quiet except for the caw of two crows that balanced on a sagging fence.

A shiver went over her as he settled the chain around her throat. She would never take it off. Never. She whispered her thanks.

"Don't you want to know where it came from?"

"Where?"

"Pampillonia's in the Mazza Gallerie."

"But Shelley, that's such an expensive place."

"I didn't say I'd paid for it, did I?" He sat back, laughing at her astonished silence. Then: "I stole it for you."

"Stole it?" she repeated. "Oh, Shelley. You shouldn't have." She shook her dark head. Her face became solemn and sad. In the voice she had used on Seth, on Donnie, when they were small, she said, "It's wrong. Against the law, against the Ten Commandments, too — "

"You believe in that stuff? In an old guy with a beard floating over the mountain, and throwing a stone tablet at that old Jew named Moses?"

"Maybe not in the stone tablet, and the old guy. But I believe in the laws. They're made to protect us. So we can live together without hurting each other. A contract to make living easier for everyone — "

"Nobody ever gave me a contract. Nobody ever tried to make it easier for me."

She took both his hands in hers. Almost crooning, she said, "But Shelley, you have to believe in something. Even if you don't always live up to it all the time. Even if it's hard. Faith is important — "

"Yeah. Okay. Now let's go to my place."

"There isn't time. I've got a big week coming up, and a lot to do to get ready."

"For instance?"

But she wasn't going to say that she had to prepare for John's return. Shopping. Arranging some kind of social thing. The putting green . . . She had to remember to remind Seth. She started the car.

Shelley said, "I kept thinking about you. All yesterday. Waiting. A long slow rotten Sunday. Wanting you. I thought about it and you, and nothing else."

The words quiet, his eyes steady on hers. "We'll go to your place for a little while," she said.

The drive didn't take long. She looked at the front windows when they went in. No curtain moved. This time Shelley's landlady didn't seem to be watching.

Something was different. Mira didn't know what. She looked around thoughtfully. The torn Japanese screen. The sagging divan. The dirty, high windows.

"I cleaned up," he said. "For us."

"But you didn't come to get me in Joe's."

He sighed, shrugged. "You haven't thought of the obvious, have you?"

"What obvious?"

He drew her to him, held her tightly. "It takes money to drink beer, to eat. You've got to pay when you sit at a bar. I couldn't just hang around."

"Oh, Shelley, I'm sorry."

"It wouldn't occur to you."

"I guess it should have," she said softly.

They fell on the divan together.

Later, with his hard arms still around her, she said, "I want you to promise me that you'll never do it again." And she touched the place between her breasts where the heart-shaped locket lay. "Promise me."

His face paled. He was still, hardly breathing. His eyes seemed blank, bottomless. And his head was filled with voices. "Promise me, Shel. You won't, you won't, will you?" And: "Goddamn runt of the litter. Didn't ever think he was mine anyhow. If you'd done what I said we'd be free and clear." And: "Let him be! He's a good boy. He's as much yours as the others. He won't, will you, Shel?" "So keep him off. I don't want him in bed peeing on me." The door slamming . . . weeping. "Promise me, Shel."

"Suppose you'd been caught?" Mira was asking. "Suppose they'd seen you? You'd be in jail this minute. Locked up for I don't know how long." She took his

face between her hands. "Locked up. You can understand that, can't you?"

His eyes cleared. The crooked grin fell on his mouth.
"But nobody caught me. And it was more fun that way
anyhow."

"Fun? Stealing?"

He said, "You can't kid me. You don't believe that
crap about the Ten Commandments. Nobody does. Just
as nobody goes to jail for a little shop lifting."

She insisted that it did happen, that people were
caught. She insisted harder that she did believe. She
went through the whole explanation again of just what
her faith was. When she stopped talking she realized
that everything she had said was a lie.

"You see how it is," Shelley told her.

"Oh, no," she said. "I couldn't ever do it."

"You could. If you wanted to."

She protested vehemently. He silenced her words
with kisses.

Three days later she stood in the silver department of
Woodward & Lothrop's at 11th and F Streets in the city.

She was frightened. At the back of her tongue there
was the bitter taste of metal. A pulse thumped persist-
ently behind her eyes. Her fingertips were cold and the
palms of her hands burned with sweat.

But she was there for Shelley. To please him. And
she felt his presence with her. She had dressed for the
adventure. She wore an old black straw hat that shaded
her face. Above its wide brim, she had tied a white
streamer. Her white dress was accented by a small tuft
of black chiffon that drooped from its pocket. Her
shoes, bag, and gloves were black, too. She was a proper
matron. Of the 1950's. She remembered that when she
was very small, she had clung to her mother's hand in

Woodies'. Now Mira wondered if her mother had ever owned a wide-brimmed black straw hat.

It was the wrong thing to think about. Even more frightened, she pressed on. She didn't consider stopping or retreating. She didn't look to see, but was certain that Shelley must be watching her. She felt his eyes, his presence. He was there.

She tipped her dark head, brought to her face the bemused expression of a woman trying to decide which of the two ladles, both silver, both heavy and carved, and proportionately expensive. She hefted one, then the other. Loathed both. Hands steady, she noted, sighing aloud. She stroked the deep gleaming traceries. "Lovely," she murmured. "But it's so difficult to be sure."

"Either one makes a lovely gift," the saleswoman told her, a bored glance drifting away down the aisle.

Either one, Mira thought. Yes. It didn't matter which. But it was too quiet here. The long softly-lit glass counter stretched on both sides of her. Empty. Still. The saleswoman waited, with nothing to distract her.

Too obvious to be safe. But Shelley had said silver. Why, she didn't know. She didn't know what it meant to him. So much she didn't know.

She made a regretful shrug. "I guess not. Somehow . . . " Her glance fell on the napkin rings. "Oh, wait . . . may I see some of those?"

The two ladles swept along the counter, disappeared into purple bags, dropped away into hidden shelves. The napkin rings appeared. Four different styles.

Soft music. The shuffle of footsteps on the deep pile of the carpet. A waft of perfume from the cosmetic department only a few paces away. It was crowded. If only Shelley had said eye shadow, or rouge. Or any one of a dozen things. But silver . . .

"Nice?" Mira said. "I suppose that the plain ones

could be initialled." A pause. "But it would still be very plain. Look like nothing. And it has to be special." She peered into the counter. "And these?" Her fingernails, freshly painted a pale rose, glistened in the light as she gestured. "Oh . . . and let me see that other one, too, while you're at it."

Five more napkin rings were placed before her. She took up each one, the diamonds sparkling on her left hand. John believed in investments. And if he could see her now . . . . She banished John. She studied the carvings, hefted the weight. If only someone else would come.

But the counter remained empty. The saleswoman close by, silent now, while a thin hand revealingly tapped the glass counter top.

Mira drew a deep breath. Shelley was watching. Silver, he'd said. For me, Mira. He'd accept that. Keep it forever. But he wouldn't let her give him five dollars for food. He wouldn't even let her talk about it. He'd get an odd job, make a few dollars. He only wanted the silver. From her. To him.

If not here, where then? Mira asked herself. She allowed her big black purse to slip from her hand. It flew open, spilling its contents in every direction.

She wailed, "Oh, dear, this just isn't my day!" And knelt quickly. One napkin ring was cupped in her wet palm. She flung lipstick and compacts and car keys into the bag. The napkin ring went with them. But, flexing to rise, she caught a glimpse of a blank staring eye. The high round mirror on which there lay the small reflection of the counter, the aisle, and her stooping body in white and black.

The carpet faded to misty brown as dizziness enveloped her. She bent her head, rocking on one dainty sandal.

No good. No. What was she doing here? John would say, "Christ, Mira, what the hell were you thinking of? You can pay for whatever you want. If this gets around, I'll be finished. Christ, don't you have sense enough to charge what you want?"

And how would she answer him?

"You all right?" the saleswoman was asking.

"Yes. Of course." And rising, her grin wry. "I'm just all butterfingers today. I guess I'll have to think over what I want. But thanks for your help."

As she turned to leave, finding breath again, the saleswoman called, "Oh, miss!"

Caught. Choked. Blood drumming in her ears. Mira swung back, the beginnings of apology on her lips. Explanations. Quiet words. Perhaps even tears. Her hand was already fumbling in her bag.

The saleswoman held out the small gleaming pill box. "You left this, didn't you?"

"Oh, yes, thank you." Relief a swift running river that dammed in her bladder. She had to go. Her thighs quivered with need. But she accepted the square of pink enamel in which she kept the pills for her migraines. She smiled, shrugged. "I told you. Not my day."

She walked slowly, casually toward the door.

Shelley was somewhere. She could feel him. Even as she stepped into hot bright sun, and relief became giddy excitement, she knew the budding of heat deep in her body. Shelley . . .

A brush at her shoulder. He was beside her, his step matched to hers. "Easy as pie?"

"I didn't see you."

"You weren't supposed to."

But she wondered. Had he been watching? Or had it been her own mind watching? If he'd been waiting outside, she could have charged the napkin ring. He'd not have known. She could have destroyed the slip and walked from the store and pretended to him.

He looked at her sideways. "Don't try to fool me. I'd see through you. I'd know."

She still had to go. She told him. "I got so scared that I almost let it happen right there in the silver department."

"Just wait a little while."

A giggle broke from her. "It was so funny. And so simple. That poor woman won't ever be able to figure it out. Me, and my butterfingers. So quick, so neat." And it was a little thing. What did it matter?

They started walking to where he had left his car. The buildings and pavements steamed. The air was heated glue, and gritty with pollution. Giggling still, she followed him. He stopped at a street vendor and bought her an orange. He stopped at another for a single pink rose. She remembered the American Beauties that John had sent her for her birthday. It seemed a long while ago.

By the time he had retrieved the car, and they were on the way out Massachusetts Avenue, she had stopped giggling and the reaction had set in.

It had been crazy. Childish. She was ashamed of herself. She said, "I can hardly believe I'd be that dumb. What for? Just to laugh for a little while?" she turned on the seat. "Shelley, admit it. You're a little bit kooky, aren't you?"

He didn't answer that. Maybe he was. Maybe he wasn't. So what? He asked, "How do you feel?"

"Relieved that I didn't get caught."

"What else?"

They had turned into Wisconsin Avenue. Familiar territory. They were on the route for home.

"I'm not sure myself," she said slowly.

"Tell me. I mean it, Mira. Tell me everything you feel."

"I've got to go," she said slowly. "You just passed two gas stations."

He said he'd stop at the next one, and again asked her to describe how she felt.

"I'm tingling," she told him. "It's a . . . what do you call it? Like I'm sailing. Flying."

"A rush," he said.

"Excited. Everything's working. I can feel my insides."

"You feel alive."

She considered, silently agreed. Alive. Was it stealing the napkin ring? Or was it Shelley?

He swerved the VW into a station.

She hurried to pick up the key to the women's room, rushed inside. It was a relief to let go. When she had, the residue of fright was gone.

She laughed when she returned to the car. "You wouldn't think a little bit of shop lifting could carry me so far."

"After a while you'll believe it, too."

"Just the same, I'm going to quit while I'm ahead."

"It'll be gold next time," he told her.

Later, in his basement room, he pulled her into his arms, buried his face in her breasts. As she clung to him, she said softly, "I'm scared for you, Shelley."

"For me? Or for you?"

"You."

"We're the same. One. From now on."

It was what she felt herself. But at the same time it was too much. The fourteen years between them . . . her family . . . "Shelley, you have to be smart about this. You know . . . you *know* . . ."

He pulled away, went behind the screen.

She heard a click. Then her voice. His. Sounds.

The blood drained from her head. A wave of trembling shook her. She buried her face in her hands. She tried not to hear the voices, the other sounds. Set up. That was the word for it. Maneuvered into a trap. Now this. Then . . . He'd refused her offer of money. Because it hadn't been enough. Now. Now he'd ask. After she'd heard how they had spoken together, panted together, cried out together. She ought to have known. What else could he want with her? She was too old for him. Old. Old.

Shelley said softly, "Mira?"

She raised her head. He had that lost look. His eyes pleaded with her. For what, she didn't know. "Why, Shelley? Why did you do that tape?"

"To have you with me. All the time."

It was true, she knew. His face, eyes, told her to believe. She did, but said, "It sounds so . . . so awful."

"I wanted you the first time I saw you. I wanted to touch you, and hug you. It began right then. When you walked into Joe's. I just didn't know how to get started." He swallowed, smiled faintly. "It doesn't sound awful to me."

"But to someone else . . . "

"Who'd ever hear it except you and me?"

She didn't answer.

But he suddenly understood. "You thought I might use it against you. But you ought to know I'd never hurt you. So don't be afraid of me, Mira."

He dropped down, lay with his head in her lap, looking up at her. Fingers stroking the chain at her throat, he said dreamily, "I wonder. Gold. Should you go to Pampillonia's, too? Or somewhere else. I'll have to think about that."

"I couldn't do it again, Shelly. I wouldn't want to."

"You don't like the feeling?"

She shrugged.

"So why not? Just for me."

"You know."

He blinked, winced. The images crowded in . . . They filled his mind, his eyes. She was wearing a gown like a rainbow, all filmy, showing the lady bumps. He was still young enough to call them that. Later he learned they were breasts and what they were for. The door opened and darkness slid in. His father moved on its current. They went upstairs. Just the two of them. He trailed after, hurled himself at the locked door. He screamed, wept. Then: "Damn kid! Now what's the matter with him? Get away from that door! Shut up!" A shrill cry. The door flung back. The kick that sent him tumbling toward the steps. His mother's arms around him. "Why can't I come in, mama?" And: "You know, Shel. You know."

Through tears, he looked at Mira, "Don't. Please. We belong together. You and me."

She leaned over him. Her hair moved like feathers on his cheeks. Her mouth pressed to his. And that made everything all right. For a little while.

But after he had left her at her car, he was restless. He went into Joe's for a beer, but didn't stay to finish it. He drove aimlessly, then went home. He counted his money. He had seven dollars. For the first time he could remember he wished he was rich. He wished he had credit cards, and bank accounts, and a thick green roll inside a silver money clip. He wished he owned a house, and had two cars. He wanted everything there was. Not for himself. But so he could have Mira, too.

He was thinking about that when Mrs. Radman tapped on the door, and called his name.

He let her in. Her hand shook as she offered him half a cherry pie. "Fresh baked today."

He thanked her.

She was a tiny eighty-five, rail-thin. Her eyes were cloudy with cataracts. She managed to survive on a pittance in the house she had paid for by very nearly starving herself for close to twenty-five years.

A few months before, Shelley had been wandering past her house. He'd just been let out on Arlington Road, had taken a short cut, hoping to hit a main highway into Washington to hitch a ride in.

He saw her trying to push a lawn mower over the high grass of the front yard.

He stopped, watched her, then asked if she needed any help.

She peered up at him, smiled wryly. "I do. But I can't pay."

He dropped his pack, rolled up his sweater sleeves and took over.

Later she fed him scrambled eggs and coffee. When she heard he was on the road, with no place to stay, she offered him a room. He chose the basement. In exchange for that, he did her chores.

Soon she found other jobs for him. He helped paint a house, and was given the old VW. It didn't run then, but he managed to get it going and had kept it going ever since. He worked when he wanted to. When he needed to. He had been thinking about moving on when he ran into Mira. He didn't think about moving on any more.

Mrs. Radman was turning to leave.

"Anything I can do for you?" he asked quickly.

"The sink . . . water won't go down any more."

"I'll be up in a minute."

"Thank you. You're a good boy, Shelley."

It took him the better part of the evening to get the sink unclogged. While he worked Mrs. Radman sat watching him, making small conversation. When he was finished she fed him a bowl of vegetable stew.

He went to bed early, fell into a deep sleep while listening to the soft sounds of the tape. Mira's voice. His. He dreamed of her. She wore golden chains around her throat and a long rainbow gown.

CHAPTER 6.

T WAS raining when John returned that Friday night, the beginning of the Memorial Day weekend.

He was always so indefinite about time and place of arrival that Mira had long before stopped going to National or Dulles or Friendship to meet him. He was in the habit now of taking a cab, and never seemed to have trouble getting one, even when the airports were crowded with holiday travelers.

He refused to carry house keys with him, so he rang the bell, a stranger awaiting to be admitted to his own home. He was a man of forty, his sandy hair shot through with gray, fatigue and age lines radiating from his brown eyes. Of medium height and compact build, he seemed dwarfed by Bull Baron, who was with him.

Ruth Baker opened the door. She was smiling. Her blue eyes twinkled. Her cheeks and lips were the same pink as her blouse. "Oh, you're soaked. Come in," she cried. And: "Mr. Baron, how good to see you again." It had been several years, but her voice showed no surprise. She went on, "Mira's getting dressed. How was your trip, John?"

He was amusedly aware that she had made up her face and brushed her silken white waves for him. As she would cook for him. As she would make certain that when he left his shirts were fresh and his handkerchiefs carefully pressed. He was master and mainstay of the house. To her generation that meant something. While Bull greeted her in his raspy voice, John kissed her cheek. The two men followed her inside. The familiar odor of the place closed in on John. It wasn't unpleasant, but it weighed on him. He always noticed it when he first came home. After a while it seemed to disappear.

"You'll want to dry off," Ruth said. She waved Bull towards the powder room. "Fresh towels there."

When he had gone, John asked, "How are you? And the boys?"

"We're fine, John. All's well."

It was the same answer she always gave. But the next morning, when the newness of his return had worn off, she would launch herself into the familiar litany. She would tell him what had broken during his absence, what needed to be repaired or replaced. Then she would tell him about Donnie and Seth. John would listen gravely, nodding agreement. The repairs would be ordered. The replacements purchased. He reserved judgment about the boys. They were as boys always were. Ruth Baker was old, and no longer a good judge. She wanted and expected too much of them.

She asked if he and Bull would want iced tea, or a drink, then asked if Bull would be staying over.

"He's just stopping by for an hour," John said. "I'll go up and say hello to Mira. Then we'll have some Scotch." He meant that he was going up to warn Mira that Bull was there. John knew how Mira felt about the big man. So did Bull. That, of course, hadn't stopped him from saying he wanted to stop by. Maybe it was why he had. Bull enjoyed showing his power.

John carried his suitcase and briefcase with him. From behind the door, he heard small rustlings and movements. He went in.

Mira swung away from her reflection in the mirror. "Hi, John. Good trip?" That was all she ever asked him. He never spoke of his business. She never questioned him. The life he lived when he was gone was separate from the life they lived together.

"Everything was as always," he answered. The same words he always used. He kissed her cheek. "It was all right here?"

She nodded, turned back to the mirror. "I see you were caught in the rain."

"It wasn't much." Then: "Bull came along for a drink. I'll drive him in to the Hilton afterwards." He went on, "I'll look in on the boys."

When he was gone, Mira blinked at her reflection. The thick mascara made heavy black fans of her long lashes. Damn the man! She didn't know if she meant Bull, or John, or both of them. Bull knew she didn't want him in her house. He didn't come often, and when he did nothing happened, but it always left her upset anyway. Maybe that's why he sometimes turned up. Because he knew it bothered her. That would be like Bull Baron.

In spite of her anger, she was relieved that those first few moments of greeting John were over. It was odd. The way it had gone between her and John. Though nothing had really happened. Nothing that they'd ever talked about anyway. Maybe he wasn't even aware of it.

There had been that twelve months when she was between seventeen and eighteen, and he was five years older, out of school, a fledgling C.P.A, who once a month still reported to his Army Reserve unit. Twelve months when they were feverish lovers, starting out for the movies, but ending up in some dark cul-de-sac to writhe endlessly in delighted discomfort on the back seat of his car. It was 1962. Small early ripples of change were already beginning to gather.

Far below the surface glamor of the Kennedy White House the cesspools were filling.

All Mira's life, beginning with her first memories, something wonderful had been expected of her. She'd always known she was special. But in those last months before she was to graduate from high school to be the first in her family to attend college, she began to see that nothing was going to happen. She would still be Mira Baker, faced with . . . what? She didn't know what she wanted to be. Even who she wanted to be. The future was a big dark question mark.

She became pregnant. She knew now that it had been a very nearly deliberate act. Then she only suspected it, wondered at herself. She could have had an abortion, but she didn't allow herself to consider it. Not because of moral scruples, not because the seed growing in her was real to her. Only because she knew John would want to marry her. And in marriage she would escape home, her parents' expectations, being a child to them.

She spent endless hours daydreaming about the two girls she knew who had dropped out of school, gone on the road, and disappeared into the far West. She was drawn to that freedom, frightened of it.

John seemed the answer. She married him, moved to a small walk up apartment in Langley Park, had Seth. She knew who she was. Mira Priest. She knew what she was. Wife and mother. The terrible year of the president's assassination rolled by while she did diapers, shopped, took long walks pushing the baby carriage while Alan walked beside her, talking of school. Sometimes he stayed to dinner, and he and John did the dishes while she put Seth to sleep.

Scarcely a year later, she was home with her parents and Alan again. John's Army Reserve unit was called up for duty in Viet Nam. He went. He wanted to go. She wept bitterly when he told her, again when he moved her and Seth back to her parents' home. He was gone for two years. She heard from him frequently, but his letters said little. On his return, he never spoke of Viet Nam. They moved back to an apartment.

He opened a small office. She worked with him, answered the telephone, greeted clients. She thought they were happy then.

She was pregnant with Donnie the first time Bull Baron came to visit. She disliked him even before she knew why he was there.

He was an exceptionally tall man, with a bear-like body, broad in the shoulder, thick in arm and thigh. His head was big, bald, with a narrow purple scar across the top of it. His dark eyes were the color of mud, set deep under ridged and scarred brows. He seemed to dwarf John, the living room, the chair in which he had seated himself, carefully adjusting thick and obvious genitals beforehand.

She noticed immediately that John was different with Bull there. He was more animated, with light in his eyes and new color in his face. In some undefinable way he seemed eager to please, to win agreement, approval.

While she prepared a meal, she strained to listen to their soft-voiced conversation. It was about places she'd never seen, people she'd never heard of. They seemed, always, to speak a language she didn't know.

When Bull left, John told her he was going to do one job for Bull. She asked what kind of job. John said that

Bull had made contacts in the Army. He was in the munitions business. He wanted John to handle the paperwork for him. The one job became two. After that Mira knew it was a permanent thing.

John traveled most of the time. Places she'd never been to. With people she didn't know. He did well. They bought the Bethesda house. Her father died. Her mother came to live with the family. She ran the house, raised the boys. Mira played tennis, swam at the country club, spent her time at bridge.

The distance between her and John continued to widen. Maybe it began at the beginning, in the moment she told him she was pregnant. Maybe when he came back from Viet Nam. Maybe when he started the job with Bull. She didn't know. She didn't care either.

The feverish joy they'd found together became memory. One night Mira found their rare joining a chore. She wanted nothing, felt nothing. By accident she learned that if she pretended John was Bull, then it would be all right. So, when he came home from his travels, John became Bull Baron in her bed.

Now she heard John go downstairs, the boys clattering after. It was time to put in an appearance.

They were in the living room. Bull sat in the biggest chair, thighs spread. He gave her the usual broad knowing smile that left his mud-colored eyes untouched. "Just as beautiful as ever, Mira. Long time no see."

She managed a greeting.

Her mother had fixed drinks for the two men. She was a tee-totaller herself, disapproved of alcohol in any form for anyone but John.

Mira fixed her own drink, ignored the look her mother gave her.

There were crackers, cheese, and olives on the marble-topped table. The television set was on. The late news.

Donnie sat on the floor close to it. Seth complained from the sofa that he couldn't see. Donnie didn't move. Seth told him to get out of the way. The younger boy jerked his shoulders irritably, shifted an inch.

Ruth said, "I don't know why anybody would be so peculiar. And I mean you, Donnie Priest."

"He can see," Donnie said.

"I'd like to hear the news," John cut in, while Bull laughed, winked at Mira.

Seth rose, took a chair at the corner.

A cross flared on the television screen. "Montgomery County police report another front yard cross burning. It took place in the early hours of this morning on Handley Lane before the home of Mr. and Mrs. Abraham L. Johnson, who, with their three small children, moved into the neighborhood seven months ago. The cross burning is attributed to a group which has previously identified itself as the White Knights, in connection with other burnings in the county. The Police Department is continuing its investigation, and attempting to learn if the group is connected to the Ku Klux Klan."

"Damn idiots," John said. He rose, made refills for himself and Bull.

When that round was finished, Bull rose. "I hate to go, but I've got to." He winked again at Mira. "A heavy date in town. But it sure is good to get a whiff of family life."

She said nothing, allowing her mother's and the boys' farewells to cover her own silence.

When the men had gone, Ruth said brightly, "I almost forgot to tell you. I asked Kit and Alan to join us for the barbecue Sunday. I was sure it was all right since they know the Weidemayers."

"That's fine," Mira told her, thinking that it didn't matter. No matter who was there, the barbeque would be boring.

Later, in bed, she waited for John, listening to the small hum of the air-conditioning unit. He might pass to her a signal that he wanted her. He might not. It didn't matter. She was thinking of Shelley. When John lay down beside her, settled close, then closer, she closed her eyes and turned to him. That time she didn't pretend he was Bull Baron. He was Shelley in her bed.

On Saturday John spent his time at golf. He complained that Seth hadn't done the practice green, and went early to the club. Mira and he had dinner at Tiberio's that night.

The Sunday barbeque was as dull as Mira had expected it would be. Burt Weidemayer and Kit talked real estate, and Burt made the mistake of asking John why he didn't buy a house in Potomac. That was the place to be, the best investment area, too. John said he had no interest in Potomac. His real reason, Mira knew, was his feeling that he wanted to keep a low profile. Armaments was legal, he had told her once, if you kept it legal. But just the same, he didn't want to be known as anything more than a successful accountant.

Dora Weidemayer complained that since she'd opened her law office she'd gained ten pounds because she no longer had time for tennis.

Kit said, "But you're not sorry, are you, Dora?"

Dora laughed. "No, I can diet some other time. It's the getting out every day. The feeling of doing something. And pitting myself against what comes along. Finding out that I'm not an old . . . old . . . " She glanced sideways at Ruth, coughed into her drink, and let the rest of the sentence go.

Mira didn't attempt to cover the lack of tact.

That was the worst part of it, she thought. The proselytizing. They couldn't do whatever it was they wanted to do. They had to make everybody else do the same. As if they felt guilty. She, Mira, couldn't sell real estate. Nor be a lawyer. Didn't they know that?

Donnie spoke softly around a rib. "What do you do when you sneak out, Seth?"

Seth glared at him, didn't answer.

"Can I go with you sometime?"

The reply was swift, fierce, threatening. "You shut up, damn you!"

Kit slid down to the grass beside Seth. "Tsk, tsk, such language." She had heard only Seth's reply. Not Donnie's question.

"The kid bugs me."

"Isn't it time you got laid back about it?"

"He bugs me, that's all."

Donnie's grin blazed across his face. His eyes sparkled. "The trouble with you, Seth, is you don't ever know when I'm kidding. Nobody ever does."

"Like the catsup in the pool?"

"Like that." Donnie sighed. "I guess you wouldn't want to talk to my mom, would you, Aunt Kit?"

"About what?"

"Letting me go back to the club. There's nothing to do around here all day."

"I won't talk to her about that. You deserve to be grounded. But maybe your Uncle Alan will take you fishing one of these days."

"That would be something. The two of us . . . "

Kit, rising, saw that Donnie was looking at his father. She took a patio chair beside him, stretched out her long legs, lifted her face to the blue sky. "Nice, isn't it, John?"

"Yes," he agreed, staring into his gin and tonic.

"Don't you ever get tired of it?"

"Of what?"

"The traveling. Coming. Going. Being away from home so much."

"I've never thought about it."

"Of course you have."

He raised expressionless brown eyes, waited.

"You must have. It's a hard way to live."

"I don't find it hard."

Kit asked gently, "Are you just saying that? Because it's what you do? Because of the money you earn?"

John gave her a quick sharp glance. "That's what you'd like to think, isn't it? I guess women always do. They want to believe that men are dependent on them, their homes. The truth is, I've never in my life done anything I didn't want to do. Not for any reason."

Later, that night, as he lay beside Mira, he heard the words echo back at him. He hadn't touched her. She hadn't turned to him. He was tired, but not sleepy. His body ached. But the ache was from this bed. This house. From Mira. Yet he had come back because he wanted to. He always wanted to return. It was home base even if it meant less and less to him.

There was one thing, though, that he hadn't wanted to do. Once in his life his control had been weak. He had learned that the man he thought he was was a man he was not. It was that single time that had tied him to Bull Baron, would always tie him to the big bald headed man. And through that bond he had learned new ways, new appetites. He was no longer willing to consider giving up what he had become to be the man Mira had married.

Virgie Evans . . . love-making to Beethoven . . . The tall blonde sophisticate who called herself a prostitute because she was one . . . She'd been in Caracas with him.

She waited now in a Baltimore hotel to meet him at Friendship when he left the next morning. Virgie, who had come to him through Bull, and from him. Her slender body having curved to his bulk. Her flesh bruised by his big hands. Her mouth burned with his kisses . . . And now she was John's.

Mira sighed. John held his breath, listening. He didn't wonder if she were dreaming. He didn't care. He turned away from her, tucked his hands between his thighs, and let himself drift. Tomorrow was Monday. Soon. Virgie would be waiting for him in Baltimore. So would Bull.

On the way home that night, Kit described her talk with John.

Alan said, "I think you'd better be careful. This meddling's not going to accomplish anything. And it might make trouble." The warning was as much to himself as to Kit. He'd noticed how aloof Mira seemed. He'd suggested that they have lunch the following week. She'd said she didn't know, was busy. She'd call him. He'd been sure she didn't intend to.

Kit was saying, "But don't you understand? John doesn't travel because he has to. It's because he wants to. It means he doesn't want to be home with Mira and the boys. He doesn't care."

"Maybe it means that," Alan said grudgingly. He, Mira. They'd been friends as well as brother and sister. She'd always leaped at the chance to be with him. There was always plenty to talk about. Or there *had* been.

"It has to mean he doesn't care," Kit said. And that would explain Mira's obvious restlessness, her disinterest. Her downright detachment. All that made Kit so uneasy. Anything could happen when a woman felt that way.

"So what?" Alan was saying. "John does the best he can maybe. It's his life and Mira's."

"And the boys'. And your mother's."

"It's none of your business."

"It is, Alan. I can't help what I see. And besides, what makes you think John does the best he can?"

"And what's that supposed to mean?"

But Kit only shrugged. Her conversation with John had left her wondering about him. Not only that he didn't really care about his family. But that there was something odd about him. And maybe Mira knew it, sensed it. And was acting on it. When anything could happen, one of the anythings was divorce. Where would that leave Ruth? Donnie? Seth? Kit knew more about those problems than she wanted to. More about the pain involved than she wanted to.

Alan's mouth was tight. He frowned through the windshield at the glaring red tail lights of the car ahead of them. He struggled not to say it, but finally the words formed themselves and spoke themselves as if they had been waiting for a long time just at the back of his tongue and would no longer be held back. "If you had enough to think about with your own family, you wouldn't be studying Mira and John so much — "

"It just happened to occur to me . . . ," she began tightly.

"It didn't just happen to occur to you. You've been considering it for weeks at least."

"The boys . . . I told you . . . "

"Donnie and I are going fishing next Saturday. All right?"

"Of course it's all right. Just remember you're not do-ing *me* any favors. You'll have fun with him, too. And I was just trying to help out. Not make you mad."

"I'm not mad. I just don't like this meddling."

"Okay. I won't be interested in your family any more. How's that?"

"Thank you. It might be a good thing."

"And if your mother's miserable, and calls me, then I'll just say I'm busy. So how's that?" Only Kit knew she wouldn't. She wouldn't be able to.

"Damn it, Kit. Are you trying to start a fight?"

"You've already started one," she said acidly.

He slowed for a traffic light, put a hand on her knee, turned to her. "Listen, I'm tired of this conversation. Okay? I want to skip it. Okay? I'm going home with my beautiful wife, and I want to make love, and I don't want to talk about John, or Mira, or their kids, any more, Okay?"

"Sure it's okay," she said, as if it was finished. But she knew it wasn't.

CHAPTER 7.

JIMMY WAS talking with the regulars.

Mira looked sideways at Shelley, spoke in a quiet voice, "I'm going to leave now. I'll meet you at the car."

Shelley nodded, silver eyes bright.

She left three singles on the counter, waved at Jim, the others, and went out. She leaned against the car fender, waiting.

He was only moments behind her. "You didn't have to do that. Nobody cares about us."

Nobody cares. True. What if Jimmy, the regulars, realized that she and Shelley saw each other away from Joe's? It wouldn't matter to them. To anyone. She thought of John, the boys, her mother. They didn't matter either.

She smiled at Shelley. "Let's ride."

"Your car or mine."

"Mine." There was a reason. She wouldn't tell him yet.

He took the keys from her, said, as they got in, "It

happened again. Both of us thinking the same thing, I mean."

"About riding?"

"Yes. It's what I wanted, too."

As they left the parking lot, Mira saw a new sign across the road. House for rent. She thought of Kit. But no. Better not mention it. Kit would be too close to Joe's. Some time, coming or going, she'd see Mira. So Mira realized caution mattered after all.

When they left the suburban traffic behind, she slid close to him His hand settled on her thigh. "You have any special place you want to go to?"

She shook her head.

"Then I'll show you a place I know."

"And we'll stop?"

"If you want to."

The road was unfamiliar. Through half-closed eyes, she watched the long sloping meadows unroll. Young corn in regular stands. The unfurling leaves of soy. Maple groves interspersed with gum trees. A farm house, its fresh-painted white gleaming in the afternoon sun. Fences covered with roses where bees and butterflies hovered. Soon it would all be buried beneath houses, concrete, automobiles. The rolling fields would be flattened, the trees ripped out, corn and soy planted over with weedy sod. Change. Plumtree Road had once slept like this beneath a springtime sun.

But the fields she examined with regret, and even the thought of Plumtree Road, seemed almost a faintly-remembered dream. Reality was the four wheels, the cushioned seat, the glints of sun thrown into her eyes.

Reality was Shelley's hand on her blue-jeaned thigh.

He said softly, "I can remember exactly how it was. The first time I saw you. I wanted to put my hands on you. My fingers twitched and burned. I kept trying to think of what to say. How to get started. To make you look at me. But I couldn't find the right words. You looked so . . . so beyond me. The way you sat. How you held your drink. Your cigarette. Even the way you were dressed. You looked so beyond me."

She smiled at him. "But I knew you were there. I couldn't have been all that far beyond you, could I? Maybe you ought to have tried 'hello.'"

"I was afraid you'd get up and walk away and never come back. Then I wouldn't have seen you again. And I wouldn't have had anything to hope for."

His voice, his words, young, believing, that had become reality for Mira, too.

He slowed, saying, "We're almost there."

The road hooked away ahead of them. At the place where it curved out of sight, water glimmered through tree tops. "My hideaway."

"You really want me to see it? If it's your secret place maybe you'd rather keep it like that."

She had wanted him to tell her he needed to share it with her, wherever, whatever, it was. Her fingers crept to her throat to touch the gold chain. She'd not taken it off since he'd given it to her. When her mother asked about it, she'd said she picked it up one day in Saks Fifth Avenue. It was her secret. She shared it only with him.

But his head jerked back as if he'd been struck. The wheel slipped in his fingers and the car lurched off the road and bumped into a shallow ditch before it stopped.

"Shelley! What's the matter? What did I say?"

He couldn't hear her over the thunder in his ears. *Secret place.* Images flickered and faded within black shadows. A small house . . . Tall redwoods standing guard over it . . . A pickup truck parked in the front yard next to a fallen fence. On the road beyond, his two brothers were rolling a black tire. Bragan. Bennett. Ten-year-old twins. "Just leave you. That's what papa said," they jeered. "Take you into the woods and dump you. Like we did the puppies." He ran screaming to the house. His father threw a beer can at him. He watched it spiral through the air, leaking a silver trail across the dusty wood floor. He tripped and sprawled, still screaming, while his brothers yelled, "Dump you in the secret place." Then his mother was holding him. And from the distance there were curses. Secret place —

"Shelley!"

Mira's fingers were tight around his wrist. He felt the nails dig in. He felt the trembling. He said, "It's all right."

"But what's the matter?"

"Nothing. I just lost control for a minute."

"But if you could have seen your face . . . "

"Sorry. The wheel slipped in my hands. I'll watch it."

"Was it something to do with where we're going?"

But he had recovered. He started the stalled car, grinned. "Of course not. I don't have secrets from you. I don't want to."

"We all have secrets."

"Even you?"

"Of course."

"From me?"

"Not many from you." She paused. "But some."

"I'll allow you some. For the time being."

He slowed at the curve, then pulled off and parked. The ground fell away from the road to a bank of steep rock. The Potomac River was wide, slow-moving at that point.

They took a narrow stony path down the embankment. It ended in a grove of trees. It was shaded and sheltered by a tall rock wall. A cluster of jagged granite dumped there eons ago. The road was lost beyond its dull peaks. Only the occasional hum of a car was a reminder that it was there.

It was as if they had stepped into their own small Eden. The air was warm, scented with earth. Tall ferns rose through dense underbrush. The river murmured below. Then, suddenly, from somewhere she heard the put-put of an outboard motor. A mockingbird sang from the top of an oak tree. A small white butterfly sailed in front of her and ducked and wheeled and flew on.

He led her straight to the rock wall, and then stopped. "I don't think anybody knows about it but me."

She waited, breathless. She felt as if something important was about to happen. Something that would change Shelley, change her.

"And soon you'll know, too." His voice lightened. "You can't see anything, can you?"

"Just the rock."

"But look." He drew her with him, turned her. They went around the base of a boulder. At its landward side, there was a dark crevasse. Sweet damp air flowed from it.

He swung sideways, flattened. She did the same. One step. Two. Silence.

"My cave."

She clung to his hand, unable to answer. He seemed so proud, joyful. It was like a mausoleum to her. She found herself shivering.

But then, he freed himself. She heard him move. Sudden light bloomed yellow, glinting against the dark walls.

His head was bent over the construction lantern. Outlined by a sharp halo. His face was streaked with shadows. When he looked up, grinning, his eyes were as bright as silver coins.

An escape that was all his. A barrier against the world. A nest in which he could hide.

"Thank you for bringing me here," she said.

He put a hand out to her.

The impulse was in her, moving her before she recognized it. She drew away. Her fingers moved at the buttons of her shirt. Smiling at him, dancing away into the shadows, she drew off her clothes. Silently, swooping and turning, swinging low into the lantern light and retreating away into the dark, she pirouetted before him. She was a nymph, floating within the cool shell of the blooming world. She was a willow, bending with a spring breeze.

She was a flame. He got up. His long black shadow fell on the ground before him as he came closer. It fell on her as he took her into his arms.

He kissed her. Long. Slow. His hands tangled in her hair and drew her head back, and he settled his mouth at her throat. Together they sank down to lay entwined in the flicking stillness until he whispered, "This is the way it should be. Only always. Just you and me. Nobody but the two of us."

Later she would wonder if the nymph who had danced in the lantern light had really been Mira Priest. Had she really undressed, danced in throbbing silence to unheard music?

But for now she was lost in his hungry caresses. And glad of it.

Shelley's eyes gleamed when he sat up.

Mira stretched, buttoned her shirt. It was time for her to leave. Soon her mother would be looking first at her wristwatch, then at the door. She would be fidgeting around the kitchen.

It didn't seem to matter. That other world, the people in it, weren't real, Mira thought.

She said, "I forgot the surprise. It's in the trunk of the car. If you're still interested."

"You're not scared to stay here by yourself for a minute?"

"It's your house, isn't it? Then why would I be scared?"

He grinned at her, slipped through the crevasse that led to the outside.

She had thought she wouldn't be afraid, but the moment he was gone, she heard small skitterings. The lantern light seemed to shrink and pale. A mausoleum. Hidden. Underground. A place never touched by sun. She shivered and wished he hadn't left her.

But he was gone only moments. When he returned, carrying the big red-and-blue hamper, she forgot the time alone.

He grinned happily. "You made a picnic for us. How did you know what we'd be doing?"

"I just did," she said.

"You see? It's what I told you. I always know what's in your mind. And you know what's in mine."

There was paté and fresh French bread, a hunk of cheese, a fat tomato, a bottle of wine.

He examined everything, smiled at the plastic knives and forks, at the cocktail napkins. He ate hugely, and fast, while she nibbled a bit of paté, a slice of tomato.

"It's the way it should be," he said when he was done. "You and me. In our home."

She smiled, didn't answer. He had given her an idea. She would cook food for him, bring it to his house. She would buy him a few small things, a broiler, an electric oven, a table cloth and napkins. She would make his basement room more home to him than the cave near the river.

She brushed her hair with her fingers, made up her face.

He watched her silently. Then: "I wish we didn't have to leave. I don't want to go back. I want to keep you here with me. Just the two of us. All the time."

A warning quiver went through her. He mustn't think that way. It was like when he had done the tape. It frightened her. But the trouble was, she felt the same. She didn't want to go back either.

But she managed to say, "It'll wait for us, won't it?"

"It always has before." He bent over the hamper, filled it slowly. He blew out the lantern flame.

They didn't speak until they were back at the car.

Then she said, "Thanks for showing me your hideaway."

"Will you come back with me?"

"You know I will." And she knew she would. If he asked her to. But she wouldn't like the place. Something about it . . . the mausoleum . . . under ground . . .

A short distance beyond the curve there was a woman. She was standing in the middle of the road. She waved thin arms at them. In the white light of the high beams, her face was gray. A pickup truck, its lights off, was parked nose in against a fence.

She ran toward the car, calling, "Listen, can you help me? I need to get my truck started. I've got my little grandson with me." As she called out, she swung back, pulled a small boy from the truck.

From behind her, a man came up out of the shadows. He moved close to the car, peered in at Mira.

His face was bloodied, as if raked by broken glass. His

eyes were dull. His lips were loose, working, though he didn't speak.

Mira gasped, "No, no," not hearing the words, not knowing that she had spoken or what she meant.

The woman said, "That son of a bitch don't have nothing to do with me," and ran to the car.

Shelley's foot came down hard on the accelerator. He spun the wheel. The car danced sideways in a tight curve. It raced past the woman, who staggered back. It shot away from the woman, who screamed after them, "He's got nothing to do with me, I told you . . . "

In an instant the woman, the small boy, and the man were gone.

Later, under the bright lights of Wisconsin Avenue, Mira said in a tired whisper, "We should have stopped for her, Shelley."

"I know."

"Why didn't we?"

"It was dangerous. Mixing into their fight. And you were scared."

"It was because of me then."

"I didn't want you to be scared."

"I didn't matter then."

Shelley winced. Somewhere in his mind a shout echoed . . . "He doesn't matter, goddamn you. I always told you to get rid of him. I knew we couldn't make it. He doesn't matter ahead of all of us . . ."

At last he said, "I don't care about them, Mira. Only about you."

"You've got to care. Everybody's important."

"No." His voice was flat, cold. "Why should I? I don't owe anybody anything. Most people are ghosts, walking around ghosts. They live their whole lives, whatever of them that they get, in some kind of a weird dream.

They think they're real. Because all they know is what they are. And they can't imagine anything else."

"No," she said. "No, Shelley, that's not how it is — "

"I'm describing you."

"Me?" She was indignant, but beginning to wonder. Was her life real? Was she real?

He blunted the sting by reverting to the 'they.' "Most people, they're just the things they believe they own. That actually own them. That's what it comes down to in the end. They're little piles of rusted refrigerators and rotting cars in the great big stinking smoking dump of the world. So why do I owe them? What do I owe them?"

Where did his bitterness come from? He was so young to have learned it. So sweet to have learned it.

She said softly, "You owe kindness, Shelley. And love — "

"Even if they never gave it to me?"

"Those people, that woman, never hurt you. And that man . . . "

"They're just examples. And you're giving me the easy answers. What's on top is what you see. And what you see is the least part. The important thing is the inside. The hidden part."

"No," she said, "you're making life too simple — "

"Why don't you say 'shit'" he demanded. "It's what you mean."

"All right. It's shit."

He laughed at her. "Your lips go funny. And it's just a word, Mira. A true word."

"It's a point of view, too."

"You're getting smarter every minute."

He pulled past Joe's, and stopped behind his VW. "And now you're going to say good-bye, and you'll never turn up again."

"Shelley, what's the *matter* with you? Is that what you want? Is that what you're hoping?"

"Not what I want, nor hope. It's just that I've said too much. Given too much away. Now you know me. You know what I am."

"And is knowing you bad?"

"It's good. But you might not like it."

"I'm afraid I like everything about you," she said softly.

But he shrugged. Then: "What does your husband do to make all his money?"

She was cautious. "He's a salesman." True, but not the whole truth. She preferred not to say the whole truth.

John had something to do with making up the contracts that dealt with the selling of death.

"What does he sell?" Shelley looked straight into her eyes, willing her to answer, daring her not to.

"He works for an armaments company."

"Armaments. Guns. Bullets. Dynamite." Shelley laughed. "So that's what pays for your pretty clothes, and your house and car and wine. That's what makes you."

"Just like everybody else."

She expected him to argue, but he agreed. "Planes. Cars. Death. Drugs. Roads. Name it. Death makers."

"Then do we go back to the jungle? Eat berries. Light fire with flint?"

"We're already in the jungle. The rest is all things. I told you."

"Then what else is there?"

"Only the inside. What we feel. Love. And I don't mean kindness, which is charity. Giving to get back. I don't mean that. I mean love. And the other part of it. Hate."

She drew a deep breath, sighed. "You scare me, Shelley."

"But you believe me."

"Believe in what we feel?"

He waited, then touched her breast. "In what we feel."

CHAPTER 8.

SMALL PINK circles glowed on Ruth Baker's cheeks. Her eyelids were red, swollen. She wove her thin fingers together as she quavered over the roar of the stereo from above, "Thank goodness you're home, Mira. I've been so worried. It's late. And I couldn't think what to do."

"Mother, I'm thirty-five years old. A grown woman. I have two sons . . . " Mira paused, cast an angry glance at the upper hallway. "Seth, turn that down this minute!" The music roared on. Mira said to her mother, "No wonder you couldn't think what to do. All that noise. How long has it been going on?"

"I was too worried to notice. It scares me when you go out to shop and don't come back."

"I am back," Mira said.

"So many things happen. Nothing's the way it used to be. When you listen to the news . . . "

"I know. I know," Mira said. She thought of a man's bloodied face, dull eyes peering into hers . . . a woman's angry cry . . . But she went to the stairs. "I'm going up to see the boys."

"So if you'd tell me where you're going . . . and when to expect you home . . . then I wouldn't worry. But not being able to guess, or even to call you any place . . . " Ruth let her words fade away. It was no use. Mira wasn't even listening. She had trotted up the stairs. What was wrong with the girl these days?

When Ruth heard the first shouted, "Seth! I want you to . . . " She sighed, went into the kitchen. She dialled the telephone, her eyes on the doorway.

"Turn that racket off," Mira was saying. "Or turn it *down*. One of these days you're going to come home and find a bunch of loose wires. I'm going to rip your whole fancy system to pieces if you don't control it — "

"You got a headache, mom?" Seth asked, his voice warm with false sympathy. He hoped she did have one. It would serve her right. Always nagging at him. Everybody knew that the music was best at high volume. That's when the vibes came through.

"*No*, I do not have a headache. But if I did get one, I'd know where it came from." She herself heard the subtle threat, and didn't like it. She changed the subject. "Where's Donnie?"

"I don't know." Seth grinned. "I'm not my brother's keeper."

"Oh, yes you are. At least you ought to be. What do you think family's for?"

"You sound like grandma." Family. What did they mean by family anyhow? Seth hid his disgust. They were phonies. The Priests weren't a family. They just lived together, not knowing each other, not wanting to. And not really that. When had his father lived with them?

Mira had heard herself. Just like her mother, she'd thought. Half her mind listened and winced. The other half had jeered at the cliche. Next she'd say blood was thicker than water. She let it go.

Her eyes lit on a poster hung on the wall. Hitler. The thin ugly face and maniac eyes. The toothbrush mustache. "Where did you get *that* thing?"

"In a place in Georgetown."

"It's disgusting. What that man stands for." She turned away.

"History, mother. That's what it is," Seth called after her with a grin. He'd waited for days for her to see the thing. He'd known she'd wrinkle her nose at it. Not that she really knew or cared what Hitler stood for. The strength. Power. She only knew she was supposed to hate him.

She heard Ruth from the hallway.

"It's all right, Kit. I'm sorry I bothered you and Alan. She just came in a minute ago. No. Nothing's wrong. She's just fine. Went up to talk to the boys. Yes, I am sure. Thank you, Kit. You're so good to me. I don't know what . . . " Again the words faded.

"Go on," Mira said from the threshold. "Don't mind me. Finish your conversation."

But Ruth said, "Good-bye, Kit," and hung up, saying quickly, "It's just that I get so nervous. Whenever you go out . . . "

"You should be used to it by now. And what am I supposed to do? Should I stay in and keep you company all the time?"

"Mira." The reproach was in the name. The pale glimmer of blue eyes, the small embarrassed smile. "Some day, when you're as old as I am, when you're seventy, you'll understand — "

"You shouldn't have called Kit. What was she supposed to do? Get in her car and track me down?"

"Track you down?" Ruth echoed. "What a thing to

say. But when you're driving . . . when you're away so long . . . so many bad things . . . it's not like it used to be."

"Never mind." Mira was tired of it. "It's all right. But why you had to call Kit . . . "

"But who should I turn to if not my children? Who cares if I worry? Who can I ask for help when I know I can't help myself?"

"Kit's not your child," Mira said. "If you'd spoken to Alan . . . "

"I did. First. He just told me to calm down. He's a man. They don't understand. Kit's different. Women always are."

"Alan's grown up to be a very understanding man, mother."

"But he's busy. He has things to do. He works too hard. And taking on the summer session . . . " Ruth was off on another worry now.

Mira let her talk about it, but didn't listen. She made herself a drink. She finished it, excused herself, and went upstairs. She heard Donnie and Seth talking in Seth's room. But didn't go in. Maybe what she'd said to Seth had sunk in. She wouldn't interrupt now.

When she stood before the mirror, she saw two small bruises on her hip. Shelley's fingerprints driven into her flesh. She touched them, smiled.

A dance in Eden . . . kisses by lantern light . . . Shelley.

Mira Priest, Judas Priest. She shook her head.

They walked together, hands clasped so tightly that it felt as if the stream of blood that spilled through her veins passed through hot membranes to course in him.

She didn't know the road. It wound through strange countryside under unfamiliar trees. The sunlight slanted thin and yellow over the horizon. But glittering stars hung over it, as if day and night were one. Shelley spoke. She couldn't understand the words. They were in a strange language, and whispered. When she turned to look up at him, he wore a stranger's face. She stopped, ready to accuse him. Of what she didn't know. At that moment a blue panel truck swept around a hidden curve. It bore down on the two of them for what seemed hours. Then it crashed, splintered bone and flesh and carried them away . . .

She sat up, the sound of the crash still thundering in her ears. Half in the dream, she heard a wail from somewhere in the distance. Reaching for wakefulness, she heard Seth yell, "Donnie."

The dream was gone. She jumped from bed, grabbed her robe.

When she reached the hallway, she heard Seth. "Donnie! What happened?"

Ruth stood at the foot of the steps, white-faced and blue-lipped, her eyes wide as a child's, murmuring, "Oh, oh, oh."

His hair rumpled, dressed in pajamas, Seth ran past Mira. "Donnie fell. I'll see."

Mira went with him.

Donnie lay moaning beside the house. A limb of the big old oak that spread its limbs between his window and Seth's was splintered and broken near him. Tears streaked his cheeks, and his leg showed bloody beneath ripped pants.

Mira leaned down, Seth at her shoulder. "Where does it hurt, Donnie? Tell me."

"Leg?" he groaned. "Everywhere."

She looked. His right leg was scraped raw. It bled from a ladder of small cuts. "What about your back, Donnie?"

"I don't know," he yelled. "I hurt all over. How do I know?"

She told Seth to get the car started. They'd take Donnie to the Suburban Hospital emergency room. At that he stopped moaning. "The hospital?"

"We have to see what you did."

"I didn't do anything — "

"To yourself. We'll talk about the rest later."

They were three hours at the hospital. The emergency room was full. A nurse came and spoke to Donnie, tweaked his toes until he jerked his legs away, took note of Mira's identification and health coverage, then disappeared. Much later he was x-rayed, disinfected, and dismissed.

He limped out to the car, chewing his lip, silent, alternately casting sidelong glances between Mira and Seth.

She said nothing until they were at home. Ruth had made some hot chocolate. She sat at the kitchen table, every light aglow, and greeted them nonchalantly.

Mira told her that Donnie was all right, as she could see. To go to bed and get her rest. Ruth protested that she was fine.

Mira put her arm around her mother's shoulder. "I can only worry about one thing at a time, Mother. Right now it's Donnie's turn. So help me by getting your rest. All this excitement is too much for you."

Ruth allowed herself to be led to her bedroom, tucked in. As Mira turned off the lamp, she asked, "What was Donnie doing, Mira? How could he fall out of the window?"

Back in the kitchen, Mira asked the same question of Donnie.

Seth, listening intently, got to his feet when Donnie said "I was just fooling around."

The dimwit wouldn't say anything. He didn't have to

worry. He muttered a 'goodnight,' and went upstairs. Not that the dimwit could fool Seth Priest. He knew what the score was. The kid had figured he'd climb out, hide. He figured he'd get into the car, and duck down. When Seth drifted out later on, then he'd have company. Seth grinned as he got into bed. From now on he'd remember to check out the back seat before he took off to meet the gang.

"You were just fooling around," Mira said. "And hanging out the window by your toenails?"

Donnie shrugged. "I guess. Something like that."

"That sounds crazy."

He gave her a tentative smile. "I guess maybe it was crazy. But I was just trying to see . . . and the windowsill didn't seem all that narrow."

"You could have been killed," Mira told him. "Or paralyzed."

"You sound just like grandma," Donnie retorted. "Always thinking of catastrophes."

"I am like grandma," Mira answered. "And catastrophe is what sometimes happens."

"But it was nothing. A couple of scratches."

"Why were you fooling around on the windowsill?"

"I told you. I just wanted to see if I could walk it."

"Not a very likely story."

Donnie grinned, yawned. "Would you believe an astral invasion? Some strange being crept into my body while I was in bed and — "

"In bed in your clothes," she said flatly. There was more to it than he was saying. She knew it. He knew that she knew. But she was baffled. He knew that, too.

Donnie's face stretched in a wide innocent yawn. He got up, limped to the door and then came back to press a kiss on Mira's cheek. "I'm sorry, mom. I didn't mean to scare you."

"But you did. And grandma, too. You've got a good head on your shoulders. Maybe you can start using it to keep from cracking it up."

When he had left, she rinsed out the cups and started for her bedroom.

She heard Seth say, "You dimwit, you can't lie to me. I can see through you any time of the week. I know what you were doing."

She paused, but the voices stopped. They didn't start again until she had closed her bedroom door behind her.

Then Seth said, "You were going to spy on me."

"I wasn't. I was just trying to see — "

"You figured you'd follow me."

"Nope, Seth. But it was a good idea. Only not mine. I wouldn't follow you."

"You'd better not, dimwit."

"Were you going out tonight? Are you?"

"None of your business."

"Maybe sometime you'll let me go with you, Seth."

"Maybe," Seth said. "Only now go to sleep."

Mira lay in bed, listening to the stillness.

Donnie was twelve years old. He was too grown up to fall out of the window. She didn't believe that he was foolish enough to have tried to walk the narrow sill in his leather-bottomed shoes. He'd been up to something. He'd tried climbing out on the limb. It had broken under him. So he'd been trying to sneak out of the house. Why?

She was still wondering about it at breakfast the next morning. Donnie was cheerful, his bruises already beginning to fade, the ladder of cuts on his leg scabbing over.

When she tried to speak of his fall, he got up and came to her. He kissed her. "I'm okay, mom."

"I'd still like to know what happened."

His mischievous grin spread across his face. "Would you believe I was sleepwalking?"

"It's a little better than astral invasion. But not much. How come you went to sleep in your clothes? And why'd you sleepwalk out of the window."

"I was reading and just dozed off. That's it."

She waved him to silence. There were sounds from outside. She went to look.

Seth was cleaning up the debris brought down by the fallen limb. The sun glinted in his brown hair. From that angle he looked just like John. John as he had been in his early twenties. But Seth was only seventeen.

Seventeen. Just four years younger than Shelley. Most of the time he seemed a child compared to Shelley. But not now. When he came inside, she thanked him.

He gave her a defensive look. "Somebody had to do it."

"And if it hadn't been you, it would have been me," she said, smiling.

"That dimwit. I can't figure him out. Did he tell you what he was trying to do?"

"I don't know what I was trying to do," Donnie said indignantly. "And don't talk about me as if I'm invisible. I'm sitting right here and listening to you."

Seth shrugged.

Donnie announced that he was going to watch television and went away.

Mira asked what Seth was planning for the day. He grunted that he didn't know. She suggested that maybe he'd like to take Donnie into Georgetown with him. He didn't seem enthusiastic, so she didn't push it.

A long hot soak in the tub relaxed her. Now she was dressed, perfumed. She told herself that the thing was not to make too much of Donnie's adventure. He was a boy, after all. And boys did get into things.

Ruth agreed. "Boys are just different from girls. That's what it is. But he did scare me nearly to death. I remember when you and Alan were young. He was always cut up from something or other."

"He didn't fall out of windows that I remember."

"No. But he fell out of that boat once. Remember when he and your father were fishing on Chesapeake Bay, and how he came back soaked through, and sunburned, and bitten all over by those gooey nettles?"

Mira laughed. "Dad was terribly apologetic. I remember that much. And you got a terrible migraine."

"Is that so? I don't remember *that*."

Ruth, once she had stopped having the headaches, seemed not to know that she'd ever had them. Mira wondered if some day she would be the same.

She stood up, got her purse.

Ruth raised hopeful eyes to her face. "Are you going shopping?"

"I might."

"I could use some underthings."

"I'll take you another day."

Half out of her chair, Ruth allowed herself to sink back. "Oh, all right." Her blue gaze touched Mira's face, then slid away. "Another day will be just fine."

Mira felt relieved when she stepped outside. It was as if she had put the burden of one life behind as she moved forward to another. But why did she think of it that way? She didn't have two lives. She had a family, and a lover. Still, what she felt was different from what she told herself. Shelley was a second life. She was another woman when she was with him.

She was almost to Wilson Lane when the guilt took her over.

Swearing, she turned back.

It was twilight now. The day was almost gone. In the kitchen there was the rattle of pots and pans.

Listening to it, Mira walked restlessly from room to room. Her mother was cleaning up after dinner. They'd had the usual little squabble about who would do what. Mira had given in. She knew her mother had to feel needed.

The lunch together had been strained. Mira, impatient. Ruth, uneasy. She'd hoped for woman to woman talk. She'd led up to it, smiling, "There's a time in every marriage when things go funny." Mira's level glance had warned her off. They'd talked about the weather, the new styles. They'd both been relieved to finish eating, complete the shopping, and return home. Mira told herself to be pleasant for the evening hours.

Seth had gone out, yelling that he'd be back early. The jalopy rattled away before she could ask what he meant by that, and where he was going. She supposed that was all right. He was too grown up to have to account for every minute of his time. She knew how she hated to be questioned about where she was going, what she was going to do. Her mother had never understood that, never would. Maybe Mira herself could try to.

Donnie was watching television. He seemed to have forgotten what had happened the night before. It was lucky he'd broken no bones. Almost a miracle that he hadn't. She remained uneasy about that. It seemed so senseless an accident. She told herself all accidents were senseless. But why was he sneaking out so late? What had he planned to do?

It was a question she didn't pursue. The migraine

came on as suddenly as always. One moment she was thinking uneasily about Donnie. The next a chill went up the back of her neck. Glimmers of light flashed before her eyes. She took her pills, knowing that it was already too late. This was one she wouldn't evade.

Gasping, she fell on the bed.

The pain lasted through twenty-four hours. A full day lost, though as it passed she was unaware of it. She couldn't speak, think, plan. She lay still, waiting for the iron band around her head to loosen. Shivering on the rack of chill. Choking on the moans that rose in her throat.

She knew when her mother bent over her, asked if there was anything she could do.

She knew when Seth turned on the stereo, then quickly lowered the blast of sound to a murmur.

She knew when Donnie limped into the room, looked at her, and then backed away.

But she couldn't acknowledge any of them.

There was no Shelley then. No meetings at Joe's. No rides in a different world. No Eden in a mausoleum.

Time passed slowly. The attack receded gradually. After a cautious wait, she opened her eyes. She turned her head with care. The room was still, the house, too. She rose when she was sure it was all right. Her body was stiff. She felt as if she'd run for miles, straining her leg muscles, stretching her shoulder tendons.

After she showered, dressed, she felt better.

She was suddenly hungry.

Downstairs, her mother fixed her a chicken sandwich, clucked over her.

Mira finished her sandwich. Afterward she wandered into the living room.

When she looked out of the window, she saw Shelley's VW parked on the road at the front of the house.

She asked herself what he was doing? Why he had come here? With the questions, she was on the move. Swiftly, silently, she went upstairs. She caught up her purse.

But the dressing table mirror mocked her. Too pale. Gaunt. She was old. And old was dying. Death. She saw herself in a coffin, hands crossed on her breast, eyes and mouth sealed. Nothingness.

She brushed rouge on her cheeks and saw her eyes brighten. When she colored her lips, they smiled.

Hurrying again, she went down the steps. The sound of the television set in her mother's room covered the small click of the door closing behind Mira.

Halfway down the driveway, she saw Kit's station wagon come down Plumtree Road. Mira slipped into the Impala and pulled out. She swung around the VW, lifted her hand to Shelley, and slowed as she came abreast of the station wagon. As Kit braked, Mira called, "Have to go out for a minute. I'll be right back."

Shelley, behind her now, beeped as if to tell her she was blocking the way.

Kit nodded at her, drove on.

Mira sped away from the house. Shelley followed her. When she stopped on River Road, he parked behind, then came to her.

"What happened?"

She swung the door open, and he got in beside her. She was going to tell him that he must never come to the house. Her life away from him had to be kept separate.

But she was disarmed.

He said accusingly, "You weren't there yesterday. You didn't come today."

"Shelley, I couldn't help that." She didn't want to explain about the headache. It was a disease, a flaw. Something that attacked the old. She said, "I had to stay home."

"Why? What happened?"

"Nothing to do with you."

"I thought all kinds of crazy things."

"I'm sorry. But you shouldn't have come to the house anyway. It's just not a good idea."

"I had to see you, to be sure you were okay." He paused. There was more to it than that. When she left him she seemed to disappear into an unimaginable emptiness. He couldn't picture her, what she did, said. She had to understand. He said, "But I need to know more about you. Your house and kids. Even your husband. I *need* to, Mira."

His intensity frightened her. It so much matched her own. They shared a single-minded need.

But she said, "You know all of me that matters. The rest is unimportant." Her voice was cool, masking her urgency. She wanted to take him into her arms, to hold and comfort him. She wanted to love him.

And it didn't matter that he'd come to Plumtree Road. The kids, her mother . . . they wouldn't notice him sitting in the VW. They were wrapped up in themselves, their own little plans. She, Mira, was just a ghost to them, as they were ghosts to her.

She put her hand on Shelley's knee. "I have to go back now. I'll see you tomorrow."

"Do you promise?" As the words came from his lips, he heard them. His eyes went blank. He was hearing soft voices from deep in his mind. Whispers. A caress. "You won't let him, will you, mama?" "No, my darling, I promise."

Mira leaned to him, pressed her mouth to his lips. "I'll be at Joe's. I promise."

His arms went around her, folded her tightly to his

pounding chest. The voices whispered on . . . "Can you stop him, mama?" And: "Nobody's going to throw my baby away." His arms tightened even more.

She said, "Shel, it's time for me to leave."

"No. *Stay.* Don't you know how it is? I don't have anybody. Just you. And you . . . you have all of them. I wish . . . I wish a tornado would come and smash your house, and smash them all. So you'd have nobody left but me."

"Shelley, no. You don't mean that. It's only until tomorrow."

"Maybe it won't come. Do you ever think of that? Maybe there won't be a tomorrow. For us — "

"There will be."

Slowly, he allowed his arms to loosen. But she didn't move. She lay against him. Warm. Soft. All he wanted, needed. Tomorrow.

CHAPTER 9.

E HAD been waiting more than half an hour when she walked into Joe's. He thought that he'd made a bad mistake when he'd gone to her house. Maybe she wouldn't want to have anything more to do with him. Maybe he'd lost her. He wished he'd waited longer, given her more time, given himself more time so the bonds between them were stronger. He wasn't sure why, but it was important that she be as dependent on him as he was on her.

She ordered her drink from Jimmy, nodded at the regulars, before she turned to smile at him.

Immediately he forgot his dismal thoughts.

"You came," he said softly.

"I told you."

Richard was morose about the Iranian situation. "We can't win. No way. No how. They got the oil. And us. And that's the fact."

Gus, the retired Navy man, peered at the bottom of his glass, then jerked his head at it.

Jimmy understood, served him.

They weren't paying attention to her, to Shelley. They never did.

She said, "I'll finish up and leave first."

He nodded.

She had worked it out after Kit had finally left. The twenty minute visit had seemed to go on for hours. Mira's explanation of why she'd raced out, that she'd suddenly needed fresh air, seemed lame even to her. Her mother had gone on and on about the migraine that had kept Mira out of commission and nearly unconscious for a whole day.

Kit said, "That's why I came over. I thought maybe there was something I could do."

"There was nothing. But thank you. And I'm over it now. Just a little tired, shaky." Mira was aware of Kit's sharp studying glance. She tried to cover her impatience. She wanted to be alone. To think. To allow her hunger for Shelley to run through her. To remember his arms tightening around her so that she couldn't breathe. To savor his need for her.

At last Kit left. Mira went upstairs. Finally alone. Seth was playing an old Frank Sinatra tape. Donnie was watching television with her mother. And John . . . John was in Tangiers with Bull Baron.

Mira filled the tub, sank into the scented bubbly warmth. Sweet steam arose in a cloud. She breathed it deeply.

In slow dreamy motions she soaped her body. Breasts sensitive even to the touch of her own fingers. Thighs quivering suddenly. Shelley needed her. She needed Shelley. To be whole they had to be together. Nothing else mattered . . .

Jimmy interrupted her thoughts to ask if she wanted another drink.

She told him that she didn't, added that she was in a

hurry. With a sideways glance at Shelley. She paid, left the bar in a swirl of skirts.

She waited through a toe-tapping ten minutes until Shelley followed after her. Breathless, she whispered, "The cave, Shelley?"

He took the keys from her. "You're sure?"

"You know I am."

He smiled at her, hugged her to him. "Okay then."

He drove slowly, an arm around her shoulder. She wanted him to hurry. She wanted him to be as eager as she was. But she didn't tell him so. She made herself wait.

There was plenty of time. The whole of the afternoon. All of the evening. She had told her mother that she was going to shop in the Washington Garfinkle's. She'd have lunch. She'd have dinner with Marye Morris, an old friend from school. The lie didn't matter because Marye wouldn't phone. She and Mira had been out of touch for years. Afterward, Mira had told her mother, the two of them might stop to see Mark Russell at the Marquee Lounge. So Mira would be late getting home. She had told Seth to be in by midnight. Donnie was going to sleep over with a friend. Everything was taken care of. All burdens set aside. So there was plenty of time.

But when Shelley parked off the road at the embankment, she hurried ahead of him down the slope and into the shade of the grove. Escape. That was what she was thinking. Escape from one world into another.

The river shone through the trees. Two gulls rose overhead, complaining about the intrusion.

Shelley paused to watch them become dark distant specks on the horizon. Then he went first into the cave.

She followed him, sun-blinded into the shadow. A shiver danced along her spine. The mausoleum. No, she told herself. Eden. He smiled at her, and opened his arms.

They kissed, paused to breathe, and kissed again. The sweetness of his smile was in her mouth with his tongue, filling her. When he let her go, the shiver danced over her again. But only for a moment. He unzipped her skirt, and unhooked her bra, and drew her panties off. Carefully, he folded her clothing, put it aside. He stood before her, smiling into her eyes, as she undressed him. When he was nude his flesh took on a glow. But shade touched it in some places. The small scars on his shoulder, the long jagged scar across his back seemed to disappear.

They fell together on the blanket, his mouth at her breast until she could bear no more, and moaned, "Wait, Shel."

Then he rose over her, smiling still. He lay his weight on her. She took him in, into her flesh. He was hers.

He had put on his trousers to go out to the car for the hamper. But when he returned with it, she still lay nude on the blanket. The lantern light sparkled in her eyes as she looked up at him.

He set the hamper down, said, "I was thinking, on the way back, that maybe you wouldn't be here."

She sat up to put out the food, asking, "But where would I have gone?"

"I know it doesn't make sense. It was just a feeling. Suppose I just dreamed you? Suppose you and me, the whole thing, was something I imagined."

"It isn't, Shelley."

"No," he agreed. But he wondered. How could he tell? His head was full of memories that weren't really memories. Maybe Mira Priest was one more of them. Maybe the grove and the cave and the locket at her throat were all just bits of the filmy detail surrounding the big question marks that reached to him from a foggy past. There was no way to know. He dismissed his uncertainties the way he always had. Deal with the here and now. Don't worry over yesterday. Don't try to figure out tomorrow.

There was roast beef. Sour pickles. Cole slaw and potato salad. Mira put out paper plates and napkins, and frowned because she had forgotten to bring a knife to cut the sour rye bread.

He pulled out a switchblade. It clicked when he opened it. Light caught on its narrow dangerous edge, flickering at her like tiny flames.

"Handy," she said. And: "You carry that with you all the time?" But she was thinking that she'd never known he had a knife. So much she didn't know of him. So much still to learn.

"You never know when you'll need one," he told her. But it felt wrong to him. The weight. The heft. Some time it had been different. He tried to remember. When he raised his eyes to her they were blank, empty, the color of tarnished silver.

"What?" she asked quickly. "What is it?"

His eyes cleared as he looked at her. The small face, surrounded now by disordered black curls. The hazel eyes shining. The pink-tipped breasts. "Nothing. Except I'm glad I know you." He bent his head to slice the bread.

When they had eaten, she lay back and laughed. "I feel good. Like a pagan baby. No worries. No rules." She gazed at the low rock that hung over them. "This is ours. Our house. Yours and mine."

"Just the two of us," he said moving closer. "In our own world."

"We'll make it good. Comfortable. I'll bring pillows,

and a down quilt for a mattress. And some candles and incense. We can get a small gasoline stove and I'll cook for you." She laughed again. "What's your favorite food?"

"Pot roast." But his voice was quiet, without enthusiasm. The cave was special. But not a home. He didn't want to furnish it with candles and camp mattresses.

She pretended not to notice. "Your favorite dessert, Shelley?"

"Apple pie."

"Do you like salad?"

"Rabbit food! What do you think?"

"I think it's good for you. It'll make you grow."

"I've grown enough," he said. "I don't want to grow any more." He grabbed his shirt, put it on.

She watched him, then asked, "What's wrong?"

He didn't answer her.

"Okay then. No salad."

Echoes. "It's good for you. It'll make you grow big and tall, like your father." He didn't want to be like his father. He hated him . . .

"Shelley! What did I say?" Mira. Her hand on his shoulder.

He hugged her to him. "I love you."

It was dark when they left the cave, but she still had time.

He drove slowly, the headlights cutting a white tunnel through the shadows before them. "We could be anybody, going anywhere."

"Yes," she agreed.

"We could be on a trip. The two of us. Can you imagine what fun we'd have?"

"We'd drive South in the winter. North in the summer."

"West, Mira. Across the Mississippi."

"You'd show me all the towns you've been in."

"Some time I will," he told her seriously. "We'll do it together."

She slid close, leaned her head on his shoulder. Together. The car was their world. Nothing existed except the two of them, floating through the dark. She was startled when he slowed, chuckling.

"What, Shel?"

"You'll see." He spun the car in a sharp turn. Their headlights went off. The sky was aswarm with stars. A moon hung over the black fringes of oaks.

The car bumped off the road into a drive. There was the glint of light on a chrome bumper ahead.

"Somebody's there," she whispered. "Let's go on."

His grin flashed. "Take a good look."

It was a hatchback. It was filled with moonlight. A couple lay in it. The girl had her dress around her hips. The man's pants were down. They looked like some strange beast struggling to be born.

Her eyes widened. She stared as if hypnotized. Rejecting. Accepting. Amused. Horrified.

Shelley gasped, "No, no." He slammed his hand on the horn at the same time that his foot hit the accelerator. The car seemed to leap ahead on an explosion of blaring night-shattering sound.

There was a scream. A curse.

The hatchback was gone. The swarming stars and low moon disappeared. They were back on MacArthur Boulevard, and heading sedately for Bethesda.

"You scared the life out of me," she said.

"Them, too."

"But why did you do it?"

"Because."

"I'd hate it if somebody did that to me, to us."

He laughed, pulled her close. "Let's stop at the house for a little while."

She wanted to say she couldn't. Suddenly a Shelley she didn't recognize had appeared on his face. But the strange-looking beast had excited her. The sudden blasting of the horn. The urgency had renewed itself. She was back in their world, Shelley's world, and hers, having briefly been out of it. She wasn't ready yet. She nodded, whispered, "Yes. Let's."

When he parked near the house, she saw a glimmer of white from across the street. She looked back at it as she followed him from the car. A sign, "For Sale by Owner . . ."

She thought of Kit, who spent hours driving the roads for likely houses. This would be one. But Mira wouldn't tell Kit about it. She'd not want Kit to know this street.

The basement room was still, dim.

Shelley gathered her to him.

They lay on the couch, legs entwined, hearts pounding together.

"This is our home," he said. "Someday we'll make it pretty. As pretty as you want. We'll have so much money that we'll put rugs on the floor, and drapes at the windows. We'll have a color television set, and a hot pool."

She had thought of that herself before, even planned what she would buy. She had spoken of bringing a few small comforts to the cave. To Eden. To her, the cave seemed right. Not to him. She wondered why.

"It would be real," he said after a little while. "If you didn't have all the others. It could be real, if there was only us."

She pressed close to him, didn't answer. She wished he hadn't said that. It forced her to remember.

"It *should* be real. That's how it was meant to be. That's why we met in Joe's, and you asked me about my tattoo. And why I wanted you as soon as I saw you. Because it was meant to be."

"If only it had happened before . . . before . . . " She heard her words, and wondered at what she was saying. If only it had happened before what? Before she married John? That was when Shelley was four years old. Before she'd had Seth? That was when Shelley was four years old, too. Burning tears rose in her eyes, spilled down her cheeks.

Shelley said softly, "I didn't mean to make you cry. I don't want to see you cry. There's no reason. We're together now, aren't we?"

"We're together," she answered. That was all that mattered.

He pulled her down so that his head could fit into her shoulder. He breathed softly on her throat, touched the locket he had given her with his lips. Finally he said, "I know what we need. Some gold, Mira. To go with this." He touched the chain from which the locket hung. "Something for me. To go with us."

"Shelley, no," she protested. "I can't do it again."

"Yes," he said. "Yes, you can. You'll see."

CHAPTER 10.

KIT RUBBED her eyes and blinked and yawned. An end of June thunderstorm was building out of the coals of a long day's heat. That was enough to have tired her.

But there had also been the Treblings' settlement. The sale had gone through as planned. She'd have her commission in a few days now. If there'd been anything wrong, she hadn't discovered it, although she had been more than usually careful because of her suspicions. The Treblings were, she decided, simply nervous people. They worried about big items and small, and their tensions had spread from them to her.

She hardly had the right to criticize them. She was just as bad. It was no short detour to go to see her mother-in-law. Yet a vast uneasiness drove her. Something was wrong. Ruth Baker had sounded so quiet on the telephone. No small chit chat. No little stories. No complaints about the boys.

Kit told herself she didn't want to know. What happened at the Priest household was none of her business. Alan would say the same.

But if there was trouble then who would help except family? John was away. The boys were still just boys. And Mira . . . what was it about Mira that bothered Kit so much? Surely she was just as she had always been. Except, and this was what Kit wasn't sure of, there were moments when she had the feeling that Mira was a sleep walker. Aware, but not aware. Moving, but not attending. Aglow, but with a certain vagueness around the eyes. . . .

At Bradley Boulevard Kit turned left on the green arrow. She drove a few blocks, recognized a narrow tree-shaded road that would take her the back way to Wilson Lane. She swung into it. A block on, she made another turn. She slowed when she saw the 'For Sale' sign in front of a house midway on the block. Owner offering. It was a good area. And lots of older people getting ready to move out. She stopped the car, made a note of the phone number and house address.

She was about to continue on her way when she heard the tap of heels, the soft laughter. Too familiar to ignore.

She waited only long enough to see the man, the woman, who approached a car across the street. A maroon Impala. Then, wishing she hadn't stayed, she drove quickly away.

Mira. With someone. That someone a man. But a man so young that at first Kit had thought it might be Seth. It hadn't been Seth. This man was taller, thinner. And this man, for all his youth, had a look of maturity about him. But not enough maturity for Mira. Only the difference in age wasn't what mattered. What was Mira doing with some strange guy? Who was he? What was he to Mira? Did he explain the absent look in her eyes, the glow in her face?

Kit wished she hadn't seen the two of them together. She knew she could be wrong. There might be any number of innocent explanations. But she felt that her uneasy suspicions were confirmed. She'd worried all along that Mira might be getting involved with someone. In a way, it served John right for putting his damned guns ahead of his family. But what about the boys, Ruth?

When Kit reached the Priest house, she found Ruth Baker standing on the door step. Her blue eyes were as big as a frightened child's. But she smiled, rose on tiptoe to kiss Kit.

"Why are you out here in the heat?" Kit asked.

"I was looking." Ruth didn't say for whom. Or why. She didn't have to.

Kit knew. For Mira. Because she'd been out so long, hadn't called. Don't waste your time, Kit thought. Mira won't be home for a while. She won't phone. She's busy. She can't be bothered with you, with her family. Kit fought down sudden bitterness. Mira had everything, and everything apparently wasn't enough. But when a woman has everything she doesn't go looking. So she didn't have what she needed. It was as simple as that. Kit remembered that she'd thought there was something funny about John. Not just that he cared more about making money than his family. But something even stronger. An empty space in his feelings. Whatever Mira did, she must have her reasons.

"You can stay a little while, can't you?" Ruth asked anxiously.

"Sure." Alan would be waiting. It would probably mean another fight, but that couldn't be helped. Ruth needed Kit now and Kit couldn't turn her back and leave her. And as for Alan waiting . . . It was just as well that she didn't see him right away. She had to think. What about Mira and the boy? Should she tell Alan? He ought to know maybe. But what good would it do? How would it matter? Except to maybe turn him against Mira. No. That wasn't what Kit wanted. She wanted to help Mira some way. Was there a way? Kit asked aloud, "The boys around?"

Going inside, she knew the answer. Seth's stereo was silent. He was out. Donnie came tumbling down the stairs to greet her with a huge hug and multiple pats on the back.

"Hi, Aunt Kit, what's up?"

It surprised her that he was so demonstrative. Usually he wasn't. She dismissed the suspicion that he was up to something. Maybe he, too, had a feeling about Mira. Maybe he was uneasy without knowing. She remembered how it had been for her. Watching her parents' nothing marriage collapse. Always scared. Always wondering, waiting . . . .

Ruth got out the cards, and Donnie and Kit settled down to gin rummy with her.

Kit saw that Ruth continually stared at the kitchen clock on the wall. It made her impatient. She knew it would be a while before Mira came home.

But pity finally made her say, "Don't worry, Mother Ruth. Mira can take care of herself."

"Of course," Ruth agreed brightly. But her eyes remained frightened.

She felt threatened. She didn't understand why. Her home, her place in life, were endangered. But the threat was unidentifiable. She recognized it, without knowing its name. She wasn't sure she wanted to. When a car pulled into the driveway, she jumped to her feet.

"It's Seth," Kit told her. "That jalopy sometimes sounds like a bomb going off."

Seth, with four of his long-legged friends, came piling in. Briefly, the kitchen was filled with noise as Seth collected six-packs of Cokes, a huge bag of potato chips, and led his troop into the family room. Donnie followed after, but was shouted back.

Face sagging, he slumped in his chair.

Ruth brightly suggested another game. He shook his head. "Gin rummy. Ugh!" Then, glumly: "But I'll bet I know what they're talking about."

Nobody took him up on it, so he let it go.

When Kit got up to leave, Ruth said, "Your blouse, Kit. What on earth! You've got black fingerprints all over your back."

Donnie choked on a smothered giggle.

Both women looked at him.

He grinned at Kit.

"Very funny," she said. "Just hope that it washes out, my boy."

"It will. Charcoal always does, doesn't it?"

So much for a twelve-year-old's affection, Kit thought, as she started home.

But she was more sympathetic than angry. Donnie and his never ending pranks . . . He had to make himself known. He and Seth weren't close. Seth was close to no one. Except maybe the boys he had brought home with him that evening. And she wondered about that, too.

She took the Beltway, remembering how she'd once feared driving it. The high speeds. Flashing lights. Cars and trucks swerving from lane to lane. Now she took it for granted, the same way she took for granted sitting alone in an empty house, waiting for strangers to appear. It bothered Alan. He thought that something could happen. Those girls in Northern Virginia murdered in the trailer office of that real estate development . . . The hold-up of the woman showing a house in Vienna . . . Kit was vulnerable, Alan said. But she didn't feel that way. A woman took her chances just like a man. It didn't make any difference any more.

She cut into the exit lane on a sharp swerve, thinking again of Mira. What was Mira doing? Was boredom pushing her? Did she miss John, a more routine marriage, so much? Kit couldn't try to imagine trying to live Mira's life. But they came out of different times, Kit knew. The fifteen years between them could have been a century in attitudes. Kit couldn't live the way Mira did. Mira couldn't live the way Kit did.

She wondered if she were being unfair to Mira. Maybe leaping to a conclusion that was wrong. Could Mira have had some business with the young dark-haired man? Okay. What business? Could she have been visiting a friend? And he was the friend's son. Walking her back to the car? Kit heard again Mira's soft laughter. No. It hadn't been that. It had been exactly what Kit had first thought, and nothing else. And she'd be silly if she tried to persuade herself otherwise.

She parked in the back lot, hurried up the stairs. Alan would be wondering. But the apartment was dark, still. She stood in the doorway, called his name.

No answer. A peculiar emptiness. Tears suddenly burned her eyes. Her hand trembled when she turned on the lamp.

The table was set for one. A note leaned against the blue coffee cup. *Dinner on stove. I went to the movies. Back eleven-thirty or so.*

She remembered then. Woody Allen at the *Langley*. She'd told Alan she'd go with him. He hadn't waited for her. What if she were two hours late? She'd been visiting his mother, his nephews. Before that she'd been working.

She put the beef stew away. She heated coffee, drank it standing up.

He should have waited. He should have wanted to know how the Trebling settlement had gone, and if it had gone. He should have wondered why she had been delayed.

And more than anything, he should have been there when she needed him. Not that she'd have told him about seeing Mira. She couldn't. It would do no good, and would only upset him, make him angry even. But she'd needed the reassurance of having him waiting. She'd needed to know at least that he was what he seemed. Solid, steady Alan. Her husband, who loved her. And he hadn't bothered to wait for her.

Anger carried her swiftly through her night time chores. She listed her stops for the following morning. She rinsed her shirt in Woolite, relieved to see that Donnie had been right. The charcoal fingerprints disappeared. But she still remembered the feeling of his arms around her neck. If Donnie were her son . . . she stopped the thought. He wasn't. She didn't want a son. Certainly not now. She brushed her hair, did her nails, and went to bed.

But she was still awake when Alan came home.

He walked quietly into the bedroom.

She didn't speak.

"Kit?"

"I'm awake," she said, her voice cold.

"How did the settlement go?"

She was glad that he asked, even if it was too late. "Okay."

"So you were worried about the Treblings for nothing."

"This time."

"Maybe you always worry for nothing."

He'd insisted she'd imagined that something was wrong with Mira. Only it hadn't been imagination. There had been, still was, something to be uneasy about. Mira was having an affair, risking everything. Kit switched on the lamp so that Alan could see her glare at him. "You certainly don't worry too much. You don't even care what I'm doing. Or where I am. Or why I'm late getting home."

"I knew where you were. At Mira's. My mother called. She wanted to tell me you were on the way."

"Then why didn't you wait for me?"

"I was angry. That's why."

Kit turned her back on him, burrowed into the pillow. She listened to his movements. His shirt whispered as he took it off. His shoes thumped on the floor. The change in his trousers pocket rattled when he put them away. The lamp clicked. The mattress shifted under his weight.

"I gather you don't want to know why I was angry," he said into the darkness.

"No."

He was quiet for a little while. Then: "I wanted you to come home to me."

"Jealous of your own mother?"

"It's not my mother you go to see. Even if you believe it yourself. It's Mira. The Priests."

"You're out of your mind!" There was more on the tip of her tongue. Mira and the dark-haired man who was young enough to be her son. Ruth's uneasiness that meant something. Donnie's pranks that meant something, too. And what about Seth's closed, expressionless face? She bit it all back. It would only give him more ammunition. He was wrong but he'd never admit it.

"I maybe am out of my mind. But it's what I think."

"Then think again. It's family. I'm concerned about your mother. *Your* mother." That was all she planned to say. But the rest came out, "*Your* sister. *Your* nephews."

If he'd asked, she might have told him, shamed at exposing Mira, hating herself even, but too angry to stop. But he only said, "You're worrying about nothing."

"Did you ever get to have lunch with Mira?" It was as much as Kit allowed herself.

He looked uncomfortable, thinking of how Mira had evaded him. At last he admitted, "She's been too busy, I guess. We'll do it one of these days."

"Busy doing what?"

"The usual. Shopping. The house."

Kit folded her lips firmly, said nothing.

"Oh, I know she wastes a lot of time. But so what? She's got plenty to waste. She's got a husband who can give her everything. She doesn't have to get out early and dig for worms like a robin."

"But I *like* working," Kit said, goaded into answering him. "I wouldn't stay home if I could."

"If we had a kid . . . "

"Alan!"

"Sorry. I know you don't want to talk about that."

She was glad it was dark now. He couldn't see the expression on her face. The 'I know something you don't know' look that she was sure must be printed there.

She said, "It's off the subject anyway."

"The subject being my sister."

"No," Kit said, very determined now. "The subject being that I'm a worrier and you're not."

He yawned. "I don't believe there's any more to say about that. Would you like me to tell you about the movie?"

"Was it funny?"

"It would have been funnier if you were with me."

"Sorry."

"At least I'd have laughed, if you were with me," he went on.

"You could have waited."

"You could have come straight home," he countered. Then: "But to hell with that," and reaching for her . . . "Let's cut the chatter and make love."

The phone was ringing when she walked into the office. She knew, even before she picked it up, that it would be for her. That it would be her mother-in-law.

Ruth said, "Kit, we just had a call. John's coming home this weekend. Can you and Alan come for dinner Sunday night?"

Kit said she'd let Ruth know, a smile warming her voice. Her mother-in-law sounded like an excited teenager. "Everything all right?"

"Fine. Just fine."

Kit put down the phone still hearing the echo of Ruth's words. Fine. Just fine. Kit knew in her bones that her mother-in-law was wrong.

When she told Alan about the invitation that night, he shook his head. "I want to go out to Ocean City for the weekend. It'll do us both good."

They were both pretending that they hadn't just managed to avoid a really serious fight. They'd stopped talking just in time to make love. After that, they'd let the quarrel go. But Kit wondered how often they could resort to that. So she kept her voice light when she said, "I thought maybe we could go to Ocean City some other weekend. After all John's home so rarely."

"We can see him next trip."

"Your mother will be disappointed." Kit's voice was still light, but now it held an edge of insistence.

"If John's around, she won't even know we're not there."

"Alan," she said slowly. "Alan, you sound jealous of him.

Alan grinned at her. "No. I'm grateful to him. After all, he took my mother in after my dad died. He's been good to her. But I don't feel obliged to drop my plans to fit with his comings and goings. We have *separate* lives, although you don't seem to think so, and I intend to live mine."

"No matter what?"

"That's right. No matter what." He put his arms around her. "Don't misunderstand me. I'm glad you care about my family, I just want you to care about me more."

Neither of them mentioned Mira.

CHAPTER 11.

THE ITEM was a small one, but it was on the front page of the Washington *Post* Metro section.

Reading it, Seth smiled. Fourteen gravestones had been vandalized in the cemetery off Riggs Road. Jew gravestones. He could still hear the deep growls of the German shepherds until they were decoyed away by the hunks of bleeding beef Mickey had thrown them. He could hear the satisfying crash of marble toppling off the crowbar. They'd planned on a bonfire, too. But a car had drifted along the road. They'd gotten out. The five of them. Punching each others' arms as they scrambled into the jalopy. The White Knights strike again. Sixteen thousand dollars worth of damage.

He laughed aloud. Sixteen thou wasn't peanuts. And nobody knew. He guessed that was what tickled him so much. Nobody knew about his secret life. But there he was, in the paper. Talked about. Important. Seth Priest, the White Knight.

Donnie peered at him over a bowl of corn flakes. "What's so funny?"

"Nothing," Seth answered.

"Then why are you laughing?"

"Because I want to, knothead."

"Crazy people laugh for nothing. And you're not crazy. Or are you?"

"*I* don't think so," Seth said.

"How can anybody tell though?"

Seth groaned. "Knock off the questions, if you don't mind."

For a moment, Donnie was quiet. Then: "What're you doing today?"

"The usual. Just hanging around." Seth didn't ask about Donnie's plans.

But the younger boy said, "Me, too. Unless I can go to the pool. The thirty days are up. Have been for a while."

Seth shoved the newspaper away, rose. He knew that Donnie was hinting. When Seth didn't take the hint, then Donnie would ask right out if he could tag along with Seth, or if Seth would go to the club with him. But Seth would say no to either. He didn't plan to kill time with Donnie. Seth was going on a scouting expedition with the White Knights. They'd cruise the neighborhood looking for houses where blacks lived. They'd hit the Jews the night before. It was the blacks' turn next. They'd drive the cops crazy.

He was at the door when Donnie did just what Seth knew he would do. He asked, "Can I hang around with you? Or can you come to the club with me?"

Seth growled a refusal and made his escape. He didn't want Donnie in on it. Twelve was too young to be trusted. He trusted no one in this world except for Mickey, and Bix, and Jim and Hark. The White

Knights. Besides, if anything ever happened, there'd be trouble. He didn't want Donnie in on that.

He decided he'd buy a *Post* somewhere, cut out the article and save it. There'd been two other stories in the past weeks. He wondered how he could get hold of the old papers. He wanted to start a scrapbook. His secret scrapbook. Then he and his gang could read over what they'd done and remember how it had been. He wondered why he hadn't thought of it before.

Peering into the mirror, he combed his hair. His face reminded him of his father. People said he didn't look like him really. But Seth thought he did. The same brown eyes. The same short, smooth sandy hair and narrow mouth over narrow chin. But that was only outside. Seth wondered about the inside. Was his father's secret life anything like the one Seth imagined? Did he get the biggest high of all from leaving his sign to frighten whoever found it?

Seth chuckled. He was beginning to see how he'd fooled himself ever since he was a kid. He'd pretended his father was something special. But now he understood. John Priest wasn't anything. He wouldn't know about highs. He was too old. He'd think the only rush there was was what he'd read in the papers about pot or heroin. And who needed that? Only people without imagination. Seth had something better. Besides, all John Priest cared about was his money, his golf game and his country club. There was more to living than that. If he only knew.

Seth went downstairs. As he passed the kitchen door, Mira called to him. But he pretended not to have heard her, got into his jalopy and drove away as fast as he could.

She frowned at the sound of the slamming door, the

roar of the jalopy. That Seth . . . but her irritation was only momentary.

John would be coming home. She had to do a full shopping for the weekend. She had to call the Hartleys to see if they'd be available one night. She had to drop Donnie off at the club.

She didn't want to do any of that. The sun was bright. A faint breeze ruffled the trees beyond the window. She wanted to ride. With Shelley. In their own small world. She wanted to ride until there was nothing left in her of Plumtree Road, or this house.

A small shiver moved along her spine. There was something else, too. She'd promised Shelley. Today was the day. Gold.

Now she wished she hadn't agreed. There was a tiny itch of fear in the pit of her belly. Suppose she was caught? It would spoil everything. Today was the day, but she wouldn't think about it. She reached for the newspaper, flipped the pages slowly, looking for the grocery ads. She didn't notice the small article about vandalism at the Riggs Road Cemetery.

It was near closing time, but the store was still very crowded. There weren't enough salespeople to handle the impatient shoppers.

Twice Mira had turned back, gone outside. Hands wet with the sweat of fear. A curious drum of warning between her shoulder blades. She'd gotten away with it before. But what about this time? And why? Why should she steal for Shelley? It didn't make sense. But she'd promised him. And it didn't matter really. The stores were insured after all. So many people did it. How could it matter if one small charm was slipped away? Twice she forced herself to return to the shop.

Now she stood fourth in line at the jewelry counter.

She tapped her foot, sighed loudly, fumbled with her purse. But that was pretense only. She had deliberately chosen the place and time, hoping for just such a situation.

The woman in front of her complained in a strident voice that she didn't know what the world was coming to. You had to stand in line to buy gas. You had to stand in line to buy a birthday present. Pretty soon you'd have to stand in line to buy your coffin. The girl behind Mira giggled. Mira ignored them both to study the counter from the corner of her eyes. Beneath the bright glass she saw a tree shaped rack of gold charms. There was a quivering in her knees, and her thighs tightened, almost as if Shelley were sliding his hard hot fingers between them. She was scared, but she wasn't going to turn back again. She couldn't. She knew Shelley was somewhere close by. She could sense his presence. She had to do it for him.

There was a surge, a grumble. The line shifted forward, re-grouped.

Mira and the girl behind her reached the counter at the same time. The saleswoman tried to divide her attention between them.

Both wanted gold charms. They turned the rack slowly.

The girl was attracted to a small replica of the Capitol building. Mira admired it, murmured that it had a good shape, her voice steady but hoarse. While the girl wrote a travelers' check, Mira turned away, saying, "I think I'll see what they have in stick pins."

Within the palm of her hand there was a small gold VW.

Relieved, all fear gone, she felt as if she were sailing as she left the shop. She had done it. And safely. Perfect for Shelley. And he was near. She could *feel* him.

But she waited for a full ten minutes at the curb, tapping her foot, staring up and down the busy street.

Then he drove up, pushed the door open. Mission accomplished, he thought. He could tell. The flush of her cheeks. The sparkle in her eyes. She'd been scared, he was sure of that. But she'd made herself do it. For him. It was a special feeling. For him. Because of him. To please him. About time.

She slid in, slammed the door. As he pulled away, she opened her hand. It was no longer shaking. "Look, Shelley."

He grinned down at the small gold VW.

"Okay?"

He nodded.

"I'm glad it's over."

"Were you scared? Really scared?"

She could play it down now. "I guess so. A little."

"Guess so? A little?"

"I was too busy thinking how to do it. No time to wonder what might happen." But she had. And she'd sweated and shivered and made herself do it anyway.

"You're getting to be an old pro."

Old. She shot a quick glance at him. Had he meant anything? No. She was too sensitized to the word. His face was joyful. He was pleased. With her. With himself. He looked at her and their eyes met.

"Let's ride," she said. "Anywhere you want. Just to go."

"We will."

They circled the outskirts of the city, going east to west in their own little world. They were insulated against the past and the present. They were together, just the two of them, with no reality except what they made between them.

There was a coursing in her blood. It was like being

148

young again. It *was* being young again. Except that then she hadn't felt this.

They stopped at a McDonald's, had thick hamburgers with melted cheese, two orders of French fries, and milk shakes. Her white skirt had a catsup stain on it when they squeezed out of the tiny booth. She thought of Donnie, closed her mind, and paused to wash away the red mark before they left.

Driving again. Twilight falling. The giant oaks black against the lavender sky. River Road. Headlights like spilling diamonds along the dark cement.

Guilt and time began to press her. She fought as long as she could. At last she said, "I ought to go home."

"Not yet. It's too early."

"I have things to do." She didn't say what things. She didn't mention John.

"We both have," Shelley said.

"You mean together."

"What do you think?"

But she was silent, waiting, hoping. She wanted him. It was a constant, but the adventure had sharpened it.

"Go on," he urged. "Say it, Mira."

"Shall we go to the cave?"

"That's not what you're thinking."

"I want to make love, Shelley."

"I want to, too."

A turn. A long winding road that ended in an empty parking lot.

She thought of the ugly humped beast that she and Shelley had watched in the hatchback. Anyone could follow the road to its end here. Anyone could park alongside and look.

But when Shelley pulled her into his arms, she didn't protest. She didn't care who saw them. Indeed, let the whole world watch. She wanted Shelley. She had to have him.

They stayed there for hours.

When they finally left, the moon had risen.

Shelley drove slowly, deliberately delaying. He didn't want to take her back to her car, to her other life. He wanted to keep her with him forever. But he didn't know how. When he tried to plan, he saw no way. It was hopeless to think of it even. He had nothing to give her. Only what he felt. He said softly, "The one bad time is the going back."

"Let's not talk about it, Shelley."

"But that's how it is. The going back. Leaving our world behind, and starting into yours. Every time it's the same. Scary. How do I know I'll see you again? How do I know I'll find you came back into our world? Maybe some time you'll just disappear, and I won't ever know what happened to you, or why."

"No," she said. "No, it's not like that. I never really leave you. When I go home . . . "

"Home?" he asked sharply. "Home? Is that place your home?"

She began again. "When I go back there, to that other place, I take you with me, Shelley. I never forget you. I never stop thinking of you and wanting you and wishing you were there with me." And it was true. No matter what she did, brief flashes of him lit her moments. She saw the boys, her mother, through a misty veil. John, an occasional voice on the telephone, was even fainter.

Shelley whispered in slow halting words, "It has to be. Somehow, someway, it has to be."

Has to be. Has to be. Echoes in her mind. Part of the long conversations she had with him when they were apart.

She made a small sound that was wordless agreement, and looked ahead. There was a high stone wall at the right. An iron gate stood open within it where a short bush-lined driveway entered the road.

As Shelley slowed an approaching car whipped into a sudden left turn just missing the VW's bumper. It was an eight seat limousine, all black, with heavy glass windows. Its tail lights winked a jeer as it disappeared into the dark.

"Big shots," Shelley growled as another long dark car whipped in front of him.

"I wonder whose house is in there," she said idly.

He had speeded up to go on. Now he slowed. A grin touched his mouth. He made a U-turn. "Let's go in and see."

"Wait a minute. It's private property, Shel."

"They may think so."

"But if there are guards . . . You don't know . . . "

"We're not going to crash their lousy party."

He parked on a small circle near the other cars, but at the outside. Easy to get out, she thought. He cut the lights.

The front door of the mansion was open. A glow of Waterford chandeliers spilled down white stone steps. One couple, then another, was welcomed in by a uniformed butler.

As the door closed, Shelley grinned, slid close to her, "We're early for the best part of the party. So let's stay put for a while."

What were they doing? she asked herself. Why were they here? What was he thinking? She studied his face. It was relaxed. His eyes gleamed.

"I want to go," she said softly. She put a hand on his knee. "Shelley, it's no good. We're going to get caught." She imagined headlines. *Wife of Arms Dealer Peeping Tom*

"No, we won't," he told her.

"I still want to go."

He drew her to him, held her tight. "But it's my game, Mira. Don't spoil it for me."

She shook her head so that her cheek brushed his shoulder, back and forth, back and forth. No. No. This is silly. What am I doing here? No. It's dangerous. Why am I staying?

But he held her and she didn't move away. She leaned against him. She felt his heart beating against her breast, and his hand go slowly, softly, through her hair.

Finally he said, "If you mean it, if you want to go, then I'll take you."

But their world, and their reality, had closed in on her again. She felt excitement building in her. She asked, "What are we going to do?"

"We'll see how the other half lives. The rich half. Your half. And how it looks from the outside."

"I don't have a mansion, Shelley."

"It looks like one to me when I stare at it from the road."

"No," she said. "It's just an ordinary house." That was what John wanted. She didn't care. It was an ordinary middle-class house. But empty. People slept and ate and spoke and said nothing there. It had a slow and uncaring pulse. It wasn't even real.

A car pulled in, a long white convertible, custom made. There was the slamming of doors, the chatter of gay voices. The door opened again. When it closed, the night became still.

"We're not dressed for it," Shelley said. "But we'll do the best we can. You'd better take off your shoes."

She stepped out of her pumps, kicked them away.

The ground was cool, soft underfoot. Pine needle carpet. Its fragrance rose up around them. She moved silently behind him. He was like a wraith, drifting in the shadows.

He heard the clink of metal first, and stopped. The pad of feet. A growled warning. He froze. She stopped breathing. The brush crackled, burst apart. A dog exploded from it, and a breath exploded from her throat.

But Shelley was quick. She barely saw the motion of his arm. There was a flying glint of light. The dog yipped once and sank down and disappeared into the dark.

Shelley moved away. She saw him kneel, retrieve the knife. She saw him plunge it into the earth, once, twice. He came back to her.

"You killed him . . . ?"

"Him or us." Then: "Come on."

He took her hand, led her away from the front steps to the low windows at the side of the house. A rhododendron hung thick dark leaves along the wall there.

He nodded to it, drew her with him. They blended with the shadows of its heavy limbs.

The room beyond the window was full of golden lights. Candles flickered on mahogany sideboards, and reflected back in quivering images from four large mirrors.

The butler was serving drinks. A maid offered trays of hors d'oeuvres. Cigarette smoke drifted over the long smooth hair of the women, the coiffed hair of the men.

It was like watching the beginning of a play. The lights on, the stage set, the actors beginning to gather. But what was going to happen?

It was like being God, too. Looking, but not participating. Weighing. Waiting. She wasn't sure she liked the sensation.

"Too early for fun and games," Shelley whispered. "Let's move on."

They drifted toward the back. Another window. The kitchen. A gleam of copper and chrome. Bustle. A quick kiss on the nape of the neck. Butler and maid.

He smiled, led her back to the car. "Next time we'll be prepared, dressed in black. And we'll start much later."

"No next time," she said as she got into the VW. But she already knew there would be. She knew by the look on his face. She knew by how she felt. His games were her games now.

He smiled at her.

"You've done that before, haven't you?"

"A lot of times. When you're outside, you have to look in. When you don't have a home you search for one."

She thought of the knife's quick shining flight through the dark. The dog sinking down. Shelley's arm rising, falling, as he cleaned blood from it in the soft earth.

"It's dangerous," she said softly. "One of these nights . . ."

"That's why I like it. You, too."

But she didn't answer that. She said, "You have a home now, Shelley. You have me. You don't need to do it any more. Because of me."

He pulled her close. "I don't have you the way I want. Not for always."

It was as if a switch was pulled when she stepped inside the door.

Something went out of her. Life.

Something rushed in. Death.

A wave of dizziness swept her. Was that how it would always be? A little while alive with Shelley? The rest of the time dead?

She stood still, waiting for her head to clear. She arranged her face, put on her at home expression. No danger here. No thrill. Only the known, safe.

There was the soft shuffle of footsteps. A door opened. Her mother asked, "Mira? Is that you? I've been so worried."

"I went to the movies." Suppose her mother asked what she'd seen? She didn't have the faintest idea of what was playing. Something on Wisconsin Avenue maybe. One of those little places . . .

Her mother didn't ask. She said, "But John's coming home tomorrow, Mira."

John. Yes. But what difference did it make? "I know, Mother."

"Did you finish the shopping?"

"You saw me unload. You know I did."

"Is everything ready for him?"

"Of course it is. Go to sleep, mother. I'm going up to bed, too."

"A nice cup of hot chocolate?"

"No thanks."

Her mother sighed. "You know, Mira, I didn't hear Seth come in."

"You were probably dozing. His car's in the drive."

"Donnie played cards with me all evening."

"Good night," Mira said tiredly.

She turned toward the stairs, but her mother came into the hallway. She was wrapped in a white robe, with fluffy slippers on her feet.

"Let me look at you, Mira. You sound funny to me."

Mira forced a smile. "Funny?" she asked, turning back.

Ruth studied her daughter's face for a long moment. There was a frown between her brows, and her mouth quivered. Finally she said, "You're my own little girl, Mira. You'll always be my little girl."

"I know, mother."

Was that the trouble? Was she trying to grow up at thirty-five? Was Shelley her growing up?

"So if you're worried about something, you can tell me. We'll talk it over and fix it. I'll understand."

"I'm not worried, mother. But you are. Though I don't know why."

She knew. Naturally she knew. But there was nothing she could do to ease her mother's fear. No way to explain. To say 'I'm in love, and it's crazy and I know it, but that doesn't change how I feel.'

Ruth's lips trembled a little, but she didn't say any more. She turned and went into her room. She closed the door as if closing it against the unknown that troubled her.

Mira was thinking of Shelley again when she slipped into bed.

CHAPTER 12.

MIRA WATCHED the four of them in the blue-tinted mirror. She decided that they looked good together. Helene Hartley wore a white dress. Her blonde hair was piled high on her head. Since she'd begun to work for her Ph.D. she had taken to glasses. Very large, and black-rimmed, they gave her round face a distinction it hadn't had without them. Mira herself had on a sleeveless black dress with a deep V neckline. A single strand of white beads hung within it. The men were both in dark worsted suits, well-shaven, well-scented, well-barbered.

But looks weren't everything. They didn't go well together. The conversation was strained. The weather, the subway construction were both taken care of over the egg rolls. After that, it was hard going. Helene complained about the university. Her husband Dirk complained that she never cooked a meal. John was sympathetic to both, but contributed nothing himself.

Mira wondered what would happen if she told the three of them about Shelley. With the thought, the impulse grew. She bit her tongue to keep from saying, "My lover would die laughing at this." She gulped tea, swallowed moo-shu pork and Peking duck. *My lover.*

Dirk leaned toward her. "Saw you and your boy at McDonald's a while back."

"Me? And Seth?" Wide-eyed over the tea cup, she waited.

"He's turned into one good-looking boy, hasn't he? Mature for his age, too."

She didn't answer. She couldn't. She and Seth hadn't been to a McDonald's together for . . . for how long? She didn't know. Dirk had seen her with Shelley. Shelley.

"You don't look old enough," Dirk went on. "Not to have a boy that age."

She nodded, sipped tea, and stopped listening. Son. It was deafening thunder. She wanted to kick Dirk, spit on him. She wanted to yell, "He's my lover, damn you . . ."

Instead she sat so quietly that John, watching her, began to frown, finally leaned to whisper, "Headache coming on?"

She denied it irritably.

"We'll get together again soon," Helene said when the evening was over.

Mira denied that, too. But not aloud.

In their bedroom, John said, "Pleasant evening, wasn't it?"

"Don't you think those people are boring?" she asked.

John gave her a disinterested look and said, "No, I don't." Then: "You sure you're not getting a headache?"

"Maybe I am," she agreed. She went into the bathroom, but she didn't take her pills. She didn't need them.

But a migraine was a good excuse. John was a very considerate husband.

"Good night," he said. He lay down, careful not to touch her, turned on his side and, thinking of Virgie Evans, went to sleep.

The morning sun brightened the avocado of the kitchen. That was one of the things John liked about the house. It was family-style spacious, and comfortable. And it always smelled of good home cooking. Now he breathed deeply of French toast. Imagine trying to get that in Rabat.

His mother-in-law turned from the stove to look at him. "Almost ready for you."

"No rush," he said, smiling.

"Oh, and I meant to tell you. I invited Kit and Alan to come for dinner tonight, but they were already planning to go to Ocean City for the weekend."

"Don't look so unhappy about it. We'll get together next time."

"But I was sure you'd want to see them."

"I do. It's always enjoyable. When they're in town. And it's convenient."

"You're such a nice man, John. Such a reasonable man, too."

He laughed softly. "Why not? I have everything I want. There's nothing to be unreasonable about, is there?"

"And that's reasonable, too."

She refilled his coffee cup, placed the French toast in front of him. He fell to hungrily.

"Mira still asleep?"

He nodded, his mouth full.

"I hope she's not getting a headache."

He swallowed, sipped coffee. Then: "She should be okay. But she took her pills last night."

"Oh." It was a sigh. Ruth retired to the stove.

When he finished eating, he thanked her for breakfast. Taking the golf club from where he'd left it against the wall, he went into the back yard.

It was a funny word. Reasonable. But he meant what he'd told Ruth. Why not be reasonable when everything was going your way? He was lucky. Or else smart. Maybe a little of both. He had everything. Bull as friend and confidant. Money in the bank, and more to come. A good home. Two sons. A pretty wife. And Virgie to keep him company on his travels. She had nothing to do with his family, took nothing from it. It was the perfect arrangement, for a man.

The grass still sparkled with rainbow dew. He squinted at the practice green. It was overgrown again. He got shears and took care of it. But he told himself that Seth was laying down on the job. He'd have to speak to the boy. But John knew that he wouldn't. He was home only a few days a month. He wasn't going to read the riot act when Mira could do it just as well or better. He'd mention it to Mira instead.

He took the practice ball from his pants pocket, and set it on a red tee. He made a few warm up swings, then stroked with all his might.

It felt good. The pull of his muscles. The relaxation and tension. He liked to do whatever he did as hard as he could. He enjoyed the strain of stretching himself to the limit, and then beyond the limit. But it never showed. He neither panted, nor sweated, nor reddened.

That was one of the things that Bull Baron liked about him. He knew John would sit quietly, legs crossed, shoulders slumped, faintly smiling, while the other men waved their arms, stamped and fumed, and argued in strident voices. When they had worn themselves out, he'd pull the papers from his brief case, and in a calm even tone, go over the figure again. He was unmoved by ideology, unshaken by threats. It was cash on delivery, at prices he quoted. Bull would get them whatever they wanted, and guaranteed an arrival date. But they had to pay. And the price was high for handguns, rifles, semiautomatics, and ammunition for all.

The contracts part of it was handled elsewhere and by someone else. John didn't do any accounting. That was just his cover. In case there was a foul up some time.

There was another reason Bull liked him. He owed Bull. As long as he lived, John would owe Bull his life. It gave the big man a sense of power. John understood. But this was a time when mere understanding didn't matter. Bull fed on his sense of power. And John was obligated to him for the breath he took.

The dawn in Viet Nam . . . the shell that had struck company headquarters had changed John forever . . . Log roof collapsing in splinters that looked like raw white bone . . . John had crouched in a corner, the grenade frozen in his left hand, the rifle frozen to his right . . . Wave upon wave of small bony knees flashing under muddy shorts . . . The towering sergeant crashing through them, thick body a battering ram to lift John, hold him, pluck grenade and rifle away, slam through a fiery wall . . . A hard overhand toss . . . The rattle of the gun . . . They were all gone in a red wet cloud . . . And then: "Baron's my name. What the hell's yours?"

It was the beginning for the two of them. Bull always asking . . . John always answering, "Yes."

When Bull came to ask him to take the one job on,

John couldn't refuse. Bull had said, "There's nothing to be scared of. It's safe and as sure as your office in town. Only you'll make a hell of a lot more money."

It wasn't the money that swayed John. Partly it was the need to prove to Bull that he wasn't afraid, would never be afraid again. But more important was another need. Unrecognized. Unacknowledged. The hunger to be with Bull. To see him . . . to be part of the life of this man who had saved his life.

Mira had hated Bull on sight. She had cried when John agreed to take the job. She had fought with him when he said he would do only the second trip. After that she'd said nothing. She'd adjusted to the idea. And why not? She had everything she wanted. More than most of the women she knew.

He was aware of her now, watching him from the window. He knew that Donnie was sitting on the back step, chin in hand. They didn't affect his concentration. He didn't wonder to himself what they were thinking.

He got the ball, set it on the tee again. He took a few small swings without hitting it. Then he gave it a gentle tap. It moved inches, dropped into the hole. He scooped it out, took a pace back, and went through the exercise again.

Donnie yawned behind his hand, and watched his father tap the white ball. It was a dumb game. A nothing game. He didn't really believe that man with the club was his father, nor that the small woman inside the house was his mother. He figured they'd adopted him some time, and been sorry they had, but wouldn't admit either the one or the other.

He'd rather have his Uncle Alan and Aunt Kit for parents. That would have made sense. They cared about him. Aunt Kit didn't know how to show it, but Donnie knew anyhow. Uncle Alan was different. He was smart, being a school teacher, and he knew boys, so he understood how it was. That day he had gone fishing with Uncle Alan, he'd talked about the way things were. Without mentioning names, as if speaking about some of his students, he said how Donnie felt. Maybe that's how Seth felt, too. All locked in, and no way out. But you couldn't tell about Seth. He was as quiet and as shut in as their father, who couldn't be Donnie's real father. Else why did he stay away all the time?

Donnie yawned again. He got to his feet, and strolled slowly around the corner of the house. He glanced once over his shoulder. His father was still stroking carefully at the dumb little ball.

When Donnie passed the telephone in the kitchen, he stopped. Maybe his Uncle Alan and Aunt Kit hadn't really gone to Ocean City. Maybe they'd only said that so they wouldn't have to come over that night. Or maybe they'd changed their minds and not gone. You could never tell. He dialled. He counted off twelve un-answered rings before he put the receiver down. It was just as they'd said. They'd gone.

Mira had been watching John, too. Soon, she knew, he'd put the practice ball in his pocket, and get the golf bag, and her car keys, and he'd drive to the club. He'd spend most of the day there. Somehow he always man-aged to find a group to join. If he didn't, he'd play through alone. When he returned, they'd have dinner.

His wallet lay on the dresser. She stared at it for a mo-ment. John always carried a thick wad of bills. Perhaps just to be prepared. Perhaps to show off. She checked to see how much was there. Seven fifties. Three tens. Some singles. He probably didn't know exactly how much was there. And if he did, so what? He'd think he'd spent some, or lost it. He'd never suspect she had helped herself. Smiling, she took two of the fifties, tucked them into her purse. She'd buy something for Shelley with them.

A few minutes later, John came in. He leaned the club he was carrying against the wall.

"I'm going to the club now," he told her. "Want to come?"

"No. But why don't you take Donnie?"

"He isn't interested in golf."

"He can go in the pool."

"Okay. I'll ask him." John took his wallet, started out.

"The club," Mira said.

"Oh, yes. Thanks." He grinned, was gone.

It was like a lollipop, she thought. That golf club. He carried it with him wherever he went. As long as he was home, she could find it leaning against the wall in any room in the house.

When the downstairs door slammed, she forgot the golf club, forgot John.

She began to think about what she would buy for Shelley's basement room.

Shelley drove slowly out of Plumtree Road.

There had been no sense in his having gone there. If Mira knew she'd be angry with him.

But she didn't understand how it was. He had nothing. He was alone. Except for her. So it was important.

He had to see what her husband looked like, and how he walked, and what he was. That man, that house, threatened Shelley.

Some time she would disappear . . . go from him . . . to them. And he'd be alone again.

He imagined himself moving slowly through the rooms. Behind him, trailing his footsteps, there'd be chaos. He smiled faintly, seeing it in his mind. The sofas torn, the rugs stained. flour and sugar and syrup puddling the kitchen floor. Suits, and jockey shorts and shoes tangled in the bedroom corners.

Then he imagined it all gone. The house fallen amid steaming and charred timbers.

A little while after he got home, Mrs. Radman knocked softly at the side door. When he went to answer it, she told him that she had a job for him. Mrs. Tealer, around the corner, needed somebody to repair her broken back step before she fell down and broke her hip. Would Shelley?

He said he'd go over right away. No reason to wait.

The job took him most of the afternoon.

All the time he cut and sanded and nailed, he kept thinking about the things he could do to the house on Plumtree Road, and pictured how they would look when they saw what he had accomplished.

Soon he found himself imagining what he could do in elderly Mrs. Tealer's house. He finished the job. She paid him, gave him milk and donuts, and promised to tell her friends about him.

On the way home, he stopped and bought two pairs of rubber gloves.

CHAPTER 13.

When John left that Monday morning, Mira drove him to Friendship Airport. On the way he told her that he'd be back for the July 4th holiday. Since it fell on a Wednesday that year he would probably arrive Monday night. He didn't mention that he was going to take three days in New York with Virgie Evans. He did suggest that she plan a gathering while he was home. The Hartleys and Weidemayers. Alan and Kit. Whoever else she wanted, if there was anyone else. Mira said she would make the arrangements. John told her to remind Seth about the practice green. She promised she would see to that, too.

It was an ordinary conversation, a long time marriage talk. But it made her uncomfortable. She didn't fully understand why until that evening.

They were in Shelley's basement room. It no longer had the dismal and dingy air of former times. The old and tattered Japanese screen had been replaced by a new one of light bamboo strung with yellow ribbons.

The sagging couch was covered by a yellow and red throw. Five thick shaggy oval rugs in crimson were scattered on the cement floor. A small round table, covered with a bright yellow cloth, stood in one corner. Piece by piece she had brought all these things to the room, remaking it for Shelley, and for herself. The shopping, the buying, had been a joy. She didn't remember those days when she had re-done her bedroom in pink. She thought only about Shelley.

That evening, Shelley said, "I'm glad you're back. I missed you."

"It seemed a long time." It had been a long time. Three slow tiring days while John was at home.

"Three days," Shelley said. "I wished I could sleep them away."

"A blur of hours," she told him.

"But did you think of me?"

She nodded slowly. Oh, yes, she had thought of him. Thought of him constantly. John's deep voice . . . her mother's happy chirp . . . had seemed to come at her from a great distance. She hadn't wanted to hear them. Had barely heard them. The casual talk in the car with John had been like an invasion of her dream. The dream was Shelley. No wonder the long time marriage talk had made her uncomfortable.

"What did you do, Mira?"

"Do?"

"With him." Shelley knew John's name, but didn't like to say it. 'Him' was easier. He knew what John looked like now. But didn't like to think of that either.

Mira said, "That's not something I want to talk about."

"I want to know. I keep wondering. I had the feeling that maybe this time you wouldn't come back to me.

You'd decide you didn't need me any more. And that would be it."

"Don't think about that."

"Why don't you tell me not to breathe?"

"Because I want you to breathe," she said, smiling. "What good would you be to me if you didn't?"

"But what did you do?" he insisted. "Three days after all."

She said, "Nothing. That's why there's nothing to tell you about." She didn't remember. The days when John had been home with her were gone now. They'd faded beyond the mists of disinterest. She was with Shelley that evening. And that was all that mattered.

"I wish I'd been there. A fly on the wall. Then I'd know," he said.

She moved from the circle of his arms. "Let's go out, Shel."

"Later on."

"Then I'll bake you a pie. Okay?" She didn't wait for an answer. She turned on the electric oven she had brought him. She gathered the ingredients she had put in the cabinet the week before.

It didn't occur to her that she was playing house with him, playing at cooking for him, at living with him.

He sat very still, watching her. He was thinking that that was how he wanted them to be. The two of them. Always together. Always. Just the two of them. And no one, no one else.

"If only we'd met before," he murmured out loud.

She turned to look at him. "Before what?"

"Before everything happened to you."

The pain caught her in the throat. A stab so intense that she gasped aloud. Before . . . before she had married John . . . When Shelley was four years old. When she could finally speak, it was only in a whisper. "It's no use talking about that. What's done is done. We have to take what we have, and be glad for it."

"A couple of hours here. An evening sneaked there."

"Shelley, please. How do you think I feel?"

"I don't know. That's the trouble."

Her fists clenched on the table top. A sift of flour drifted to the floor. She stared at him across the distance between them. "I want you. I want you all the time. Every minute I'm awake. And in my dreams I want you, too. Just suppose . . . suppose for a minute that we'd never met."

"And you hadn't asked me about the tattoo."

"And there hadn't been the hold-up at Joe's. If we hadn't met . . ."

"By now I'd probably be in Albuquerque or some place else. I'd have moved on. There wasn't anything to hold me here."

"And I'd still be sleepwalking . . ."

"Okay," he said. But he had the lost waif look on his face. His gray eyes were filled with doubt.

She wiped flour from her hands and went to him. She took his face and held it. "Don't look back."

"And don't look ahead either. That's what you're saying."

"Nobody can look ahead. Nobody ever knows what's going to happen." She returned to finish the crust, made up the chocolate filling, and put the pie in the oven.

When she went back to him, he was smiling. "You've got flour on the end of your nose."

"And you've got a pot to lick, if you want to." Seth, Donnie, had always hung over her when she baked. Wanting the pots, hurrying her. Her mother had watched, offered suggestions. It seemed to have happened in another life.

"I'll take you up on it," Shelley said. But he didn't move. He kept smiling at her.

Finally she said, "What're you thinking?"

"About what we're going to do after a while."

"Are you going to tell me. Or tease me?"

"You'll see."

Later, after he'd scraped the pot clean, and had the pie, he led her to the VW. He drove slowly past the Tealer house, noting the lights at the windows, then went on.

Mira leaned against his shoulder. Her home, her family, seemed far away now. This was her world. The time when she was gone from Shelley had no reality. This was where she, Mira, was herself, and breathed and hoped and lived. The other was zombie time. Routine. Habit. The rut worn by unwilling footsteps. Death.

She paid no attention to where the road took them. She was briefly aware of the bright windows of houses, of shadowy streets, of flashing turn signals and headlights glaring like angry eyes through the night. But all these were simply a part of the world in which she and Shelley floated.

He stopped the car, said, "Want to get out?"

She followed him.

They were in an unpaved alley. A white fence surrounded property that abutted it. The air was scented with roses. A glimmer of dark windows shone through heavy foliage.

He took a black shirt, black trousers from the car. He handed her rubber gloves. "Put these on."

When she asked why and what for he only repeated what he'd said.

"It's your game, Shel, isn't it? I don't know . . ."

He laughed softly.

She hesitated. A game could go bad. Some time they

171

could get caught. But, no question, she wanted the adventure too . . . the feeling that came after. She wanted it, and didn't want it. In the end the wanting won. It would make her part of Shelley. He waited silently. At last she smiled, pulled the shirt and trousers on. She drew on the gloves. Now they were like twins, both dressed in shadow. Except that one was tall, one was short. He bent to kiss her, and his eyes seemed to glow like new-minted silver.

She could have told him that she wouldn't go with him. She knew that. She knew that if she had, he'd have given in. They'd have driven away together. But she didn't want to refuse him. She didn't want to refuse herself either.

As she followed him to a side window, the small ember of curiosity inside her grew larger. He paused for a moment. The window slid open. He climbed in, looked around, then leaned out to say softly, "Come on."

She managed to hook a knee over the sill. He pulled her the rest of the way. With her heart drumming in her ears, she trailed him. They toured the empty house quickly, going from room to room with the small flashlight he carried, making a pale path for them through the dark.

She didn't know who lived here. But they were clearly well off. The drapes were good quality, the furniture contemporary and unworn. There was color television, a stereo with multiple speakers. It could have been the house on Plumtree Road.

They were upstairs, in a small study, when Shelley suddenly swept all the books off the shelves. "So perfectly in place," he said laughing. "So well taken care of. And private and safe. We'd better let them know that somebody's been here, hadn't we?"

It reminded her of Goldilocks and the three bears.

'Who's been sleeping in my bed? Who's been eating my porridge?' Mira wondered if she remembered her mother reading her that story, or if she remembered herself reading it to Donnie or Seth. 'Who's been sitting in my chair?' But what did it matter who? Someone had. Someone . . . Nothing was safe. Nothing inviolable. Not for anyone. Not at any age.

Her curiosity became a familiar elation. She found herself smiling, almost giggling. She felt as if she'd taken something strong and sweet that had flooded her veins with electrical currents. They'd come softly, and unseen, to walk through somebody's life. They were here now, within it. That somebody ought to know.

She opened the desk drawer, upended it. Stationery and stamps floated silently to the rug. She put her fingers through the mesh of the drapes, and tugged hard just once. The weave ripped. The rings opened. The drapes came slithering down.

She went ahead of Shelley the rest of the way. Her eyes glinting, her cheeks flushed, she trotted from room to room, leaving a trail of debris behind her. It never, of course, occurred to her that she was actually bringing a shambles to the house on Plumtree Road.

Whatever she missed, Shelley found and destroyed. For him it was a labor of love . . . he was ruining all houses that he'd been shut out of all his life, all that he had hated and that had hated him. Yes, a labor of hateful love.

As silently as they had come, they slipped away. They made love at the foot of the property where the air was scented with roses. The mocking birds sang as they drove off.

Later, at home, she soaked in the bubble bath. The sweet hot excitement still churned through her.

It was insane that she should play his games. But they were his gift to her. The adventure, the challenge. The danger of discovery. The being young that she had missed because she'd been afraid to be, was what he gave her.

He led her back to the time she had wanted but turned away from out of fear. To those golden days when she was seventeen, and didn't know who she was and was afraid to try to find out. She was still afraid, but now the bright excitement she had once only imagined was strong enough to give her the courage she had lacked before.

But by the time she had stepped from the tub, wrapped herself in a thick towel, the burden of the house was on her. Escape was only temporary. The haven of Shelley's arms a memory.

Her mother. Donnie. Seth. John, returning for the holiday. That was how it was. How it would always be.

She lay in bed, glaring fierce-eyed into the dark.

Twice in the next week Shelley led her in forays against secluded and empty homes.

She listened silently, laughing inside, when the invasions were mentioned on the television news.

But then the game palled.

They met at Joe's Cafe, and spoke a few words to each other, and left separately to go riding for hours.

"If it was just us," Shelley said once, "then this is how it would be."

They spent hours in his basement room. One night he said, "If you weren't tied to somebody else then you'd never have to go home. And I could wake up with you in my arms."

They began to weave fantasies together, each stroking in a detail that led to another one until they had formed complete tapestries for each other.

Mira had no family. She was alone. That was the basic premise. Shelley was alone, too. He had always been alone. They joined forces. It wasn't choice that brought them together. It was fate. Before, both had been spinning in separate orbits. And then they met and made their own universe. They had a van and traveled when they wanted to. When they were tired they stayed on in some quiet and sunny place where warm breezes ruffled the fronds of tall palm trees. They visited every town he'd been alone in, and he wouldn't be alone any more. He'd have Mira.

"Just don't go back," he said. "Forget them. We'll start out in the morning. We'll drive away. We can be a hundred miles from here before they miss you. And you'll never be sorry. The two of us, Mira."

It always came back to that. The fantasies sank under the weight of those words.

It was what she wanted. Time was so short. To waste it, living without love, was the same as dying. It *was* dying. But there were the boys. Her mother. And there was the matter of money. Shelley shrugged that away. They'd manage somehow.

She knew better. To go on as they imagined, they had to have resources to support them. It was too late for her to take to the road with nothing and suppose that they could survive. She was too old to fool herself that way. Within a few short months, Shelley would begin to wonder why he'd ever loved her, wanted her. And soon he would leave her. She knew that they had to have money to give them the freedom which was part of their enchantment with each other.

With each meeting now the fantasy of being together always grew stronger. But how?

They spoke of it constantly. And she, alone, continued until the dream developed its own reality. There was a place, though, where it faltered, broke to shards, and fell in on itself.

How. Without money, they would have nothing. So, privately, she found herself imagining how to put the shards together. The untempered passion she felt for Shelley was the furnace in which, slowly, the shards were melded.

John. Her mother. The two boys. These were her problems. Her enemies even. Or at least the enemies of the Shelley-Mira person she'd become . . . *they took her from Shelley*. She was nothing to them. A voice. A body. But they kept her from Shelley. Without them to burden her, she would be complete and alive. With them, she moved slowly and surely toward her grave.

She began to feel as if she were looking at everything through a thick barrier of smoked glass. She saw only single dimensional figures. She heard their voices, but muffled and distorted. Need, plan, worked endlessly within her mind. She held long silent conversations with John, her mother, the boys, explaining it to them, begging them to set her free for Shelley.

But while those conversations went on, she moved through the routine of days as they had always been. She shopped for the house, agreed to the meals her mother planned. She arranged for the Hartleys and Weidemayers and Alan and Kit to come for the Fourth of July when John would be home.

One day, noticing her mother's sad silence, she took her out to lunch. Ruth brightened for a little while, responding to the pleasant atmosphere of the Magic Pan. But then, over a second cup of coffee, she began to wilt.

Mira had been speaking about the weather, knowing

her mother's disinterest but unable to find another top-
ic.

Ruth cut in to say, "I wonder what's wrong with Kit
these days."

"What do you mean?" Now Mira was disinterested.
She didn't care much about Kit.

"She doesn't drop by as much as she used to."

"Of course she does."

But Ruth knew better. She depended too much on
those visits not to count them. Not to know when there
were fewer. "I wonder if I could have offended her in
some way."

"Oh, mother . . ."

"I mean it. I can't understand why we don't see more
of her." Ruth paused, added, "And Alan, too."

"You still miss your baby boy, don't you?"

A frown deepened the wrinkles between Ruth's
brows. "I'm serious, Mira."

"You're imagining things. You have to realize that
Kit's a very young woman. She doesn't have all that
much in common with you."

"We have lots to talk about," Ruth said defensively.
"Lots. She tells me about the movies she sees with Alan,
and her friends, and . . ."

"And of course, she's very busy this time of year."

"Not so busy that she can't come to see me."

"But she has." Mira took a deep breath. "The trouble
is you just expect too much. She and Alan have each
other. That's enough for them. They don't need anybody else. They don't want to be bothered with us."

"I feel it in my bones . . . there's some reason . . ."
Ruth said, obviously unconvinced.

"Of course there's a reason," Mira exploded. "Kit's
jealous. Pure and simple and silly. Alan can't give her
everything I have. That's why she works so hard. To get

more, to compete with me. As if I care what she does. But it eats at her. So she tries to stay away."

Ruth shook her head, said nothing more for a little while. Then: "You don't go to the club to swim or play tennis, Mira. How come?"

"I got tired of it," Mira tried to answer lightly. "It happens, you know." But she was thinking that she ought to have realized her mother would notice the change in routine. She went on, "I'll get back to it one of these days." She knew she wouldn't. She couldn't. . . .

She was relieved that the check came, and they could leave the restaurant, and go home. She spent only a little while there before she left to meet Shelley at Joe's Cafe.

Because, always, no matter what else she did, that was how she ended up. With Shelley.

A day before the July 4th holiday she was with him. "What will you do for the next few days?"

"Wait for you," he said. Words whispered in his mind. "Waiting. Always waiting. Can't you move it? That damn kid!" He shook his head to clear it. The buzz of distant words faded. "For you, Mira," he said.

"Besides that."

He shrugged. "Maybe a couple of jobs. Some errands for Mrs. Radman. I don't know. And I don't care. I won't be alive until the holiday's over."

"You don't have to make it harder than it is."

"Sorry." He folded her into his arms, whispered, "It's just you and me. Nobody else in the world."

"Just us," she agreed, slipping into the game. "And tomorrow we're going to get into the VW and ride."

"Mississippi. There's a place in Biloxi that has the world's best barbecue."

"And then maybe New Orleans . . ."

"I always wanted to go to Antoine's."

They went on until it was time for her to go home.

Abrupt awakening. For the first time, conscious rage flamed through her. Rebellion, too. Damn them all.

But John was due in that night.

She kissed Shelley, a long lingering kiss that would have to last until they could get together again.

This time he let her leave without protesting, without trying to delay her.

CHAPTER 14.

THE FAREWELL in the parking lot where Shelley had driven her to pick up her Impala bothered Mira through the next few hours. Shelley had been too quiet, acquiescent. As if he had given up hope.

She wondered about it as she had dinner with her mother and the boys. She considered it as she soaked in her bubble bath. She was doing her make up, still thinking about it, when Seth banged at her door.

"Mom!" he yelled. "Do you know what flight Dad's on?"

"Stop shouting." She opened the door, stared at Seth. "What's wrong with you? You know I don't want to be disturbed when I'm getting dressed."

"The flight, Mom."

She realized that he was white-faced, shaking.

"What's the matter?"

"There's a plane from San Salvador. Can't get its landing gear down. I heard the flash just now."

She spun by him, dashed downstairs to the television set. "I don't know the flight. But San Salvador . . ."

"Yes," Seth whispered.

Mira glared at the comedy in progress. "Damn them! Nothing now. Just that flash. And then . . . then . . ."

"The airline," Seth said.

She ran to the phone. As she dialled, she heard her mother's footsteps. She was asking the voice at the other end for word when Ruth began to weep, crumpling into a chair like a small broken doll.

There was no news. The plane was still circling. She would be notified. Please stand by. Please don't call. Don't panic. Everything that could be done was being done.

She put the phone down on the empty reassuring drone. It rang instantly.

Alan's voice. Deep. Concerned. "Mira, is that John's plane?"

She choked out a whispered, "It could be. San Salvador. There can't be too many flights. But I'm not absolutely sure he's on it. You know that some times . . ."

"Mira," Alan cut in. "Just take it easy."

"Yes, yes, I'm trying to."

She left the phone, took a chair close to her mother, who was moaning. "I wonder where Donnie is? He should be with us."

"He'll be here soon."

"I'll find him," Seth said, getting up.

Mira nodded numbly.

A few minutes later, Seth returned with Donnie. The younger boy was subdued, silent, red around the eyes.

Soon after, Kit and Alan arrived.

Kit made coffee. Alan sat with the boys. They tried, at first, to make conversation, but finally gave up.

Mira was grateful for the silence.

For the next three hours, they waited. Spot reports came over television once an hour, reporting the plane's position, reporting the decision to dump fuel, the condition of the passengers, requesting that relatives stay in their homes and wait for further information.

Gradually, as the numbness wore off, Mira began to think, to feel. The pain of relief was insupportable. She had loved John. She wept for him. She wept with a bitterness that scalded her throat and heart. She wept for what had once been, and was no more. She was free. And she wept for that, too. Her mother. The boys. She could manage that. There would be plenty of money. First the funeral. And as soon as she could get everything settled . . . .

The last spot news reported only what had been said before.

Alan was pacing the floor.

Kit sat silently, holding Ruth's hand.

The phone rang.

"Safe emergency landing . . ." More words. Explanations. Reassurances.

Even as Mira heard them, she caught the excited flash coming from the television set.

She murmured thanks, put down the phone, and turned to the others. "It's down. Everybody's all right."

"When will he be home?" Ruth asked, her voice shaking, her eyes feverish in her ashen face.

"I forgot to ask," Mira said. "He'll probably call."

It was an hour before she spoke to John. Two and a half hours before he arrived home.

Kit and Alan had waited. They had a small celebration in the early hours of the morning.

Ruth fixed sandwiches. There were drinks. John told them coolly about the hours in the air. The child who screamed continuously. The hysteria of two middle-aged women, the aplomb of a teen-age girl. The calm of the pregnant one. The men who prayed, eyes fixed and staring over clasped hands.

He himself was unaffected. He'd flown too much to be upset by non-workable landing gear. Either it was okay, or it wasn't. They got down, or they didn't. He had simply waited the time out, leaning back, eyes closed for the most part. Not even thinking.

But when he slid into bed beside Mira later, he reached for her with a violence she hadn't known was in him. She shut her eyes, imagined that he was Shelley. When John was finished, he rolled away from her and was instantly asleep.

She lay awake through the rest of the night. She had wept for him when she thought he was dead. Now, dry-eyed, she wished that he was.

She arose late, and alone.

The room was quiet, except for the hum of the air-conditioning unit. But from downstairs, she heard the sounds of preparation. She sighed. Her mother was already at it, getting the dinner on, counting forks and knives, and casting thoughtful glances at the sky. Would it rain? If so, they'd have to eat indoors. The dining room table would have to be set up. Was the cloth wrinkle-free?

Her mother's concerns.

Mira wanted to stand at the top of the steps, to shout that it didn't matter. Let the damn cloth have wrinkles. Let the roast burn. None of it mattered.

She didn't have to look to know where John was. It would be business as usual with him. By now he'd have been fed his favorite breakfast. He'd be out at the practice green.

His trousers were hung as neatly in the closet as always. As if nothing had happened the night before. As if he hadn't had a small brush with death.

She hardly remembered now her anguish when she thought he was gone, her wish that he had been. She was exactly where she was when Seth came pounding at her door to ask what flight John was on. And she still wondered why Shelley had been so quiet, so acquiescent when she told him good-bye.

She was thinking of that when she took John's wallet from his trousers, and without knowing why she was doing it, drew out a twenty and two tens. A good thing he carried so much cash that he'd never be sure of what he had. He'd never miss it. He hadn't missed the hundred. And she might need it. Might need it, although she didn't know what for.

She was dressed when he came in.

He leaned the golf club against the wall, ran a hand through his hair, said he was going to the country club for a couple of hours. When she reminded him about the company coming, he told her he'd be back in plenty of time.

After he left she took the golf club downstairs and put it away in the closet where it belonged in its bag. She knew she'd do the same thing a dozen times while John was home.

In a little while Helene Hartley called. They'd heard John's name mentioned as one of the passengers on the San Salvador plane. Was he all right? She wanted to know. Would the dinner go on as planned? Mira said yes to both questions. Moments after she'd hung up Dora Weidemayer called, and Mira went through the same thing again. She hoped that was the last of it.

But that evening the Hartleys and Weidemayers

wanted only to talk about John's near miss. Then to describe their own fearful moments in flying.

Donnie provided the necessary interruption by slipping out for a few minutes. He was back, smiling innocently over whipped dessert, when the two twenty-one gun salutes went off at the foot of the back yard.

The blasts so startled Ruth that she dropped her coffee cup.

Mira helped her mop up, then rounded on Donnie, who kept saying, "I'm sorry. I'm sorry," while his unrepentant eyes shone with mischievous joy.

John sat back, saying nothing.

It was as if he wasn't there, Kit thought. Or as if he was a guest. Pretending it had nothing to do with him. Pretending he hadn't noticed. Just as he ignored Seth's sullen and silent face that openly proclaimed his resentment at being ordered to be where he didn't want to be.

That would be difficult for Mira. Kit watched as Mira absently wove slim fingers through the gold chain at her throat, and remembered the sound of soft laughter, the tap of high heels on concrete. She'd assumed Mira was having an affair with the tall dark-haired boy. Seeing John behave like a visiting stranger in his own home made Kit's suspicion appear even more probable. But she knew she could be wrong. She could have leaped too quickly to an unwarranted conclusion. After all, she'd only seen Mira walking with someone that single time. So what? She herself had been seen dozens of times walking with men other than Alan. That was work though. What reason could Mira have? The thing was, Kit realized, she didn't care. Whatever Mira did was justified, all right. All Kit wanted was that she be okay.

At home, later, she waited for Alan to say something about the evening.

But he didn't. He made a pot of lemon tea, dug out cookies, and settled down with the newspaper.

She washed her hair, put on pajamas, and got into bed with a book. She didn't read it. Instead her thoughts went back to the Priest house. Mira was there in the flesh, but so obviously absent in spirit. She had been that way for months now. Ruth, watching her daughter come and go, must sense that just as Kit sensed it. The dark-haired young boy . . . .

Alan came in then, sat on the edge of the bed. He yawned, stretched his long arms. "You were quiet over there tonight."

"Was I?"

"My mother thought so."

Kit had seen Ruth and Alan in quiet conversation, Alan listening intently.

He went on, "She was asking me if she'd offended you, Kit. Because you don't go there the way you used to."

"I still drop in," Kit said, putting her book aside.

"But not as often."

"Not as often," she agreed. "And you know why. I'm tired of fighting with you about the Priests. And that's how it ends up."

"We don't *have* to fight, you know."

"You can close your eyes, and play dumb, Alan. But I can't."

"I don't know what you're talking about, Kit."

"Yes, you do. You just don't want to think about it. Nor try to do anything about it."

"Mira," Alan said shortly.

"Yes." Kit bit off the word, folded her lips tightly. That was enough. She wasn't going to say any more. Mira was *his* sister. Not hers. It was up to him. Not up to her.

"My mother's concerned about Mira," Alan said abruptly.

"I'm afraid she has reason to be." No more, Kit warned herself. Not another word.

"Why do you say that?"

"You know why. I've told you. She's adrift. Doing nothing. Hardly even aware of your mother, or the boys. Something's obviously wrong."

"Women!" Alan shook his head. "Imagining. Troublemaking where there's no trouble. I can understand it in my mother. She's bored, But what about you, Kit? Are you bored, too?"

"No," she said coldly. "I'm too busy to be bored. I don't have time for that."

"You don't have to be so busy. You could quit that damned job of yours, and stay home, and have a baby."

She threw the book on the floor and sat up straight. "You think that's the cure," she said angrily. "That'll take care of everything. Well, okay, then tell me why, when Mira has two sons, she's so unhappy."

"Mira?" Alan's voice was deep, angry. "You're projecting, aren't you, Kit? You're the one that's unhappy."

"You won't listen," she shouted. "And you won't look. Yes. Mira's unhappy. And I don't blame her. She's only got a tiny piece of marriage, or life even. She's entitled to more. So I can understand whatever she does to try to make it better. But I'm worried about her. Can't you understand that? I'm just worried for her. Not imagining. Not projecting. Not judging. I'm scared."

Alan's eyes narrowed, his mouth thinned. "Wait a minute," he said, almost spitting the words at Kit. "Just what the hell are you talking about?"

"If you cared about her you'd have realized. But you

don't want the responsibility. Either of caring. Or trying to help her."

" 'Whatever she does,' " Alan said. "You were hinting. Say it straight out, Kit."

"I think she's having an affair. I don't like telling you. But I can't help it. I haven't said anything before because I thought it was better not to. For Mira's sake. But I think she is. And I know you should talk to her. See if you can do anything for her."

Alan was red-faced. His eyes flared with anger.

"Jesus, you're sick. You're the one that needs help."

"I'm sorry, Alan."

"Sorry. You say a thing like that about my sister, and then apologize, and I guess that's supposed to make it okay."

"I'm sorry for her. Not for telling you."

"Okay. Maybe you'd better tell me what makes you so sure you're right."

"I saw her with someone." Kit went on, described the street, the 'for sale by owner' sign. The tall, dark-haired boy.

"So, on the basis of that one time . . ."

"And she's so rarely at home, Alan. That's why your mother's so lonely. Mira's in and out, day after day. Night after night. Your mother sees that. She's worried, too."

"I don't believe you," Alan said. "It's all made up. What you want to think. Because you resent Mira." He stood over Kit, glaring down at her. "You've always been jealous of her, haven't you? You've always wanted to turn me against her. But I'm telling you now, Kit, it won't work." And he turned, went out of the room.

They spoke politely to each other the next morning. He poured her coffee. She buttered his toast. Both pretended that nothing had happened. But both knew something had.

CHAPTER 15.

THE REGULARS were in Joe's Cafe.

Jimmy said, "How's it going with you, honey?"

"Okay," Mira told him, a glance at the place where Shelley usually sat.

"Good holiday?"

She nodded, wishing he would keep quiet. She didn't want to think about the past few days.

"Plenty of fireworks your way?"

"Too many." She remembered Donnie's sly innocence after he'd set off the twenty-one gun salutes. And the way Seth had laughed. And John's bland obliviousness.

"Damn near drove me crazy," Jimmy said. "Cherry bombs all night long. A couple of those burning crosses the night before. Brought a dozen cops in with sirens. And would you believe it? Another vandalism. A house catty-corner from me. A man's afraid to go to the grocery store these days."

Richard asked for a drink. Jimmy served him, continued the monologue.

But Mira stopped listening. Shelley was late. She began to think he wouldn't come.

A worm of worry began to gnaw in her. She had to see him. *Had to.*

She could go to the house, but she didn't like to do that by daylight. It exposed her too much. She had the feeling that the half-blind old woman upstairs would be watching. And the neighbors. Children playing on the lawns. She imagined over-the-fence conversations. "She's in her thirties at least. Maybe even more. Surely old enough to be his mother." "Well, she's not his mother! I'll bet you that. If she knew how it looks . . ." She knew how it looked to a waitress in one of the places they'd stopped to eat, saying, "Your mother want catsup?" Mira had been in the ladies' room, was returning, when she heard it. The words had made her physically ill.

But time spun on. Desperation pushed her. She had to see him. Never mind half-blind Mrs. Radman, the children, the neighbors. Damn what anybody said or thought. She had to see Shelley.

She finished her drink, pushed aside the untouched sandwich. Jimmy protested that she was leaving too early, but she paid him and went out.

Shelley wasn't waiting for her in the parking lot. Another hope gone. So she'd have to go to him.

The lawn had a bedraggled look. The windows were as dirty as always. As Mira tapped at the side door, a blue jay swooped from an overgrown forsythia bush.

She watched it peck for worms, tapped at the door again, her hand shaking. There was no answer.

Mrs. Radman came around the corner of the house. At that distance she looked a little like Mira's mother. Small, slightly bent, white-haired.

Mrs. Radman peered at her. "You looking for Shelley?"

Mira nodded. Did the old woman recognize her? Was she wondering what Mira wanted there?

"He's not home. He hasn't been for the last couple of days."

"Couple of days?" Mira repeated. Frightened, and trying to conceal it, she thanked the older woman, turned away.

"I can't think where he's gone to. And without telling me. But I guess he'll be back. He always has before. I have a job for him. If you see him, tell him I have work for him to do."

Mira nodded, made her escape, hurrying back to the car. Once there, she sank into the seat, and tried to think. But she was bogged down in incoherent flashes. What did the old woman mean? He'd always come back before? Where had he gone? Why had he gone? Was it for good? Had he left her? What had happened? Why? Had she lost him? Where to look? Shelley, Shelley . . . .

She started the car, and drove away. She saw that the old woman was watching. She turned the corner, left her behind. Where now?

She drove aimlessly for an hour before she decided to go to the cave, although she had thought of it almost at once. It was a last resort. She might not find him there . . . .

But she did. He lay with his arms folded behind his head. A lantern burned beside him. He didn't speak, nor look up at her when she crouched beside him. "Shelley, what happened?"

"Nothing."

"No 'hello'? No 'I'm glad to see you'?"

He turned his face away.

"Something must have happened," she said. "You

didn't come to Joe's. I went to your place. Mrs. Radman said you'd been away for a couple of days. She has work for you."

"I haven't been away. I was here all the time."

"I didn't know that."

"You weren't looking for me."

"I couldn't help it."

"You don't want to."

She lay down beside him, cuddled in close. "I do want to. More than anything. But there's no way I can be with you every minute."

They were no longer speaking about her search for him that afternoon, but about being together. Always. They were moving again toward the fantasy. She tried to stop them. She told him about the holiday time. The landing problem of the plane that John had been on. About waiting those long hours for him to come home.

Shelley said, "I guess you were glad he didn't die."

Mira didn't answer. There were some things she couldn't say. Not even to Shelley. Some things she couldn't even allow herself to think.

"He should have," Shelley was saying.

An echo of feelings she remembered, but still she didn't speak.

"I wish he had. Him. And all the other ghosts that take you away from me. I wish they were all dead!"

"No," she cried. "Shelley! No!"

He was silent for a moment, sighing. Then, eyes closed, he told her quietly, "It can't go on. I can't, only having part of your life. Being the outsider, looking in, and wanting more. I want all . . ." He waited. "Or nothing."

"No," she said, pressing herself against him, clinging to him now. "No."

"What then?" he asked, not moving nor responding

except for the two words. What then? he asked himself. He was light-headed. He hadn't eaten for three days. He hadn't slept. He had lain in the shadows, listening to voices echo in his mind. To bits of old conversations, old quarrels. To shrill screams, and the sound of weeping.

She knew only that he looked genuinely tormented. His gray eyes were dull, sunk in bruised-looking hollows. His mouth seemed cracked, dry, bitten, as if his teeth had worried at his lips. "What then?" he said again.

"I don't know. I can't think. Not now. Just give me time, Shelley."

She had once thought that she felt as if she were standing on the brink of some unknown chasm. Without knowing it, she moved a hair closer to it in that moment.

"There's a way," he said quietly.

"What do you mean? Tell me."

But he didn't answer. Eyes closed, he sighed, moved away from her.

She pressed her lips to the tattooed "Mother" on his forearm. She pulled his shirt aside and kissed the small circular scars on his shoulder. "Trust me, Shel. I love you."

"Do you? I don't know. I think you like it how it is now. You, with everything. And me. Me, with nothing. And nothing to look forward to either. Except being alone again."

"That's not true . . ."

He asked softly, "Then what are you going to do about it, Mira? How long do you suppose I'm going to wait for you?"

It was three weeks before she saw him again.

At first, she didn't believe that he could have simply picked up and gone away.

Every morning, after her ritual bubble bath, she dressed carefully. By noon she was at Joe's Cafe. She had her two martinis and tuna sandwich as usual. She waited, one eye on her wristwatch, absently answering Jimmy's comments, nodding at Richard and the other regulars. She went to the cave.

Twice she went to Shelley's basement room. She didn't see Mrs. Radman. She tried to peer through the dirty windows, but could make out nothing of what was inside.

She didn't know that he was there. He stood just feet away on the other side of the door, and she didn't sense his presence. He listened to her tap, and nodded. But didn't speak.

When she had gone, he lay down on the couch, and looked at the things she had brought him. The new screen, the round table and chairs. He thought of how they had played at living together. Now she would learn what it felt like to be alone. They belonged together and nothing could stand in the way. Now she would know that she needed him as much as he needed her. He dozed and dreamed, and heard voices floating on pale mists . . . "Mama, no, *wait*, Mama . . ." And: "Shel, I can't help it, it's the only way left, oh, Shel, Shel, I love you . . ."

Mira didn't guess that he was inside aching, dreaming, crying as he slept.

She gave up, hurried home. The second time she collapsed with a migraine that came with a burst of thunder and seemed to go on forever. The hours, days, weeks passed. She moved slowly, only half-noticing her family. They were like blurred ghosts who spoke out of an immense stillness. She was a blurred ghost who an-swered, but hardly knew what she said.

There was a part of her that whispered . . . This wouldn't have happened if John had died, by now he would be buried, she would be signing papers, gather-ing together what she had, her mother and the boys would know she was soon going away, if John had died . . . Another part of her listened in horror, and told her she was losing her mind, was half way to being crazy. How could she think such things? How?

John came home unexpectedly. He didn't explain why. She didn't ask. Though the weather was cool, drizzly, he played golf as usual, left his club behind wherever he happened to be, insisted one night that they go to Dominique's for dinner, and afterward made love to her as if he were thinking of something else.

She was relieved when he left. She felt as if she'd es-caped from some terrible danger. She didn't allow her-self to wonder what it might have been.

She waited, numbly sinking into despair each day, awakening with reduced hope each morning.

And one day, at noon, when Jimmy had just put a drink before her, Shelley was suddenly there.

They exchanged the usual casual greeting. He or-dered a beer. Jimmy asked where he'd been lately, Shel-ley's answer was vague. The two men talked baseball, with Richard and the other regulars chiming in.

Mira listened, but didn't understand their words. They didn't matter. Nothing mattered to her except that Shelley was back again. She was alive again.

Heart pounding, pulses tingling. She knew she sim-ply couldn't do without him. She wouldn't give him up. No matter what else she lost, she'd learned she couldn't lose Shelley. He was right. There had to be a way. They belonged together.

Later, when they were alone in the basement room, they made love, a love somehow sweeter for the absence before. He was almost shy returning to her, importunate, tender, then close to violent. His moods mirroring her own.

After those hours, they sipped wine, smiling at each other. "This is how it should be," he told her, and she answered, "Yes. And this is how it's going to be too."

"How?"

"I don't know yet. But I'll figure it out."

He didn't ask any more. He didn't say any more either. Not then.

The next day she went to a bank in Rockville. She opened an account using a different name. Mary Morgan. A different address. One in Rockville. She deposited the cash she had taken from John's wallet at various times, the money she collected by charging most of the household expenses usually paid for in cash. It amounted to over a thousand dollars. She didn't know why she had done it, or what she would use the money for. She was just getting ready. But the amount was trivial. She studied her jewelry. She didn't dare sell the rings John had given her. The rest of what she had was of little value. Still, the gold chains and bracelets her father had given her years before would bring something. She gave them up without regret, and banked the proceeds, too.

The end of that week, when she met Shelley, he said, "We haven't done anything exciting lately."

"And you have an idea, haven't you?"

"Let's go for a ride."

She let the quick excitement take her. He parked near a big house in Potomac. Its windows were dark. The carport was empty. The nearest neighbor was half an acre away, and screened from view by thick trees.

They watched for a little while. If someone came to challenge them, they would look like lovers. But nothing moved. No dogs barked. No traffic drifted down the road.

They crept to a window, listened. All was quiet.

"Ready?" Shelley asked. She nodded, he drew on gloves. He worked at the window. It stuck, then suddenly gave. When it did, a shrill whistle exploded from within. Piercing. Ear-shattering. Terrifying. Lights suddenly blazed from behind drawn drapes.

Shelley jerked her down, pulled her with him.

Within seconds, they were at the car. He shoved her in, climbed in himself. Gravel shot out behind them, as he drove away.

She lay back, gasping, shaking. But she saw that his face was alight.

"Somebody was there," she said finally. "What if we'd gotten inside? What if we'd been there when he came down. And he'd found us?"

"I'd have killed him," Shelley answered, patting the pocket where he carried his knife."

"Shelley!"

"Would have had to."

"Oh, God, no, what a thing to say —"

"I always do what I have to, Mira."

He thought of the three weeks he'd been away. He'd made himself do it. Never wanted to. But made himself. Roaming around Baltimore, Philadelphia, at last New York. He'd thought of nothing, no one, but her. Made himself stay away. And in the end, he hadn't wanted to come back. He'd thought of going on to Chicago, further west. Back to where he'd been the year before. But he'd wanted to come back too. So he'd made himself do it.

199

Shivering, she moved closer to him. "It was too close, Shelley. We could have ruined everything for us."

"It's always a chance. That's where the excitement comes from. The chance. That's why we do it."

"Too close," she repeated.

But she remembered. If you broke into a house, you could get caught. You'd be desperate. You'd do anything to get away safely.

"When we go," Shelley told her, "you won't need much. Not the way we're going to live. We don't want to be burdened with a lot of junk."

"Yes. Just some jeans. A few skirts."

"A bikini." He grinned. "I want to know how you look in a bikini."

She laughed, but at the back of her mind there remained the memory of the house they'd broken into. The sudden burglar alarm. The lights flashing. There was no burglar alarm in the house on Plumtree Road. There'd be no flashing lights. . . .

She was quiet on the drive back to her car. There had to be a way . . . .

He said, "I know what you're thinking about."

She didn't answer.

"Want to bet?"

"No," she said, barely audible. "Maybe you *do* know."

"If he'd died —"

"Shelley, don't *say* it."

Shelley grinned. "You want it. You just won't talk about it. You think, but you're afraid of the words."

She swallowed hard. A pulse trip hammered in her temple. Her fingers trembled. "It didn't happen," she said at last. "So there's no use —"

"But it could."

A man, awakening in an invaded house . . . a trapped stranger, driven to panic . . . no, she couldn't, impossible . . . she really was losing her mind even to be able to see such images . . . "There's got to be some other way," she said finally. "Not that, Shel. Never that."

"Then tell him you want out," Shelley said. "See what happens."

"And then?"

"Leave him. Leave everything. I told you. We can get along."

Maybe it was possible, she thought. And there was the money in the bank. Mary Morgan. Waiting for her. But how long would that pittance last. And what then? Soon she'd lose Shelley. And everything would be gone.

"I have to think," she told him.

"That's the trouble. You think too much, Mira Priest. You'll think your life away." And, when he kissed her good night at the car, "Don't think too long. It'll only make it worse. Believe me."

It was eleven-thirty.

Ruth was dozing in front of the television set in the family room. Donnie lay at her feet, sound asleep.

Mira turned off the set, and the silence immediately awakened Ruth. As she smiled at Mira, the front door bell rang.

"Who on earth?" Ruth asked, instantly alarmed.

Mira hurried to look through the peephole. She opened the door to let Kit in.

The younger girl's blonde hair was disheveled. Her face was pale. But she smiled at Ruth, nodded nervously at Mira, saying, "I hope I didn't wake you up."

"No, no, of course not," Ruth told her. "But what's wrong?"

"Nothing, Mother. Really, nothing." Kit's quick reassurance rang false. But when she said she'd be grateful for a cup of coffee, Ruth went with dragging footsteps into the kitchen.

Kit, with her eyes on the doorway, spoke softly. "I'll let you decide if your mother should know, Mira."

"Know what? What's this about?" Mira demanded.

"Seth's in trouble."

"Seth?"

"Alan's with him now. He called us half an hour ago."

"But where is he?"

"The Montgomery County Detention Center. I'm sorry, Mira."

"Where?" Mira had never heard of the place, didn't know what it was.

"It's a jail," Kit said quietly. She was remembering the shrill ring of the telephone. It had cut through the tense silence in the apartment. Alan had been reading in the living room. She had been pretending to read in bed. They hadn't quarreled. It was just the way it was between them now.

She had jumped up as Alan answered the phone. She heard his startled exclamation, his questions. She immediately began to dress. Without knowing exactly what was wrong, she got ready to go with him. He'd explained on the way.

"*Jail?*" Mira was saying. "Are you crazy? What would Seth be doing in jail?"

"I wish I were crazy," Kit answered.

"But what's the matter? Did he have an accident? Was he drinking?"

"Nothing like that," Kit said hastily. "He's not really hurt."

"Then what?"

Kit knew that she should have just said it straight out. Told it quickly, gotten it over with. But it was so hard to say. She drew a deep breath, kept her voice soft.

"You've read about some cross-burnings in the neighborhood, haven't you?"

"Yes, but what have they got to do with Seth?"

"Mira, this is going to upset you, but you'll have to know. Seth, and some of his buddies, call themselves the White Knights. They've been driving around. Setting fires. Damaging cemeteries. The police . . ."

"That's ridiculous," Mira said angrily. "I don't believe it. Seth wouldn't ever do a thing like that. You know he's been raised better —"

"He admits it, Mira."

Mira felt the blood drain out of her head. She leaned against the wall. "He what?"

"I said he admits it."

"I'll have to hear that with my own ears. I just can't believe —"

"You will hear it in a little while." Kit drew a deep breath. "Alan will probably get him released on bail. He'll be bringing Seth home soon. With any luck."

"Bail," Mira repeated. "You mean as if he's a common criminal?" Shivering, she went into the living room. She turned on a lamp, sank into the green velour chair. "God, what's John going to say?"

"It's not the most serious charge in the world," Kit said. "But it's not trivial either."

"A foolish boy's prank," Mira said softly. What else could it be? Seth hadn't learned to hate blacks at home. He hadn't been taught it at school. He didn't hate anybody. So it was just something to do, something exciting . . . she had felt the same sweet-sour sensation herself, hadn't she? She knew, without admitting it, why Seth had done it — she shook her head to clear the thought away. She mustn't consider that now. She must concentrate on Seth. What to do? How to handle it? John would be furious. He was always careful of his good name.

Aloud she asked, "Besides what Seth said, do they have proof?"

"They were caught at it, Mira."

"Caught?"

"The police have been watching pretty carefully. They set a trap."

"You mean they'd been following Seth? Watching this house?" Alarm bells went off in Mira's head. If they'd been watching, following . . . what about her?

"No, nothing like that. They didn't know about Seth until he walked into the trap. What they did was have some black people move into a house. They were obvious about it. And then the police waited."

"That's not very honorable —"

Kit frowned. "It's one way to put a stop to a really ugly thing, a dangerous thing."

"But nobody ever got hurt." She was talking to herself . . . she and Shelley hadn't hurt anybody either, but if they'd been discovered . . .

Kit was saying, "I'd better warn you that Seth made a fight of it. He got a black eye. One of the boys has a concussion."

Mira got to her feet, paced the floor, arms folded at her waist as if she were suddenly cold. "I can't believe it."

Kit said, "Alan and I've had a feeling lately that something might be bothering Seth —"

"I don't know what you're talking about. He's the same as always. Quiet, like John. Not saying much, just like John."

"Just a feeling," Kit went on carefully. "Boys at that age . . . sometimes things bother them."

"Nothing's bothering Seth. He doesn't have that excuse."

"He'd probably hide it, if something were, Mira. Maybe now would be a good time to try to do something about it."

"I will. Only . . . only what . . ."

"A specialist maybe. It would have to be someone who isn't involved with him. A person who can be objective . . ."

"You mean a psychiatrist, don't you?"

"Yes," Kit answered.

Mira burst out laughing. "Oh, for God's sake. There's nothing mental about Seth. He was just stupidly playing around. You take a bunch of boys, and they get together, and the next thing you know, they're into some kind of mischief —"

"It's the kind of mischief, though, Mira."

"Excitement," Mira said abstractedly now . . . "feeling alive, testing against the edge of danger . . ."

Kit watched Mira for a moment, seeing the expression on her face. Mira seemed to know what it felt like, could understand Seth's experiences in a way Kit never could. Peculiar. It made her uneasy, damned uneasy. Finally she said, "You ought to find out why he thought he had to test himself that way."

"What can they do to him?"

"I don't know. I think there's a fine. Maybe a jail term. Malicious destruction of property, for one thing. But it's a first offense, so maybe . . ."

From the doorway, Ruth said, trying to sound cheerful, "Well, now, here we are. Coffee and cupcakes. Isn't it lucky that I baked today?"

Both women looked at her.

She dropped all pretense of cheer, asked quickly, "What's the matter?"

Ruth put the tray on the table, straightened slowly. "I can see by your faces. Tell me —"

The front door opened, closed. Footsteps came toward the family room. Alan. Then Seth.

He grinned. "I can see you know. Good news travels fast, doesn't it?"

Ruth cried, "Your eye! What happened? Oh, Seth, Seth . . ."

He ignored her, kept his eyes on his mother's white face.

She pushed herself up, asked softly, "Is it true? Did you do it?"

He laughed.

She sank down, buried her face in her hands and wept.

He fell back, staring. "What's the matter with you? You know you don't care what I do."

CHAPTER 16.

'D HAVE sworn that Seth was more . . . more solid," Alan said. "It's hard to believe he'd do a thing like that. Oh, yes, some idiot impulse. Once . . . just because. But the planning . . . It's so disgusting. And frightening, too."

"Maybe it's not all his own fault." Kit glanced at her husband's grim white face, then looked away. "What do you think will happen to him?"

Even as she asked the question, she was thinking about how it was between Alan and her. The civility that masked a bone-deep coldness. She wondered if it was going to be that way forever.

Alan was saying, "I don't know what'll happen to him. We'll have to see. I hope they'll drop the charges. But who can tell? And if they don't, then I hope for a suspended sentence."

"Do you know a good lawyer? Somebody with the right Rockville connections?"

"I don't, but I'll ask around." Alan's mouth twisted. "The thing is I feel he *ought* to be punished. Not get away with a slap on the wrist. He doesn't have an ex-

cuse, Kit. Nothing can explain it except sheer rotten-
ness."

"You always said there were no rotten kids."

"That was different, and you know it."

She said slowly, picking her words with care, "I don't
think Seth's any different from the kind of boys you
were talking about when you said that."

"Of course he is. Those kids are deprived. They've
got nothing. Not real homes. Often not enough to eat.
Nobody that cares about them. Seth's always had everything. Including parents that love him."

She ignored the almost defiant tone to ask, "Are you
really so sure, Alan?"

"Damn it, Kit, don't bring that up again —"

"I have to, Alan. For Seth's sake. If you turn against
him he'll have no one."

"I'm not going to turn against him. But remember,
he's got his parents —"

"And I'll say again what I just said. Are you sure?
With John away so much —"

"A man's got to earn a living. What's he to do?"

"And Mira . . ."

"I don't want to hear that again, Kit." He was remembering his sister as a young girl, the eagerness in her
face. He was remembering her wedding day. "And besides," he went on, "there's no connection. Seth's seventeen years old. She can't lead him around by the hand,
take him to school and home, babysit him every night."

"Yes." Kit had to agree.

"And you don't know it's true anyway. She could have
been with a casual acquaintance."

"Let's drop it," Kit said wearily. "I was only trying to
tell you that maybe Seth wasn't all to blame for the trouble he's in. He's going to need somebody, Alan."

"I think you've been waiting for something like this to throw that in my face again."

"I'm not going to fight with you, Alan." There was nothing to fight about any more. There'd already been enough of that. She wished now she hadn't mentioned it.

"The trouble is," he said, "you don't really *want* to be a woman so you resent any woman who does, like Mira. You have to make up these things about her —"

"Forget it, Alan. I won't talk about it any more."

"And I'm not going to stop talking about it until I understand and you understand what you're doing."

She got up. Slowly, distinctly, she said, "Then you'll be talking to yourself." She went into the bedroom, closing the door behind her. Hand still on the knob, she stood shivering. It was such a final sound. The end of something. Then the outside door slammed shut. Alan had gone out. That was a final sound, too.

It was four days later. Alan and Seth were in Alan's car, on the way back to Bethesda. "You've been lucky this time, Seth. I hope you know it."

"Sure." But the boy's face was closed, expressionless. More than ever he looked like John.

"You remember what the judge said. You keep in mind those people. They've got a right to live. Wherever they want. You don't have the right to scare them."

"Sure," Seth said again.

"And if anything happens . . ."

"I know, Uncle Alan. I heard the man. Jail for this bird."

"It's not funny, Seth."

Seth shrugged. "You want me to cry? Wouldn't that look pretty funny?"

"Not if you meant it. If you were really sorry." The

trouble was, Alan knew, that Seth didn't seem to regret what he'd done. Only that he'd been caught.

Seth didn't bother to answer Alan. He was only wondering how soon he and the White Knights could get together. Maybe a couple of them would be scared, fall by the wayside, but he was pretty sure of some. They'd feel like he did. He'd show the world. Nothing was going to stop him. In his mind, he saw a cross flare sky high. Nobody could miss it, ignore it. He almost laughed out loud.

There was only another week of summer classes, but Alan didn't want to wait. As soon as he'd finished for the day, he'd driven to the Priest house. He had papers to correct, tests to make up, but this was important. He should have done it long before. He only hoped it wasn't too late.

Mira, dressed to go out, greeted him. He went into the kitchen to say hello to his mother, chatted with Donnie for a little while.

But when Mira picked up her purse, he said, "I have to talk to you."

"Not today. I have something I want to do, Alan." She wasn't meeting Shelley. But she had planned to buy him a new outfit, a surprise.

"Every time I say I want to see you, you tell me you have something else to do. I know you're a busy lady, but it's important, Mira."

"All right." She sank into a chair. "Talk."

"Not here. Let's go out. Get some lunch."

"I can't, Alan —"

"You should have been with us at the courthouse. Seth needed you."

Mira frowned. "Listen, Alan. The less said about that the better. If I could have been with Seth I would have.

But the whole thing made me sick. He was better off without me. And you did better than I'd have been able to."

"Seth needs his parents' support, Mira."

"Are you blaming me for what he did?"

"No. Of course not. But . . ."

"But . . ." she repeated. She got up, went to the kitchen door. "Mother, do you need anything from the grocery store?"

"Flour," Ruth answered.

"There's plenty in the pantry," Mira told her. She was consciously playing the housewife role, diverting Alan by it. She'd show him that he was all wrong. Seth was Seth's problem. You couldn't always blame the parents. He had everything. It was his own fault. Nobody else's. And she'd told him so while she ripped that awful Hitler poster down from the wall in his bedroom.

"I didn't see any flour there," Ruth was saying.

"You didn't look in the right place, I guess." Mira found the flour, and her mother immediately emptied it into the avocado cannister. Some spilled on the floor.

Mira cleaned it up, knowing that Alan was watching, waiting.

When she rose, her face was flushed. It was no use. She knew he'd follow her from room to room, follow her when she went out. He was determined to have his talk. "All right," she said. "You can take me out for a drink."

He had his little speech planned. On the way to the Red Fox he went over it. He was so busy with that he didn't notice that the bartender there greeted Mira as if he knew her. Alan ordered the drinks, hoping they would make things easier. Mira looked impatient, defensive, and on the verge of anger.

He talked about a boy at school, in trouble. A boy from a broken home. How hard it was for him.

Mira listening politely but didn't comment.

Alan spoke of the difficult times. Not just for kids growing up. But for women. For men. No one knew exactly who he or she was any more. What role to play. How to live.

She met his gaze with a level look, said nothing.

He spoke of the hard years, when expectations begin to fade and the wide horizons begin to shrink. And hope is what people remember, but don't have any more.

It surprised her that he knew about that. She stirred restlessly, signaled the waitress for another drink. He saw Mira's hand shake when she gulped it down. He saw the brightness come into her eyes.

Finally she said, "You're a good brother, and dear to me. Just as you've always been. But this conversation is ridiculous. And it has nothing to do with Seth, which is what you said you wanted to talk about."

"It does, Mira. Indirectly."

She said softly, "The trouble is that you don't have a family of your own." She saw his lips tighten, and went on, knowing that this was the best way to deflect him. She didn't want to hear any more of what he had to say, she needed to stop him any way that she knew . . . "If you had your own kids, you wouldn't be so attached to Seth and Donnie, would you? And you wouldn't think you could do a better job than I've done." She carefully didn't mention John. "You can criticize me because you don't know about being a family. You and Kit . . . what do you have? A bed you sleep in together. And that's all —"

"I haven't been criticizing you, Mira."

"Yes, you have. In the same way that Seth's stupid behavior has to do with me. Indirectly. I think that was your word, Alan." She hurried on, still trying to divert him. "And as for you and Kit . . ."

"We have a marriage," Alan said. "Maybe we fight sometimes, but we still have a marriage." He didn't notice the implication. Maybe Mira and John didn't.

But Mira did. She ignored it. She said, "At least you think so. I suspect that Kit's behind this whole conversation. She's been feeding you all kinds of nonsense about me. I can guess why, too."

"You're being unfair to her," Alan heard himself, wondered. He'd said almost the same thing to Kit, and now he was defending her. And he knew he was right now, in this moment, as he had been wrong before. Kit's feeling about Mira had been accurate. When she'd seen Mira with a young man it had only confirmed what she'd suspected before. He'd been wrong. He'd known Mira all his life, known her too well to be fooled by her if he was honest with himself. She was hiding something. The something was an affair. She didn't want to talk about it with him. She couldn't. Let it go. He couldn't help her when she didn't want to be helped. All he could do was hope she'd come to her senses without ruining her life.

Mira shrugged. "Think whatever you like, Alan."

"I'm only trying to help —"

"I know that, I appreciate it."

But it was as if she were miles beyond his reach. He knew nothing he could say would get through to her. He touched her hand. "Listen, if there's anything I can ever do . . ."

"Thank you." She said it very quietly.

He dropped her off at the house, and drove directly to Kit's office. She was out, but he got a list of houses she might be showing. He found her at his third stop.

It was a small estate with stables and outbuildings and a formal garden. Kit was showing a young couple through the dining room when he interrupted to ask if he could speak to her for a moment.

She agreed immediately. There was such urgency in his voice, and it was so unusual a thing for him to do that she knew it must be important. She left the couple indoors and led him outside.

"I wanted to say I love you," he told her.

"Oh, Alan . . ."

"I've behaved like a nut, and I'm sorry."

"You've spoken to Mira, haven't you?"

"Yes. I felt I had to. Because of Seth. But it's no good, Kit. She's in no mood to listen."

"I'm sorry —"

"I should have paid attention to you —"

"There's nothing we can do," Kit said.

"Except keep out of it."

"Which we'll do."

They smiled at each other. They didn't have to say any more. He went home. Kit went back to talk to her clients. That night they made reservations for the long Labor Day weekend. They'd be extravagant, stay at the Carousel. They'd do every single thing they wanted to do.

But Kit saw the shadow in Alan's eyes. They'd made up one more time. Only it wasn't over. Alan wished that he didn't know what was going on. The knowledge lay like a weight on Kit's heart. She wished now, too, that he didn't know. At least that she hadn't been the one to tell him.

It was two weeks to the holiday. She wondered what would happen before she and Alan could get away.

It was easy for Mira to dismiss the talk she had had

with Alan. He had been upset about Seth. He had had to blame someone. She was Seth's mother. So who better to blame? And what she had told him about Kit and himself was true.

By the next day Mira had put it completely out of her mind. She dressed carefully in tight blue jeans, a tight sleeveless silk shirt. She wore long white dangling earrings and flat white sandals. All for Shelley.

She drove to the parking lot, and sat in the Impala. She waited.

It was more than half an hour before Shelley drove up and parked beside her.

She had spent the time dreaming, half awake, half asleep. She'd forgotten Seth's trouble, Alan's questioning eyes, her mother's anxious pretense that all was well. Instead of the paint-blistered facade of Joe's Cafe, she saw the long white beaches of Padre Island that Shelley had described to her. She saw herself dancing languorously, her body golden all over, and Shelley watching, lean, muscular, reaching for her, while the terns made circles overhead.

It was only when he got in beside her that she came fully awake, and said, smiling, "You're here."

"Let's ride."

"Just what I was thinking."

"I know." As they drove out of the lot, she looked back. "I'd just as soon never see that place again."

"Joe's?"

"Joe's."

Quick hurt. Bewilderment, too. "But Shelley . . . why? It's where we met. If not for Joe's . . . It'll always be special to me."

"Sure. Only what does it mean? So we met there. So what?"

"So it's everything, that's what. And I wouldn't give that up. Not for anything."

"Sure," he repeated. But this time it sounded like a question. She wouldn't give it up, give him up. Not for anything. But what then? Where were they? He answered himself. They were nowhere. How come she didn't know?

"Don't spoil today," she said softly, recognizing his mood, and seeing ahead to what was coming. "We have so little time together."

"Today's like any day," he told her. But when he went on, his voice was softer, warmer, loving. "We're together. We're driving. We'll stop and make love." His voice got deeper. "I'm going to kiss you all over, and taste you. And it's going to be perfect. The way it always is."

"Yes."

"And always will be."

"Yes." And: "Always."

That was how they moved into the fantasy again. But on that day the fantasy developed a further dimension.

They passed a car stopped at the side of the road. Its hood was up. A man was changing a tire.

They slowed, then drove on. Shelley said dreamily, "He could always prove where he was, couldn't he? Stuck out in the middle of nowhere with a flat. Anybody ever asked him, he'd be able to say that's where he was. And get people, people like us maybe, who saw him, to say so too. If he ever had to."

She didn't know where he was heading. "Why would he have to?"

Shelley shrugged. "You never know. Maybe he just wanted to be sure he was away from home when something happened. Or at least to make it look like he was away from home. It would maybe take some doing, but he could manage it all right."

"You mean like having an alibi, don't you?"

"Sure. It's easy to set one up. You just have to think about it a little."

"Somehow, though, there'd have to be someone to pick him up. He couldn't just stay there, could he?"

"Maybe he could. But if not, then a pick up could always be arranged."

She didn't want to talk about it any more. Quick frightening images tumbled through her mind. She imagined a dark road. The glint of moonlight. Shelley . . . coming for her . . . But she couldn't stop herself. She said, "What do you suppose that man has done that made him need an alibi?"

"He was desperate. Locked in a prison. He couldn't live that way any more. So he got rid of his wife. Of everything that bound him. He had to, to save himself. So he did."

In this oblique way, Shelley had told her what she must do.

Mira swallowed. She wanted the fantasy to end. But it had its own reality now. They'd gone too far, it was too late . . . Shelley had burned the thought into her brain and bone and flesh. "But how?" she barely whispered. "And how could a man ever get away with it?"

"There's a million ways. He probably picks the simplest. Makes it look like a burglary. Then goes out and gets himself a flat. And then comes home and discovers what's happened." Shelley smiled. "Easy as pie. Nobody the wiser. And a few months later, he marries the girl he loves."

And so, indirectly, he'd suggested the means.

But Mira asked, "And what about everybody else? The wife . . . it's her fault. Only the others . . ."

"There aren't any others."

But there were, she thought. There were. Her throat

closed against a rush of nausea. When it subsided she put a hand on his thigh . . . "That's not such a good story. Let's think up another."

"Sure," he agreed. "Then you'd better start it, since you don't like mine."

"Well" she began, "the man's in love with the girl all right. So in love with her that he'll sacrifice everything for her. To be with her. Because she's life to him. And he wants her like he's never wanted anything before, and knows he'll feel that way as long as he lives. So he's salting away what he can, so they'll have enough for a new life together. And eventually, although it takes time, he's willing to wait, and she is, too, he gets a divorce, and they go away and live happily ever after." She smiled uneasily at him. "How's that?"

"Not bad, except for the time part. And that's not good."

"And if there's no other way?"

"There's plenty of ways. I told you. Like a couple of nights ago a house burned down in Gaithersburg. And only one of them got out. One out of six. The rest of them, they died." Then, after a brief silence, he went on, his voice soft, faraway, a child's whisper from a dream . . . "They all have to go, Mira, so we can be together . . ." And this time the *they* didn't mean the people in a house in Gaithersburg, but the ones in the house on Plumtree Road . . .

Mira's gasp was a cry. Her teeth chattered. Small prickles leaped along her bare arms. The nape of her neck went cold. This was crazy. To talk like this . . . he was putting death into her mind, and she was allowing him to do it . . . "You're frightening me, you're saying things I can't stand and don't want to hear and won't listen to any more."

He was silent. She *had* to. She had to, for him. He

didn't know why. It just had to be. Then he told himself that it didn't make sense, what he was thinking, he didn't want her to do anything. Finally he laughed, "It's only a game, Mira. Another one of my games. Like going shop lifting. Or on a peeping tom deal. Or messing up a neat house. Just talk, honey. And you fell for it. But there's nothing to get scared about."

He believed what he was saying. His random 'She has to. Has to,' didn't mean anything. Not any more than the random nightmares meant anything. The scar on his back suddenly itched. He slid down, rubbed hard against the seam in the seat. He didn't even realize himself what he had been doing. Not really. He'd been putting the idea into her mind . . . pushing her forward step by step to the unthinkable edge . . . to the place there would be no return from.

"When you talk about leaving me," she said, "that's not a game."

"No, I guess not."

"And it'll happen some time."

"I guess so." Why lie? Some time, yes, he'd be on the road again. Alone. But that wasn't what he wanted. He wanted to be with her. Except it couldn't be. Because of him. John Priest.

"I couldn't stand it," she was saying. "I'd rather be dead. Even thinking about it, wondering when it'll happen, makes me want to be dead."

"Not now," he told her. "You can't go dead on me now. I want to make love to you. We'll go to the cave."

He took her hand from the steering wheel, curved it at his groin. She stroked gently at the thickening bulge beneath the zipper.

CHAPTER 17.

THE DARK road. A man fixing a flat tire. A glint of moonlight fading as he went home to find . . .

The images spun like tiny leaves in a whirlpool. They were constantly with her. They remained fresh and sharp and painful as the Labor Day weekend approached, and the time for John to return home came closer. Along with the images, like background music, there was the deep soft sound of Shelley's voice, whispering. Whispering . . .

She tried to bury images and voice, but they kept coming to the surface again. And they led on. As if Shelley were in her mind, guiding her thoughts. What must happen before she drove to the dark road and got stuck there with a flat? Why would she have been out late? She'd been to the club, had gone for a drive alone. No. John would be home for four days. Why would she go out alone? They'd quarreled. No. They couldn't have quarreled. Some time John would go into Washington. She'd meet Shelley then. They'd go to the cave. And . . .? It went nowhere.

With Shelley guiding her, she began at a different place. John and she had been out. He'd surprised an intruder. And . . .? Nowhere again.

And all the while she prepared for his homecoming as she always did. She stocked the bar, the refrigerator, the freezer. She agreed that she and John would attend a dinner party at the Weidemayers on the Friday night of his arrival. She had her hair cut, and took her mother shopping to buy a new dress. She made certain that Seth and Donnie both had trims, that the practice green was perfect. She warned Seth not to tell John about his run-in with the police, and promised Donnie that she'd break his neck if he let anything drop. To ensure that nothing did, she called Helene Hartley, arranged for Seth and Donnie to spend the holiday weekend camping out with the Hartley boys.

On that Thursday she managed to spend the afternoon with Shelley. They met at Joe's as usual, and drove to the cave. The grove was scented with honeysuckle, golden with sun, dappled with shade. She undressed and danced, while the mockingbirds actually made music for her and three crows cawed from a low limb until Shelley brought one down with a well-aimed rock. Later, in the chill shadow of the cave, they made love, and he said to her, "I want you, I want you . . ." holding her tighter . . .

She wished a tornado would strike over the holiday weekend and blow the house, with everyone in it, away. She wished a fire would leap through the night and burn it to the ground. Then she and Shelley could be together . . . She didn't remember that he had wished the same before.

The headache began as she drove back to Plumtree Road. By the time she went inside, she was near blind with pain.

Ruth said, "Mira, what's the matter with you? You're pale as a ghost."

She was barely able to answer. Her jaw felt frozen. Her tongue felt like a lump of ice.

"Not when John's coming home," Ruth groaned, wringing her small hands.

"It'll be gone by tomorrow." Mira got the words out, climbed the stairs slowly. She took her pills and went to bed.

She heard Donnie slam the bannister. Later she heard Seth come up. She couldn't summon the strength to talk to them.

She dozed, steel slivers of pain probing at the edge of consciousness, and the images forming in her mind again. A man fixing his tire . . . the black night . . . the empty road. Slowly more images developed, a swirl of gently falling leaves, each distinct, each separate. No horror now. No terror. No feeling.

John lay in bed, unmoving. Then he got up, startled. There had been some sound from below. A gray mist filtered through sealed windows and doors. Shadowy. Silent. Drifting across a dark screen, blurring the moving figures that loomed against it.

Still no horror. No terror. No fear. Nothing but a dark road, and waiting at the end of it, Shelley.

But pain struck lightning behind the screen, and the figures glowed there red. They were blurred no longer. They lay limp and broken at the foot of a blank wall, and the red was the color of blood that gushed from wounds in their flesh.

Mira awakened. Retching, weeping, she dragged herself from the bed. The floor seemed to quiver beneath her feet. The walls of the room seemed to pulse. Firecracker explosions seemed to burst in her head.

The limp bleeding images wouldn't go away. Her

mother. Donnie, Seth. John. No, *no*. All a sick dream. The migraine. The pills. A nightmare compounded of pain and pills. She didn't want that. Not even for Shelley. Except she heard him whispering close beside her. He was with her, had been with her even in the dream. Weeping still, she opened her bedroom door. Her mother was talking to Donnie. Seth chimed in. Mira eased the door closed, fell on the bed again. It was only a bad dream. Just a dream.

But it was all there in her mind when she awakened again. The headache was gone. The pills had worn off. Only the swirl of drifting images remained, bloody, gruesome, terrifying. She had tiptoed to the brink of the unfaceable, seen the possibilities beyond. Shaken, she told herself that she must forget it. It had been a dream, now it was over. But she sensed its meaning . . . which was death to all the people she loved. Sensed it and couldn't examine it. Instead she only thought of Shelley. . . .

Still, nothing would have happened except that when John came home on Friday afternoon there was a Montgomery County police car in the driveway of the house.

John paid off the taxi, caught up his bag, and went inside. Hurrying, but not showing it. Strung tight, but looking casual.

Two young blond officers in uniform got up to greet him.

Ruth lay wilted in a chair, her face ashen, her lips almost blue, her eyes swimming with unshed tears of mortification. "Thank God you're home," she whispered. "I didn't know what to do."

"Where's Mira?" was the first thing John asked.

"She had to go out. Some last minute shopping, I

think." Ruth was too frightened to dissemble. She blurted, "And I don't know where. I never do."

John raised his brows, looked at the policemen. "What's this about?" They were in uniform, so they weren't Treasury men. It had nothing to do with him. Not that he had anything to worry about. He and Bull were strictly legal, or very nearly so. Just the same they preferred not to be noticed. Their business was better kept *their* business.

"Your son is Seth Priest?" one of the officers asked.

John nodded.

"Do you know where he is now? We'd like to talk to him."

John said, "You can see I've just returned from a trip. Hadn't you better explain what all this is about?"

"There was some trouble, John. While you were away." Ruth got it out, wrung her thin white hands. "Seth . . . it was some boys he was going around with —"

"Vandalism, Mr. Priest. He was arrested for doing malicious damage. Burning crosses on the front lawns of a number of homes occupied by black people. Sixteen thousand dollars worth of damages at a cemetery."

"And . . .?" But John was looking at Ruth.

"Alan went to court with Seth. His sentence was suspended. But he's on some kind of probation."

John transferred his cool gaze to the policeman. "If that's so, then why are you here now?"

"A couple of incidents took place in the last two nights. More of the same. We want to ask him some questions."

"You mean because of the other thing?"

"We'd just like to know where he was last night and the night before."

"He was here," Ruth said, her voice shaking. "I saw him go up to his bedroom. I heard his stereo until late.

Then he went to sleep. That was night before last. Last night, too. Only Mira had a headache, so he didn't play his stereo. But he was here."

"Did you go to sleep, too?" the policeman asked.

"Yes. Of course. I need my rest."

"And what about Mrs. Priest? Seth's mother? Where was she night before last?"

"At a movie, I think she said. And last night . . . the headache —"

John cut in, "There's nothing else we can tell you."

"Except where we can locate your son."

"I don't see why you need to talk to him. You know he was home."

The policeman got up. "We're just doing our job, Mr. Priest. I hope you understand that. Whenever one of these things comes up, we've got to check out anybody who's been involved in that kind of situation before."

"If it's been resolved you shouldn't be harassing my son," John said coldly.

"A couple of questions, Mr. Priest. That's not harassment."

When the police had gone, John asked, "Was Seth really home as you said?"

Ruth whispered, "I suppose he was. He did go upstairs. And the one night I did hear the stereo . . . not the other . . . but I told them, Mira's headache . . ."

"You sound doubtful —"

"No. It's just that I was so frightened. The police. John, in all my life, and I'm seventy years old, we've never had police in our house. We've never had trouble."

"What's been going on around here anyway?" he said disgustedly. "Seth knows better."

Ruth rose shakily. She tried to smile. "Boys do these things sometimes, John. Let me fix you a nice cup of tea. You must be tired after your trip. And Mira will be home soon, I know. And then she'll tell you all about it."

He didn't answer her. He went to the phone, called Alan. Alan explained what had happened. Moments later, John spoke to his attorney. When he put down the phone, he was frowning. That was the only sign of the anger he felt. The attorney had said that what happened was to be expected. Both now, and in the future, too. The police had Seth's name. It was as the officer had said. It was only logical, and completely legal, that they would check Seth out whenever a crime came up that was similar to the one the boy had been involved in. That was that. And there was nothing John could do about it. Except hate it. He didn't want the police to know the Priest name, the address, to visit the house every time they had an urge to. But he didn't see how he could prevent it either. His attorney wanted to talk about Seth, what John planned to do to make sure the boy stayed out of trouble. John didn't know. He hadn't thought about it. He told the attorney that he would. And he would talk to Seth as soon as he could. But Seth didn't return home.

John drank the tea Ruth had fixed him, then drank a straight Scotch. He changed clothes, went out to the practice green for an hour. When Donnie returned from swimming at the country club, he sat on the steps watching his father. As soon as Seth drove up, Donnie disappeared inside.

John called Seth into the back yard, told the boy that he knew about his recent run-in with the police.

Seth even grinned. "Mom's going to be sore. She wanted to wait for you to be in a good mood."

"My mood doesn't matter. I want to know what you thought you were doing."

Seth shrugged. He'd been bawled out by his Uncle Alan, by his Aunt Kit, by his mother, and grandmother. The police and the judge had had their big deal comments. He figured he'd heard it all. Not that it took. He and the boys had already been out twice, just the three of them though. The others were scared shitless to get anywhere near him. He didn't need them or anybody. And he wasn't scared. He was busy thinking about that night. Once, maybe, he'd have tried to explain how his heart had gone out with his father to shadowed places and followed him into danger. How he'd tried to be like his father. But he was old enough now to know his father would never understand. Seth yawned.

John insisted on an answer, but didn't get any. Finally he turned his back on Seth, went to the practice green and started swinging.

By six o'clock, when Mira returned, he was his usual unruffled self. He accepted her kiss, returned it. He didn't mention Seth, the policemen's visit until later, when they were alone.

She had bathed, powdered, scented herself. She wore a sleeveless black dress, its neckline high, its back swooping in a deep V. She sat before the mirror still feeling Shelley's hands on her breasts, the taste of his mouth on hers. What was left of the day before. It would be so long until she could touch him again. She sighed as she leaned forward, delicately applying black eyeliner, knowing that John was watching her.

He still held the golf club that he'd absently brought upstairs with him. His hands stroked it unconsciously as he asked, "What's this about Seth?"

Slow, deliberate voice. Unemotional. But accusing just the same. She resented it, felt a quick heat burn her cheeks.

But her hand was steady at its work. She said, "My

mother must have told you the minute you put your foot in the door."

"No. But some policemen were here."

"Here? Today?" She put down the brush, turned to John. "Why? What for? It was all settled. Alan said so. And he was there."

"It's never all settled, Mira."

She stared at him.

"Something happened last night, night before last. They wanted to question Seth."

"But he'd never do it again. It was a child's prank. A kind of game really. For kicks. Alan straightened him out, you can be sure."

A child's pranks. For kicks. A game. Like the games that Shelley had taught her. The games that had become like some deep and necessary drug to her. A drug like Shelley. She needed them, and him, as she needed air to breathe, food to eat, sleep to renew herself.

"You think so?" John was asking.

"Think so?" she echoed. Then: "Of course."

John said softly, "And you didn't go to court with him. You sent Alan. He needed you, Mira. You're his mother. Having his uncle there wasn't enough —"

"I *couldn't* go. It was . . . you don't realize how upset I was." She stopped there. She hadn't dared to go with Seth. She didn't trust herself. She was frightened for him, ashamed of what he had done. But she was afraid that she'd break out into some awful hysterical laughter. Laughter might burst through her tightly-clenched lips . . . like mother, like son . . . did Seth feel the excitement she had felt? But at least Seth was still only half grown while she —

"You can't duck everything because it upsets you," he said coolly.

"I'm sorry, I couldn't help it." She glanced at her

wristwatch. "Don't you think you'd better start to get ready? It's cocktails and dinner at the Weidemayers. And we're going to drop the boys off at the Hartleys' first. We'll be late."

"Drop the boys off at the Hartleys'? Tonight?"

She thought of the trouble she'd gone to just to keep John from learning about Seth's trouble at the wrong time. It hadn't worked. Still, the arrangements were made. She said, "Helene's kids have set up the tents for camping out. I don't want to disappoint them, John."

"I'd sooner lock Seth in than let him go out for a good time now."

"You can't do that. You've no right to act as if he's a criminal. Boys get into funny things sometimes. You must have done the same. When you were less than perfect."

"All right," he said. "Since it's settled with the Hartleys, Seth and Donnie can go. But what about last night? Do you know where he was?"

"Home," she said promptly.

"How do you know?"

"I was here, too."

"What about the night before?"

She tried to remember. When she did, she turned back to the mirror. She'd been with Shelley. They'd played no games that night. They'd spent the time together making love. Making love so that he left his taste in her mouth and his hand prints on her flesh where they lingered still. "I was out for a while. But my mother told me Seth was home."

"I want you to keep a close eye on Seth from now on, Mira. I can't afford to have him get into trouble —"

"You can't afford . . ." She dropped the lip brush, slammed her hand on the dresser top. "What kind of thing is that to say? What about him?"

"I'm saying he's got to stay out of trouble. I don't want my name in the papers. I don't want anybody, and by that I mean *anybody*, taking a second look at me. I'm a settled quiet businessman who travels a lot. Period."

"Of course. But what —"

"And I want to keep it that way."

"I told you I was sorry."

"That doesn't help. Not me. Not Seth."

His words ended the conversation.

He put the golf club in a corner. He gathered his clothes, went into the bathroom. Soon she heard the sound of the shower.

She went downstairs to wait for him.

Ruth asked anxiously. "All right, Mira?"

"Of course."

"I didn't know what to do. It was so awful. In all my life, we never . . . not policemen, Mira."

"I know. I know."

"I'm sure Seth really was home last night. I saw him go upstairs."

"Yes," Mira said. "He did. I heard him."

"And he's upstairs now."

"Yes. I know."

"He's very hard to talk to, Mira. I tried. But he just stares at me. I don't know if he's listening or not. And sometimes he laughs."

Mira said automatically, "Let me take care of it, Mother. Seth's not your problem."

"My grandson." Ruth was indignant. "He is. I care." And then: "And John's very angry. He doesn't show it. But that only makes it worse. He's terribly angry, Mira."

"You'd better let me handle John, too," Mira said.

"But Mira . . . Mira, I'm scared. The way things are nowadays . . . how do you know . . . what can you do . . ."

Her mother came closer, leaned against her, snuggled to Mira's warmth as if *she* were a child seeking reassurance.

Mira hugged her briefly. "It's going to be okay, Mother. Don't worry."

Though he hadn't been enthusiastic about going to the Hartleys, Seth was ready. Donnie had been counting the hours since he first heard of the plan, and was plainly relieved that it hadn't been changed.

Mira kissed her mother good night, whispered, "Don't worry," before the four of them left the house.

There was a brief argument when Seth suggested he drive Donnie and himself in his jalopy. John said nothing doing, and that time Seth was smart enough not to insist too hard. Then they got underway.

The Weidemayers' house was brightly lit, the gathering in full swing by the time Mira and John arrived.

Dora introduced them to the few couples that they didn't already know, and Dirk got them drinks. Then both host and hostess left them to fend for themselves.

They separated, relieved, to mingle with the other guests.

Mira smiled, chatted. The talk was of real estate prices, the upcoming campaign, inflation . . . It was a typical Washington dinner-party.

Each new face asked the same question. Conversation began, as always these days, with "What do you do?"

"I live," Mira said, smiling into the face of an auburn haired woman her own age. And thought: But I'm the last one left who does, and I'm the only one who knows it . . . and, God help her, she wondered where Shelley was . . . .

John, suddenly at her side, said sourly, "My wife is a lily of the field. She neither toils nor spins."

"Lucky wife," the auburn haired woman answered, "But I'd think it boring. My work takes all my time."

"And what do you do?" John asked.

"I'm a sociologist."

"How exciting," Mira murmured, but the woman had already drifted away.

At dinner, Mira sat between a man who was a lawyer, and another who was in insurance. The two women across from her were professionals, too. Everyone there was either into law, or studying for it, she decided. Or else in English literature. Or working on their theses. There was a girl who acted in a little theater, another who wrote novels. She felt out of place, she hated John for embarrassing her. She ate little but drank a good deal of the wine.

Some time between the stuffed mushroom appetizer and the chocolate mousse desert she found herself shivering. It was as if a cold wet sheet had snugged itself around her back and shoulders. Her fingertips felt numb. She searched her purse for the pill box she always carried. It wasn't there. She resigned herself to the migraine she knew was coming, and drank more wine, and decided that she was what she was.

The question: What was she?

"We have to talk about Seth," John said as they pulled into the driveway behind Seth's jalopy.

She did not answer him. A vise was tightening at the back of her neck. Now her vision was dimming. The pills. The pills. She hurried ahead of him.

Upstairs, John went into Seth's room. Mira said he'd been home the night before. She sounded certain. But John wondered. From what the police had said . . . He

233

went to the window, looked out at the big oak. He was sure he knew how Seth had gotten out that night, all the other nights. He knew why Ruth and Mira had thought the boy was in his room when he wasn't. The sneaking out made it even worse. A sneak and a vandal.

Mouth tight, fury burning in him anew, John went into the bedroom he shared with Mira.

"Maybe you'd like to know that locking Seth in wouldn't have helped anyway. You were right about that, at least." His voice was still even, cool, but the rage was in his eyes.

"What are you talking about?"

"The tree."

"The tree?" she echoed, unable to think. There was something she knew she ought to remember. The oak tree outside Seth's room . . . and Donnie falling . . .

John glared at her. He wasn't going to take it, he told himself. He knew exactly what he wanted. And he was going to have it. A good home to return to, a wife to run it properly, sons he could be proud of. And Virgie Evans waiting for him in New York this time. He wasn't going to let it break up because Mira wasn't doing her job.

He said quietly, "What have you been doing Mira? How come you haven't noticed that something was going wrong with Seth?"

"You can't watch a boy his age every minute. Just as you can't keep him under lock and key."

"You should be able to keep an eye on him. If you're paying attention . . ."

The accusation in his cool voice was too much. She wouldn't let him blame her. He was in it, too. "I suppose it's my fault he's never really had a father at home to look up to. I told you to go running off with Bull

Baron. I told you to keep yourself a stranger, to Seth, to Donnie, and to me, too?"

"Where would you be if I didn't work for Bull, Mira?"

"Maybe I'd be a happy woman —"

"Not you," he said. "You'd find plenty to bitch about. No country club. No nice house. A stinking job in some office. And what about your mother? Who'd take care of her?"

"I'd have a real life," she said, her voice suddenly low, tight. "I wouldn't be watching the world pass me by. You'd rather travel with Bull, be with him, maybe even *be* him, than stay at home as a husband to me, a father to the boys . . ."

His eyes glittered at her, there was a flush high on his cheekbones. "A real life? You?" Contempt now in the cool voice, in the small hand gesture. "What would you *do*? You're a nothing, Mira, a parasite living off me. That's all you've ever been, from the day I first screwed you. That's what you are now. A *nothing*."

What was she? She remembered that she had wondered. Now she at least knew what this man thought. She was a *nothing*. But to Shelley, she was his *love*. There was only one way now. Too late to change it. She almost thanked the auburn haired woman she'd spoken to at the Weidemayers'. Only one way to go now. And with that knowledge, a profound relief. A calm . . .

Mira drew a slow breath, said quietly, "I guess this has been coming for a long time . . . John, I . . . I want a divorce . . ."

The word hung in the air between them. She imagined she saw it written in flaming letters. He heard it as a deep resounding drum that echoed on after her voice was still.

He stared at her, then sat down on the edge of the bed. Its inner springs sang out. The sound reminded her of when she and Shelley made love on the couch in his basement room. The rolling creak-creak of the springs and the sudden thrum as they both hung suspended together before their bodies dissolved as time dissolved.

His glittering eyes measured her. Cautious. Calculating. What was behind this? Finally he said, "So now you want a divorce. I wonder why? You've been content for seventeen years. What's different now?"

"It's been building in me for a long while," she told him. "I need . . . I need . . ." But she knew she mustn't mention Shelley. She went on, "I just need to be free, John. Time seems so short suddenly . . . like I said, the world passing me by . . . all I ever wanted . . ."

"You're free now. Who says you're not?"

She shook her head slowly.

"You'd better level with me, Mira. I want to know what's going on." There was a threat in his voice now.

She heard it, but kept shaking her head.

He was thinking of the derisive amusement he would see in Bull's eyes as the big man commiserated with him. Poor old John. So Mira was getting a divorce. Poor old John. Hell, that's how women were. Bull had always had some snide comment about Mira. How did she manage alone so much? She was such a hotpants. A man could smell her wanting half a block away. John must sure be busy when he was home. It had never been challengeable. Never direct. But always there between the two men. John had been above it, too confident to care. And he'd had his Virgie Evans, hadn't he? That proved the man he was. But now he knew better. And Bull would, too. And Bull would never let him forget it. And that day in headquarters company, flame and explosions, would rise up out of the mists of the past . . .

"You've been playing around, haven't you?" he said. "There's some man you want."

She didn't answer him. She saw Shelley's face in her mind, and the face beyond that that she only dimly sensed was there. Half-boy. Half-man. Adult, but child. Sweet, Tender. Stern. Sullen. Demanding. Giving. His scarred body that had become a part of her.

"That's why you want a divorce."

"No." She had to deny it. "I just want to live, that's why . . ." And it was true. Because that's what Shelley meant to her. Living . . . .

He eyed her. "Suppose I said 'okay'? How would we work it out? There's your mother. The boys. There's also a matter of money, the house. Well? I'm waiting."

"I don't know," she said. But even as she spoke, she did know, she remembered . . . She had to have money to go with Shelley. Else she wouldn't be here, in the pink bedroom now, allowing John's eyes to whip her.

"What do you think you're worth to me?"

She backed away from him. The room slowly spun around her. A flash of wrought iron shelves with African violets in bloom, a glint of triple mirror over the beruffled dressing table. The pills were beginning to take effect, creating in her a sense of distance and a sense of closeness at quick intervals. But the vise was still tightening at the back of her head and pain probed gently at her temples. She didn't know what was happening. It seemed to her that when she left the Weidemayer house with John she had stumbled into an interminable nightmare.

"Now let me think," he was saying. "I ought to be able to work it out without the use of a calculator. We've been married seventeen years. We've screwed maybe an average of twice a month, give or take a couple of extras when I was home for more than the usual days. It wasn't the highest quality screwing. But it was all right. As extras. Let's call it twenty-five bucks a throw —"

"*Shut up.*" But her vision was narrowing; she saw only a tunnel with John's face at the end of it. A gray mist was gathering. A soft cloudy twilight that held faint flickers of lightning.

"Maybe that's a little high," he went on, "considering that you've aged. But all right, I'll let that go. So we'll make it twenty-five bucks a wriggle. Twelve months to a year. For seventeen years. I figure that for somewhere around ten thousand dollars. That sounds right, doesn't it? I'll give you a check in the morning before you take the boys and your mother and move out." In the face of her silence, he asked, "What's the matter? Doesn't it sound good enough for you?"

"I should charge you for housekeeping," she gasped. "And for baby-sitting your sons —"

"You weren't doing much of a job. Look what happened while you were running around with your new man."

"While *you* were running around with Bull Baron."

It stung in a way John didn't understand. He stiffened, said, "With Bull? My dear, you underestimate me. Two can play at your game, you know. I have a girl. Have had for several years. She's young, Mira. Very young. Twenty-one or so. Unlined. Unmarred. The most beautiful body I ever saw."

Twenty-one, like Shelley . . .

"And you know what she does with her beautiful body? She sells it to the highest bidder. Which is me. And I'm delighted to pay. She's a whore. She loves to fuck. To Stravinsky and Brahms and Beethoven. And I like it, too. And I also know precisely what I'm getting. I wonder if your new man does. Does he know how old you'll be in a little while? Time's going fast you told me.

You're right. I guess you've got a few good years left in you. But what then?"

A few good years . . . time passing . . . what then? Mira could see the young whore. The curved white flesh. The silken smoothness of belly and breast and thigh. A blackness gathered in the corners of the room. Shadows floated toward her. The young body became her own. In Shelley's arms.

"Are you sure you know what you're doing?" he was asking. "You'll *never* be young again —"

Pain exploded in a great white flash that momentarily shattered the gray mist. For an instant John's hating face blazed at her, then faded again to a distant blur.

He went on, but she heard nothing beyond those words. "You'll never be young again."

Skin like crumpled tissue paper . . . sagging breasts and mottled thighs . . .

She felt Shelley's presence. The beat of his heart in hers. His pulse in her throat. His hunger as hers. He was with her, in her. They were one. And he whispered in her mind, telling her how she could live, live and be part of him . . .

She moved slowly, a puppet animated by invisible strings. Small careful steps took her around the foot of the bed to the wall where John had left the golf club. Her right hand closed around it. Fingers clenching until the knuckles were white. She felt Shelley pressing them.

John was still talking when she turned. Her arm lifted. It swung the club with all its might. The room rocked with a silent thunder. Lightning danced and faded before her.

His mouth opened wide in a soundless shout. Eyes glittering at her as they rolled up, he fell forward, hit the floor with a crash, but to her it was no more than a muted whisper. A pool of blood formed instantly beneath his shattered head.

She held tightly to the club, breathing in long shallow gasps. The lightning was gone. It was done. The fantasies she and Shelley had woven together as stories were merged into a single truth. The dream she had once dreamed continued on. The soft cloudy twilight floated before her.

Now, she thought. Now. *Now*. And it was Shelley, Shelley enfolding her, who whispered the words to her . . .

The pearl earrings she had worn that night at the Weidemayers' . . . She grabbed one off the dressing table, the other from where she had dropped it on the rug. She must throw one away. She'd thought she'd lost it in the Weidemayers' drive, had returned to look. On the way back . . . Shelley told her what she must say next, what she must do. She took her purse, and the Mary Morgan bank book. She pulled on a neat white glove (it was familiar, like a rubber glove she remembered wearing) and rubbed the shaft of the golf club with it, not looking at its bloodied head. Not looking at John either.

It was the old nightmare still. The same throb of pain. The same cloudy twilight.

Beyond the closed door, there was a sound. She clutched the club tightly, turned off the lamp, and went into the hall.

Stiff. Slow. A puppet still. A nightmare walker, with Shelley at her shoulder.

Sudden light, golden and revealing. A shuffle of footsteps. Her mother's, but she attached no name to them. She was beyond names . . . identities . . . all except Shelley's, which was her own . . . As she went down, the gray mist closed in again.

Ruth wore her white robe, her fluffy white slippers. She stood in the open doorway. "Mira, is that you? What's the matter? I heard something fall."

For an instant Mira was her mother's daughter again, the child made uncertain by the face of authority. Diminished. Doubtful. Frightened of losing the older woman's love.

But her mother's lips shook in her ashen wrinkled face. She whispered, "*Mira*, what are you doing?"

The dam inside her had broken. She was carried with the tide. It was the nightmare she had once had when they all lay limp and bloodied before a blank wall.

She swung the club with all her might.

Ruth crumpled soundlessly to the floor.

CHAPTER 18.

THE HOUSE was still. Empty.

It had all been slow, silent, happening to someone else. She and Shelley together. But he was gone. Gone with the gray mist and the pain. Now Mira heard the click of the air-conditioning unit, then the slow tick of the clock. Time.

She dropped the golf club, but didn't hear it fall. She hurried into the kitchen. Clutching her purse in her left hand, she dumped flour and sugar and salt on the floor, poured milk from the refrigerator over it, dancing away from the sticky puddle so there'd be no footprints left behind. She swept the potted plants from the windowsills, and the decorations from the avocado walls. Grabbing the scissors, she ran into the family room to rip the pillows. She swept the lamps from the tables and flung them onto the feathers that veiled the rug.

She was like a whirlwind, spinning in an enclosed place. Rising here, dropping there. A whirlwind that left chaos behind. Mindless motion practiced before in strangers' houses. This house become a stranger's too.

And the plans drawn like road maps in her mind. (Shelley had told her it would be the simplest way. A man had come home to find . . . She was that man.) She had discovered that she missed an earring. She thought she remembered brushing it as she got into the car in the Weidemayers' driveway. She decided to see if it was there. John was already undressing, so she went alone. She didn't find the earring. (She must remember to throw it away.) When she started for home she took a short cut, and suddenly a tire was flat. She waited an hour, hoping for help. At last it came. (Shelley.) A young man stopped, fixed her tire. (She must remember to give Shelley the Mary Morgan bank book, in case the police searched her belongings.) She came home, and found . . . And thank God the boys were gone for the night . . . . It was the last time she thought of Donnie and Seth.

She took the scissors with her when she closed the back door. A few swift sawing motions cut the telephone line.

The house on Plumtree Road was dark and silent when she drove away.

She parked at the corner, because even now, at this late hour, the landlady might be peering from behind the curtained window. She mustn't see Mira.

A quick, breathless race through the shadows. She tapped at Shelley's door. Gasping, she whispered. "Hurry, hurry. Shelley, hurry!" and listened for his footsteps. But there was only silence. A stir of breeze in the bushes near the door. She tapped again.

The door opened, creaking. Shelley stood there, peering at her, eyes sleepy.

She put her hands on his bare chest, thrust him aside, and went in.

It was dark. She picked her way through the shadows to the couch, and sank into it, saying, "There's not much time."

"What's wrong?"

She heard him move. A lamp spilled light on the rug she had bought for him.

"What happened, Mira?"

She said, "It's done, Shelley."

The sleepy look disappeared from his eyes. The beginnings of a smile on his lips faded. "What's done?"

She raised her right hand and looked at it. Then she looked at him. "We're free, Shelley. We can be together now."

He stood over her, still, unmoving. He tried to hear the distant murmurs in his head as he asked, "What did you do?"

"There's not much time. We have to go. We have to do it the way we said."

"Said?" he echoed.

"The flat tire. You stopping to help. Then I'll have to go home. I went out again to look for an earring I'd lost. And while I was out, I had the flat tire. You remember, and that's when it happened. While I was out."

"You're not making sense," he told her. "What flat tire?"

"The one that gives me an alibi." She heard the quaver in her voice. It echoed in a shiver that chilled her body. "The way we talked about," she said again.

His silver eyes were blank looking into hers. "We talked about?"

"*You* and *me* . . ." She scrabbled in her purse, drew out the bank book. She thrust it at him. "You've got to keep this for me. It'll all be over in a few months. We can do it if we're smart and careful. Just the way we talked about . . . "

He strained to hear the voices in his head. They were coming closer. Now he remembered. Not the past months when he had fed her the need and the means, and gently edged her along the path of no return. That part was gone. He was in another time. A time long ago. Flashes. Heat and pain. Shouting voices. Hatred. He remembered a terrible night. A dawn as red as the blood that covered him. An agony that left a scar on his back that never faded, a wound in his soul that never healed.

He was back in the dream that wasn't a dream. But he spoke to her, said, "Mira, why? Why?"

"For you."

So he was guilty again. And time had stopped. He was a small boy. Waves of hate submerging him. Sinking in dangerous currents. Pain beyond bearing. He was covered by an icy sweat, and his teeth chattered. Quick chill tremors flickered on his skin. Maggots of terror swam through the blood in his veins. He had done it again. Was guilty again. Waves of hate submerging him. Sinking in dangerous currents. Pain. The voices. Terror. And the knife in his flesh after. Tears. Whispers. The blade warm through the fold of rainbow gown.

"Shelley!"

"Yes." His voice was only a whisper. "We'd better get started, hadn't we?"

He dressed quickly. Trousers. Shirt. Blue sneakers.

She put the bank book in his hand. "Better have it with you."

He nodded, buttoned it into a back pocket. He turned off the light, locked the door behind him, as they went outside.

"You can drive?" he asked.

"Yes. But let's hurry." She was thinking ahead now. To the worst part. To walking into the house on Plumtree Road.

"You're sure you can drive?"

"I have to, Shelley."

"That's my girl." He held her against him, his strength feeding hers, as he walked her to the shadows where her car waited. When she got in, he said, "Wait for me at the corner. I'll lead the way."

"Where to?"

"The road right next to the grove. Our special place."

"Is that all right?"

"Yes."

She considered. A short cut from the Weidemayers'. It would do. She slid the pearl earring from her purse. She'd have to throw it away somewhere along that road where the brush was thick and the honeysuckle overgrown. She put the keys into the ignition. "I'll be waiting."

When she tipped her face up, he bent to kiss her. She said, shivering, "It's going to be hard. We won't be able to meet for a while. Remember that I love you."

"I'll remember," he said softly.

He didn't look back as he walked away. He got into the old tan VW, started it, and switched on the lights. By then, she was waiting at the corner. He swung ahead of her and went on, keeping her in sight in his rearview mirror.

The road was still empty. A cradle moon hung over the tree tops. Occasional light flickered from draped windows. He drove slowly, carefully, making his way into another time . . . into a moment when *she* held him close, weeping over him . . . blood on her shoulder and cheek. Bennett's blood. Bragan's. "There's no other way, my darling," she was saying . . . "He was going to do something terrible to you, I had to stop him. But how can I leave you behind? You, alone? How? No other way." And his "mama, no," as he'd uttered it in a child's voice a hundred times before . . . .

He had been born into hate. He knew it long before he knew the word. The big man was his father. The big man couldn't stand to look at him. The twins, Bennett and Bragan, were accepted. But never Shelley. The big woman, mama, would have been accepted too. Except for Shelley. She stood between his father and him, was pulled one way, then the other. She cried. She berated Shelley. She protected him. And cried again . . .

The familiar curve. Empty in the moonlight. He slowed, pulled off, and stopped.

He was waiting when Mira pulled in behind him.

She came and leaned against him. He felt her body warmth, her trembling. Her eyes were closed. She breathed with her mouth open, shallow life passing between her lips, spilling out again.

"You'll do it quickly, won't you? There's not much time. I have to get to the house soon."

"Don't worry." He felt invulnerable. He knew he could do what he had to do. He was the instrument . . . It was why he had been the only one left way back then . . . The feel of the knife haft beneath the fold of his mother's gown . . . her hand and his pressed tightly together . . . She'd saved him for last . . . And he'd had to do it . . . her or him . . . As she held him, kissed him, wept over him, crying, "No, not you, Shel. Not you," he fought her, only dimly aware of what she meant, hardly aware that it was her strength and not his that had thrust the knife into her chest, and never realizing then or in the years to come that suicide was what she'd intended all along . . . the hot blood . . . the stumbling walk into a red dawn . . . a small boy crying at the edge of a road, and pointing over his bowed shoulders at the silent house . . . the foster homes . . . the years when voices echoed from a distant dream . . . and then — Mira, who made the dream so very real once again . . .

"Come with me," he said, sliding an arm around her waist. "Come on."

She cast a bewildered look at his shadowed face. "There's no time, Shelley. The tire . . . we have to hurry . . . too much to do . . . As soon as I can . . ."

He shook his head, drew her with him, stumbling in the dark. She'd thought she knew every stone along the way, and every shadow too. Here they had made love under the trees while butterflies fluttered over the honeysuckle. Here she had danced for him, even though she had never danced before.

He stopped, looked up at the stars. Then he went on, pulling her with him.

The cave. The special place that was theirs.

The chill of the cold granite walls seeped into her. The mausoleum. That's how she had thought of it. He lit the lantern. Pale rays showed tear tracks on his face.

"We can't stay," she said.

Holding her tightly to him, so tightly that she could feel his erection, he murmured, "Mama, why? Why did you do it?"

"*Shelley*? It's Mira. Mira. Shelley, can you understand me? I'm Mira." All struggle useless. All hope.

He didn't hear her protest. He went on, body crushed to hers, arms locked at her waist, "You killed them, didn't you? You killed them all for me . . ."

She stared into his blank eyes, mesmerized, numbed. She thought, for you, Shelley. For you. And our love. It's what you wanted . . . what you told me —

And he was saying, "Like that other time. Him. Papa.

249

And Bennett and Bragan. You killed them, and then you came to kill me."

"*Shelley* . . ." They had talked it over together. They had planned it, one detail from him, one from her. A game . . . a game . . . playacting a dream . . . so they could be free . . . And now, this . . .

"But I had to live," he was saying. "I had to. I had to be the last one left. To punish you . . ."

Blank eyes, focused on a past she could only guess at, picture because of the words he said. And arms like linked steel around her.

Shelley, the lost waif . . . Shelley, the man . . .

They were both gone from her.

It was a madman stranger who held her, whispered at her. Told her how it had been that last night.

"Mama, it was so terrible. Your weeping. The way we all hid in different rooms, trying to get away from the sound of it. And then, after those words and shouts and screams. Then, that awful silence. It was worse than anything. That silence. And your soft footsteps coming, going. Coming back. And how you held me . . . the knife hidden in your gown, and cried over me and said you had to do it. The pain that raked me, and my screams. And then . . . then . . ."

She made one last effort to get through to him, a last effort to retain her sanity, her hope. "I'm not your *mother*," she said. "Shelley, listen, *listen*. I'm not your mother. I'm your sweetheart. Your lover. Not your mother. *Not your mother* . . ."

Tears wet on her face. Fists pounding his chest. Kicking, screaming, struggling.

There was the glint of his knife at the end of an arm. His arm. The blue tattoo, mother.

It was for this moment that he had gone stumbling through the years of his life, always hearing voices from a distant red dawn, from the dream that was no dream. It was this that he'd craved, sought, made come true.

His face pressed to her lips, and he whispered, "Mama, I love you," at her mouth.

"And I love you," she murmured. But in her mind she was saying, "No, no, no . . . I will not die, no, not now, not here, not for this, no . . ."

And one of her arms reached greedily around his neck, cherishing him, clinging to him. One stretched for the hand that held the knife. Her fingers grinding on his. Her body pressing to his. He, slowed to hesitation by the dream, by her complaisant touch, waited too long. Her tongue was sliding between his lips when she thrust the blade into his side.

He staggered, clung to her. The blank silver eyes flickered, lantern light fading from them.

She pulled free.

He swayed, casting a huge shadow behind him. Arms still reaching for her, he fell.

A rattle came from his throat. To her ears it sounded like a word. "Mama."

She grabbed the knife and her purse, pulled the bank book and the VW keys from his trouser pocket. Leaning across his unmoving body, she blew out the lantern. Then she ran as fast as she could.

CHAPTER 19.

A T FIRST Kit didn't understand what she was seeing. The flickering images moved across the white screen pulled down on the wall. In bright color the woman knelt. Then the man. They heaved and strained separately. They fell together, writhing in a tangle of arms and legs. Other figures appeared. There were joinings and re-joinings in varieties of angles. When, finally, Kit understood what was happening, she didn't believe it. How did she come to be there? Why would anyone think she'd want to see this?

She turned her mind off, and closed her eyes tightly, and shrank in the big easy chair, wishing that she and Alan had never run into the Taggarts on the boardwalk. Wishing that they hadn't come to Ocean City for the weekend.

A fat hand dropped to her knee. Pudgy fingers began a slow tarantula walk up her thigh. Without looking she reached down. She caught a thick wrist and flung it away, careful not to touch the hairy flesh beneath a sleeve cuff. Even that minute contact with K.C. Taggart made her feel soiled. She rubbed her fingers briskly on her skirt.

At the same time she heard Alan cough, saw his slight movement, and knew that Sue Taggart had made the same approach that K.C. had made to her.

It started several hours earlier while she and Alan were walking. The hearty greeting . . . "Long time no see. Where you been all these years, you old son of a gun!" Then came the introductions. "Sue, meet Alan, a school buddy of olden times. And I mean just that. Olden times all right." And: "K.C ., this is my wife Kit." A foursome talking uncomfortably. Then drinks together. Later on, dinner. A graceless attempt at withdrawal shouted down by the Taggarts. The condo with thick, wall to wall carpeting, and two views. The incense perfuming the air. The pot offered, refused. The porno film.

All prelude to a fat hand on Kit's thigh. A slim one on Alan's.

He coughed again.

It was time to go.

Yawning loudly, Kit rose. She opened her eyes, but kept them averted from the screen on the wall. She didn't want to know what was happening now.

"I'm sorry," she said. "I hate to break it up, but it's been a long day, and the sun's gotten to me."

Alan was on his feet, too, moving quickly toward the hall, the foyer, the outer door. "Yes, late. It's been swell seeing you, K.C. Meeting you, Sue."

His voice made a lie of the words. Kit smiled to herself. At least she and Alan agreed on that. He had hated the smell of the incense, the offer of pot, the porno film, just as much as she did.

The two Taggarts protested, but weakly. They already understood that they'd wasted an evening. No orgy was to be forthcoming. Kit and Alan didn't want to play their games.

The elevator dropped twenty floors in seconds.

Alan scrubbed a fist through his short dark hair, said, "Sorry, Kit," as the doors opened.

She shrugged. "What are you apologizing for? Obviously a lot's happened since you last saw K.C."

"In ten years a lot can. And I hope it's another ten years before I see him again."

Outside the breeze was off the ocean, salty and wet and clean.

Kit raised her head and sniffed to clear the incense fumes from her nose and throat. Her hair veiled her face, curtained her eyes. She swept it back as she got into the car.

"I should have known what to do," Alan muttered, a hand poised over the ignition key. "There are ways to deal with situations like that. But I let it buffalo me."

The self-deprecating edge in his voice filled her with quick anger. He was at it again. Even after everything that had happened. Now, if he dared mention John Priest . . .

"Let's go," she said, more sharply than she intended.

The silence held until they were parked in the motel lot. Then Alan said, "Damn it, Kit. The whole weekend's spoiled."

"Not unless you want it to be."

"I should have punched K.C. in the nose."

"It might have made you feel better, but what would it have accomplished beyond that?" Without waiting for his answer, she went ahead of him to the door.

Inside, sheltered from the night, she peeled her blue shell over her head, stepped out of her white skirt, kicked off her pumps. "I'm for a quick shower."

He didn't answer her.

She stepped under the hot spray. The soap was lavender scented. The wash rag was rough. It was good to scrub. Maybe the weekend wasn't spoiled, if they didn't let it be. But that night was. That night, which ought to have been perfect, was wrecked. If Alan touched her, she would throw up. If she didn't, she would scream at him. It was different, maybe, for men. But for women, for her, the pictures were sickening. Maybe men responded to them. Everyone said so. Not women though. Not her. Kit scrubbed harder. What about Sue Taggart? More scrubbing. Then rinsing in cold water. The images remained in Kit's mind.

When she left the bathroom, Alan went in.

She got into bed, feeling almost good again. It was the same for him. He'd been upset by the porno film, too. She savored the knowing. It was close to have their feelings touching. They needed it. Too often lately he'd stood on one side of a big pit, she on the other. They'd glared at each other across the distance.

When he came out, his hair glistened. He looked fresh, clean. There was a twinkle in his eyes. "I guess we'll recover."

"There's nothing to recover from."

He turned out the light, lay down beside her.

After a while he said into the dark, "Twenty-nine years old and acting like an embarrassed kid. I guess I really should have punched him in the mouth."

"You did the right thing. You got up and left. And that was fine."

"I guess it was fine as far as it went. But it didn't go very far. He should have known how I felt. Letting you in for that garbage."

"Letting us both in for it."

He went on, "Maybe history teachers don't punch people in the mouth."

"Maybe civilized ones don't." Her voice was even, but she was beginning to struggle with anger again. He was going to mention John. Or Mira. Or maybe both of them.

But Alan said, "If I were a different kind of man —"

She cut in, "Alan, not now. I don't want to hear about it now." But it was too late.

He was launched, on his way. "If I were, you'd be more sure of me, more secure with me."

"I don't want to get into it."

"But it's true, Kit. The reason you don't want to have kids yet is that you're not quite sure you really want me. You could have anybody. We both know that. You picked me. But you haven't really made up your mind. Even though you finally did give in and marry me. When you do really make up your mind, and you know you want me for good, then you'll pitch out your pills."

She had flipped to her stomach, buried her head in the pillow. She muttered into the starched cloth, "Just tell me why you had to ruin it."

"We have to talk about it some time."

"Not now."

"You take Mira and John . . . even with the trouble now . . ."

"You'd better leave Mira and John out of this."

"But if you were married to him —"

"I'm not. And I don't want to be."

"All that money, Kit. Wouldn't it make you feel safer. Wouldn't you be ready then?"

"*No*, no, no, no . . . it wouldn't make any difference. There's things I want to do. When I've done them, then I'll be ready."

"Okay," Alan said. "I wasn't trying to make you mad. It's just that I realized maybe you were right to feel the way you do."

"You're twice the man John Priest is. And you know it, too. You just want me to say it."

"For God's sakes, Kit."

"I'm going to sleep."

"Escape. Why won't you face it?"

"I'm sleeping, I can't hear a word you're saying."

"That's funny. It's the first time in months that you haven't wanted to talk about John and Mira. Or my mother. Or Donnie and Seth."

"There's a first time for everything. But if you want to fight about them again, okay. I'll wake up, and we'll fight."

"No, thanks. Not this weekend."

He drew her close, settled her against his shoulder. But, holding her, he wondered about Mira. How come she needed to have an affair? She and John seemed to have everything. What did she think she missed?

Kit lay against Alan, stiff, waiting. If he tried to make love to her, she wasn't sure what she'd do. But it would be something. The porno images were still in her head. She wouldn't be able to contain herself. It was the film, and the pot, and K.C. Taggart's creeping tarantula hand. It was the way Alan spoke of himself. And how he sounded when he mentioned John. And the business about Mira and Seth and Donnie. And how Alan tied them all in to Kit and the job and starting a family. The one had nothing to do with the other, but he didn't see that.

But he was silent now, and still.

Kit lay curled against him. After a while the warmth of his body spread to her. She pressed closer, whispering into the dark, "I love you, Alan."

Monday night. The end of the long Labor Day weekend.

258

It had been a slow drive back. Lines at the bridges and traffic lights. No sign of a gasoline shortage.

Kit's face was sunburned. There was sand in her shoes. The apartment was warm, and smelled of the end of summer to her.

It was too late to call Alan's family. To say hi, and how are you? And we just got back. Kit thought of it, even went to the phone, then decided to unpack and go to bed. Tuesday morning would be soon enough.

But she and Alan rose half an hour after the alarm went off. They had juice and coffee together. Then he hurried out to deal with school's opening day, and she sped to the office.

Though she was busy showing houses most of the day, she managed twice to call the Priest home. There was no answer.

By late afternoon she was tired. She wanted to go home. She was anxious to be with Alan, to talk to him about his day at school, her day at work. She wanted to re-establish the sense of closeness they had shared in those few too-brief moments in the past few days. Even their similar dislike of K.C. and Sue Taggart. It was a way of trying. And if she didn't try then it was all over. She could snuggle close to Alan, and whisper, "I love you," into the dark, but she knew, and soon he'd know, too, that the distance between them was becoming too great to bridge. Still, she had to stop to see the Priests.

Autumn was in the air when she went to her car. But she was too uneasy to savor the gentle fading of the blue twilight, to admire the sky still scarred red though the sun was already set.

Someone should have been at home in the Priest house. Ruth. Or Mira. One of the boys. Even if John had left again, there ought to have been somebody to answer the phone. Concern nagged at Kit like a low level toothache. She realized she had felt it for most of the day. Ruth Baker was virtually housebound, very lonely. The conversations were important to her. They spoke nearly every morning. Ruth enjoyed giving Kit a detailed rundown on the family, even though, in recent weeks, Kit had tried to discourage her from that. Besides, the older woman would have been concerned that Kit and Alan would be driving back through the holiday traffic. Why hadn't she called?

But as she drove away from the office Kit told herself that Ruth was probably busy pampering John's every whim. The boys would be occupied with the start of school. And Mira herself would be doing whatever she always did. Kit didn't want to know what that was. Not any more. She was determined to mind her own business. No matter what.

Starting for home, she insisted silently that there was nothing to worry about. But when she reached the turn off for the Beltway, she slowed, sighed, and passed it. There was no use going home to Alan when half her mind would be wondering about the Priests.

Plumtree Road was quiet when she turned into it. She stopped at the foot of the driveway, and looked up at the dark house. She saw that the car was gone. Only Seth's cherished jalopy was parked at the side of the garage. The family must have gone away together for a few hours, Kit told herself. She turned on the ignition, started away, then jammed on her brakes. As she had pulled off, she'd seen, from the corner of her eye, an accumulation of newspapers scattered on the front steps. Papers. Too many of them.

She cut the ignition, and got out of the car, and hurried up the driveway. John was much too meticulous to go away for a weekend without stopping delivery. A pile of newspapers was an open invitation to anyone driving by. And besides, he'd only been home since Friday. An immediate trip was unlikely.

At the steps, she paused, counted. Four. Saturday. Sunday. Monday. Tuesday.

She knocked at the door. When there was no response she hammered at it with a doubled fist. Nothing. Ruth was an elderly lady, nearing seventy. Had she been taken ill? Had she had a fall? And there was the trouble that Seth had been in. Had something happened? And Mira . . .

Kit jumped the four steps and went on tiptoe to peer into the front window. The drapes were tightly drawn. She couldn't see into the living room. The thin reflection of her anxious face looked back at her.

Alan. She wanted Alan. He would know what to do. He would tell her not to let her imagination run away with her. She thought of that as she hurried through the dusk-shrouded yard past the practice green to the back of the house. The jalousie blinds were tilted. She saw a small angle of the family room.

She sucked air in on a sharp gasp at the sight of a gashed sofa pillow, its stuffing curled like white entrails around the shards of a broken lamp base.

Wrong. Something was terribly wrong.

She wanted to run away into the falling night. She wanted Alan's arms around her.

But she stumbled away from the window to try the back door. It swung open under the touch of her cold fingers. Unlocked. It couldn't have been, shouldn't have been.

She stepped into eerie silence. Into darkness.

Shadows. Stillness except for a faint distant hum. The air heavy with an odor she couldn't identify but that made breathing distasteful. It was noxious. She choked, found the light switch next to the door.

The ceiling globe spilled pale rays on the off-white carpet. A haze of feathers from the torn pillows drifted over it. There was a pile of spilled dirt, bruised green leaves from a shattered potted plant at one corner. The chairs were slashed. The three table lamps lay broken, as if they had been flung against the fireplace wall.

Run, Kit's mind told her. Run, Kit. But after a single frozen moment she made for the stairs. "Mother Ruth. Where are you?"

No response. The silence was thick, blanketing, edged with that faint distant hum. The air was hot, stale.

Kit paused for a quick glance into the kitchen. Unbelievable chaos. It was empty now, but looked as if a tornado had whipped through it. Broken crockery glinted on the floor under a drift of sugar and flour. The table lay on its side. The pots of philodendron had been swept from the windowsill and lay amid black mounds of dry earth.

"Ruth!" Kit screamed the name. She felt like a child crying through a bad dream.

She ran through the foyer, cast a single quick glance into the shambles of the living room, and rushed on toward the bedroom where Ruth Baker always slept.

In the hall something caught at her ankle. She tripped, nearly fell, but found her balance just in time. She glanced at it as she kicked it aside. John's golf club. A funny place for it to be.

But she went on until she reached the threshold of Ruth's room. There Kit saw a mound of white on the floor. A mound of white. Still. Unmoving.

Kit fell to her knees. Brown. The pale carpet. The wall. Ruth Baker's white robe, and her white hair. Brown . . . blood long dry.

Kit cast a single glance over her shoulder at the golf

club, then jumped up, ran for the steps. "Mira . . . John —"

He was sprawled on the floor. His head was black, the carpet beneath it black, too. Black flies crawled and hummed in his open mouth.

Kit backed from the room.

Seth. Donnie.

Their rooms were empty, undisturbed.

"Seth! Where? What? Donnie!"

Kit threw herself down the stairs. As she went back through the hall she saw the kitchen telephone, grabbed it, dialled 911 twice before she realized that there was no dial tone. She dropped it, ran outdoors. She broke through the hedge, ran in darkness toward the closest house.

She banged on the door. "Help me, call the police, something happened, I can't find Mira. I can't find Mira, I tell you. . . ."

CHAPTER 20.

THE MOBILE laboratory arrived half an hour after the first two police cruisers sped into Plumtree Road, their blue dome lights spinning, sirens shrieking in counterpoint to the blat and wail of the rescue squad ambulances.

Soon huge portable lights laid a brilliant glow over the front and back yards of the split level house, and the rescue squads pulled away, empty and silently past the clusters of whispering neighbors who had gathered on the road.

Alan, bogged down in opening day paperwork, was still at school, where the call from the police finally reached him.

A deep slow voice said, "Is this Alan Baker? You're married to Kathryn Baker? Your sister is Mira Priest?"

Alan said, instant alarm bells going off in his head, "Yes, it is. What's the matter?"

"There's been trouble at the Priest house, Mr. Baker. You'd better come here."

"My wife?"

"She's waiting for you." The slow voice softened. "Here. She wants to say something."

"Alan." His name was a whispered plea.

"What happened?"

"Alan . . . my God . . . it's terrible . . ."

The policeman said, "She's too upset. We'll take care of her, Mr. Baker." A click.

Alan stared at the dead phone. Fire, he thought. Gas explosion. Something.

He set out immediately, weaving through the heavy Beltway traffic at seventy miles an hour. Tires screaming, he cut off at the River Road exit.

Plumtree Road was blocked by two police cars. Alan jerked to a stop.

"Can't go in," he was told. "Unless you're a resident."

"It's some trouble at my sister's house. My wife is there." Ahead, Alan could see the glow of the lights, the blinking domes, the clustered neighbors.

"Your name?"

Alan gave it. "What's happened?"

"Bad trouble."

When the scout car had moved back, Alan drove through. He saw the mobile laboratory, the men in uniform moving through the yards, faces intent over bright torches.

He ran up the steps. Once again, he was stopped. When he gave his name, he was directed next door.

It seemed an eternity before Jonathon Black let him in. They had met occasionally before, spoken across the back yard hedge. But they, like most of those who lived in the area, tended to keep to themselves. Alan didn't feel he knew them.

Jonathon Black said, "Your wife is in the living room."

"What happened?" Not waiting for a reply, he hurried to Kit.

She sat alone in the middle of a twelve foot oyster white sofa. Her face was more pale than the light fabric. Her eyes had the glitter of high fever. Her long slim legs were crossed, but one knee jerked visibly, and her fingertips trembled.

Whatever it was, it must be even worse than he had supposed. He crossed the distance between them in two quick steps. He sank down beside her, drew her into his arms. "Kit," he whispered. "Kit, Kit." That was all.

Mary Black, standing at the window, soundlessly left the room then.

Neither Alan nor Kit noticed her go.

Kit said, "Alan, you have to prepare yourself. Your mother. John. They're dead. They're dead, Alan . . ."

He couldn't take it in. He couldn't force himself to know what Kit was talking about, even though he had seen the lights, the policemen, the mobile laboratory.

"Oh, God, so terrible," she murmured, trembling against him.

He tried to make his voice calm. "What happened, Kit?"

She pressed closer. "Alan, we don't know, someone was there . . . in the house . . . a golf club . . . so much blood . . ."

"And —" he forced the question " — and Mira? The boys?"

"They don't know yet. They haven't . . . haven't . . ."

"Their bodies?" Alan asked.

"The car . . . it's gone."

"The car," he said slowly. The obvious struck him immediately. He winced as if it had been a blow to his heart. Mira gone. The car. But what about the boys?

"We don't know," Kit said. "Do you understand me, Alan?"

"We don't know," he repeated. "Anybody could have been there . . . taken the car . . ."

"Forced Mira to go . . ." Kit said.

It was what he wanted to believe. "Yes. It would have had to be that way . . ." Mira, and the boys . . .

And the police are looking now . . . they'd have to be sure . . ."

An officer came to the door. "We've just had a call in. Some people named Hartleys have heard a first flash. The Priest boys are with them. They came last Friday for the weekend. They were supposed to be picked up this afternoon."

"And Mira?" Alan asked.

The officer shook his head. "The Hartleys will keep the boys as long as you want." He went away.

"Donnie," Kit whispered. "Seth. Oh, God."

"We'll get them as soon as we can."

"At least we know they're all right."

Alan managed to pull himself together. "And you?" he asked softly. "What about you? Are you all right?"

"Yes." Her voice was flat, expressionless. She was thinking of the young man she had seen with Mira. Of her uneasy suspicions suddenly made concrete. "I'm all right, Alan . . ."

She said the same thing over the next few days. Even as her hands shook, and dark circles deepened around her eyes, and the color faded from her cheeks, she insisted that she was all right. She had to. Alan began to look like a walking dead man. Donnie and Seth were silent moving ghosts. Kit and Alan had gone to the Hartleys, picked them up. Seth had been gray-faced, but unemotional. Donnie wept and trembled. Kit put them into the bedroom, took the living room for Alan and herself. She watched over them, brooded over them, tried to make them feel safe. But all four of them felt caught in a nightmare together, not able to wake up, and worse, not able even to reach out toward each other.

But first there was that awful moment when Alan asked how Kit was, knowing it was a crazy question, and she said, "I'm all right, Alan," and added, "I'm sorry I couldn't find Mira and the boys."

Before he could answer, a detective appeared in the doorway. "I'll need to talk to you, Mr. Baker."

Alan hugged Kit. "I'll be back."

He went into the kitchen with the officer. Then, because Jonathon Black was there, the two men went out into the back yard. They stood together in the rim of light.

"I want to go over," Alan said. "I ought to see . . ."

"Better not." There was a faint sheen of sweat on the policeman's forehead. He wiped it away with a hand-kerchief.

"My wife . . ."

"One of you is enough." Then: "At least we know where the boys are. And we're looking for your sister now, Mr. Baker."

"Yes," Alan said. "The car being gone . . ."

"Don't jump to conclusions."

Alan nodded, relieved, though he wasn't sure why. If Mira had been abducted . . . he wouldn't let himself think it —

"Is there anything you can think of we should know?"

Alan shook his head. He was remembering what Kit had told him. Mira, and some boy, walking together. Kit's suspicions . . . He dismissed the idea. It was impossible. Not Mira. If Kit had seen what she claimed, then it was coincidence. It had nothing to do with the bloody house next door. A golf club . . . don't jump to conclusions, he told himself.

He wanted to cry, but couldn't. He wanted to curse, but couldn't. Finally he asked, "When can I take my wife home?"

"Soon. They'll get her statement down first. She'll need to sign it." The man waited a minute. Then: "I'm going to have to ask you some questions. Are you up to them now?"

Alan nodded, but when the questions came, he couldn't make sense of them. "Where were you Friday night?" "Who were you with?" "Who saw the two of you?"

"Is that when it happened?" Alan asked. And: "How do you know?"

"We think so. Because of the newspapers. And the car has been gone that long, according to the Blacks. We'll be more certain after the autopsies, though." And then: "What was your relationship with your family? Get along all right? See your mother often? Your nephews?"

Alan finally got it straight in his head. They were checking him out. Checking what Kit said against what he said. He tried to keep heat out of his voice when he answered, but it was there. He described Ocean City, the motel, the Taggarts. He explained how late they'd gotten back Monday night, how Tuesday was the first day of school for him, and he'd left in a hurry, worked late, and Kit had been running late too . . .

The policeman asked, "Your wife always get uneasy about your mother and sister? She over here often?"

"She's always visited frequently. Mostly because of my mother." Was this real? Had it really happened? Was

Kit sitting inside on an oyster white sofa, shivering while she waited for him to come back to her?

The questions went on for a long time. Between them, and Alan's answers, there were small silences filled with the sound of the men going slowly through the back yard under the glow of portable lights, the growl of automobile motors.

When the session was over the policeman said, "We'll let you know."

"But what —" Alan stopped. He couldn't go on. He wanted to ask what had happened, what the policeman thought had happened. It was no use. The policeman didn't know any more than Alan himself knew. Neither of them must jump to conclusions. There was still the young man that Mira had been walking with . . . her strange mood these past few months . . . By now that would be written down in Kit's statements, made real over her signature. He was sick at the thought. "The bodies . . ." he said finally.

"We'll let you know about that too."

Soon after, two blanket wrapped stretchers were carried from the house next door.

A few minutes after that Alan and Kit were sent for.

There was no time to speak on the way over, and none for the next hour.

A detective led them through the family room, and up into the foyer past the chalk marks that showed where Alan's mother had fallen, and then slowly, through the rest of the rooms.

"Anything you can tell for certain is missing?" he asked. "Anything you notice is gone?"

There was so much chaos it was hard to know. But finally Alan and Kit agreed that nothing appeared to be missing.

"One thing we don't see is a woman's purse . . . one

that's being used. With house keys and car keys and the usual make up," the detective said. "Do you know where your sister generally kept it?"

Neither Alan nor Kit knew, but they agreed that Mira did habitually use a purse. And finally, after a second search, and a study of the handbags in Mira's closet, Kit said that she thought a small white purse was gone. She told the detective where he could find a spare set of house keys and a little later the detective told Alan and her that they could go home. The house would be locked up and sealed by the police. Someone would want to talk to Alan and Kit again, and would be in touch.

Outside the road was dark. But clusters of neighbors were still waiting, and as Alan led Kit toward his car a man thrust a television mini-camera at them, another crowded close to ask, "What happened in there? What's going on? Are the police looking for anybody yet?"

And there was more: "Is this Priest the one that was on the San Salvador plane that nearly crashed?" "Is Seth Priest the kid in trouble over burning crosses in the county?" "What's your relationship to the Priests anyhow?"

Kit ducked her head, and Alan shouldered a path through for them. He drove slowly through the crowded way, passed the police blockade, then sped away. They stopped briefly at the Hartley house to pick up Seth and Donnie, hurrying away from an avalanche of horrified questions. It was a relief to get to the Beltway, to leave Plumtree Road behind.

It wasn't until the next morning that he realized he had not managed to leave Plumtree Road behind when he left it. The front page of the Washington *Post* had a large story, headlined ARMS DEALER DEAD IN BI-ZARRE BETHESDA KILLING. Along with the subhead, WIFE MISSING, was a picture of Mira. There was another of Kit and Alan leaving the Priest house. Alan hid the paper from the boys.

The early television news had the same story, again with a photograph of Mira, and shots of Alan and Kit.

Alan got a substitute to take his classes. Kit called the office, was told to stay at home until she felt ready to return to work.

They sat down to have coffee together, but the phone rang. It was K.C. Taggart. "Hey, feller, what the hell's going on?" he demanded. "I've had the cops here. Damn near scared me out of my skin. Me! With cops knocking on the door at 7:20 am. And Sue, boy, is she sore. What's happening?"

Alan briefly explained.

"Murdered? Your mother? Your brother-in-law?" After a moment's silence, K.C. said, "Well, hell, you two were with us Friday night. So that lets you out. But what do you think happened?"

"We don't know." Alan tried to cut the conversation short. "I'm sorry you were bothered."

But now K.C. wanted to talk. "It's okay. Any time, any time." Then: "You find them, Al?"

"Kit did."

"A mess, huh?"

Alan didn't answer that.

"Something must have been going on," K.C. said. Good old K.C.

It led Alan to think of Mira and the young man again. Did that mean anything? He still hadn't spoken to Kit about it, asked if she'd told the police, what they'd said. The night before, when they'd finally gotten home, he'd put her to bed with hot tea and Tylenol. She'd gotten up only a little while before. Big-eyed, she watched him, while he spoke to K.C., saying, "Listen,

I'm sorry about the police. I don't think they'll bother you again. Now I've got to go."

K.C. started to say something. But Alan didn't wait. He put down the phone. It rang almost instantly.

When he answered it a strange voice demanded, "This Alan Baker?" and at Alan's, "Yes," went on, "You sonuvabitch killer. You ought to be strung up —"

Alan broke the connection, sagged back.

"What?" Kit asked quickly.

"Crank call," he told her. Then, as he was about to ask her what she had told the police, there was a knock at the door.

"I guess we have to see who it is," she said tiredly.

He nodded. When he opened the door, the same detective to whom he'd spoken the night before was there.

He said, "Good morning. Sorry but I have some more questions to ask you. And your nephews."

Alan got Donnie and Seth.

The detective studied them for a little while before gently suggesting that Seth tell him about Friday night. Seth's voice shook as he said he didn't know what to tell. It had been like any Friday. Except his dad had come home. And oh, yes, his dad was sore because he, Seth, had gotten into some dumb trouble. Otherwise there was nothing to tell about. It was the same for Donnie. When the detective was finished he sent the boys out.

Then he spread a look between Alan and Kit, seated himself, and asked about John Priest's business. At Alan's look of surprise, the detective explained that sometimes arms dealers got into trouble. Maybe John had enemies. Did Alan know about John's affairs? But neither Alan, nor Kit, could give any information on John's work, though both mentioned Bull Baron's name. Then the detective took Kit point by point through her statement. No mention of her suspicions of

Mira. Not a word about the young man she had seen Mira with.

Alan asked himself how he could ever have doubted Kit, questioned her motives. He must have been crazy. Or a fatuous ass. When the detective had finally gone, Alan said, "You left something out, didn't you, Kit?"

She met his gaze. "I realize that. But . . . But . . ."

"It might be important." It hurt. He had to say it anyway.

"I know. I thought of that. But . . . oh, Alan," it was a sob, "I just couldn't . . . to put it into words . . . and maybe I was wrong . . . it's up to you . . . to you . . . if you don't want . . . if you think . . ."

He drew her into his arms. "I'll do it. A little later on. I'll drive over there. And . . . just in case . . . in case it's important, I'll tell him."

Jimmy hunched over the Washington *Post*, his round face intent, frowning. "It's her all right." He looked up at the regulars gathered around the bar. "No doubt about it. It's her."

Cable demanded, "Well, what're you going to do?"

"Mind your own business," Richard said. "It's got nothing to do with you."

Gus, staring into his glass, muttered, "Used to go with that kid, Shelley, that sat a couple of seats away from her. She'd go out. Then him. They'd drive away together."

Jimmy stared at Gus. "I never heard you say so many words in all the time you've been here."

Gus didn't reply.

"I never saw you paying attention to anything."

Gus still didn't answer. He drained his glass, pushed it to Jimmy, who automatically gave the ex-Navy man a refill.

"Better to stay out of it," Richard said.

Jimmy's frown deepened. "I don't see it. Her, and that kid, Shelley. She was just about old enough to be his mother. I'd sure like to know what happened."

A day later Mira's Impala was found at the side of Canal Road where she had left it. The area was immediately searched. Nothing was found except some old tire tracks, and six or seven rusted beer cans.

The same afternoon the police heard from Jimmy at Joe's Cafe. He, and the regulars, were asked to come in to give their statements, also to work with a specialist who built composite photographs.

By the time they had a likeness of Shelley that satisfied Jimmy, and the others, Alan had spoken to the detective who was handling the Priest case. The man listened, nodded, said, "Yes. We just heard about it. I was going to call you. I can see why you didn't speak up before. But you should have."

"Do you have any ideas . . ."

The detective shrugged. "We haven't found your sister, though we've got her car. Nothing's missing from the house, except her purse. There was this boy . . . Shelley Davis. We'd better find and talk to him."

"You told me not to jump to conclusions," Alan said.

"I'm still saying the same thing," the detective answered, "but where, exactly did your wife see Mrs. Priest and this boy?"

Alan named the street.

The detective nodded, shuffled papers on his desk. "There's an all points bulletin out on your sister. If she's findable, we ought to locate her soon." And then: "You can make the arrangements for your family. Whenever you want to. We're finished with that part of it now."

That part of it was finished. But the nightmare

wasn't. The Priest house had to be guarded night and day from the depredations of souvenir hunters. Neither Donnie nor Seth wanted to go out. They said people looked at them when they tried it. Kit worried about them. What would happen? How would they manage? But one evening over dinner Donnie asked, "Aunt Kit, is there a school around here?" "Just five blocks away," she answered. She saw Seth was listening, blank-faced as always. She looked at him. "And a high school, too." He didn't answer, but his rigid shoulders dropped. They'd be okay, she thought. Eventually.

And when Alan returned to school to take up his classes, the students stared at him, and whispered behind their hands. At Kit's office it was the same. Her co-workers stopped talking when she entered a room. Her clients eyed her, plainly not quite certain they wanted to go into empty houses accompanied only by her.

Whenever Alan or Kit left the sanctuary of their apartment with the boys, newsmen and television people surrounded them, asking the same questions over and over.

When John Priest and Ruth Baker were buried, hordes of cars trailed the small funeral procession to the cemetery, spilled over the grounds, jostled Alan and Kit, and Donnie and Seth, and even Bull Baron, who had flown in from Dublin.

Afterward, he said, "I don't like all these questions."

"Nobody does," Alan told him.

"It's got nothing to do with me . . . you think they'll ever find Mira?"

Kit's hand crept into Alan's. She pulled him with her toward the limousine. "Never mind him," she said. "We'll never have to see him again."

The boys sat up front, close together. Both wept.

Alan got into the back with Kit. As the limousine

moved slowly out of the cemetery, he leaned back, closed his eyes, "I never want to see anybody again," he said in a whisper.

"I know," Kit answered. "That's how I feel too."

He opened his eyes, looked at her. "Except you, Kit." He took a deep breath. "You've been in it with me all the way. Only you."

"We've been in it together," she told him.

He moved closer to her. "It'll be over. One of these days. We'll find out what happened."

"We'll be okay, Alan. You and me, and the boys. We're going to be okay."

Tears burned his eyes. So many that he had lost. But he still had her. He still had Kit, and a future. And at least he was alive. . . .

An officer, canvassing the street where Shelley had lived, knocked on the door of an old house. He waited a long while. When it opened, he smiled, tipped his hat. "No need to worry. Just a question or two."

"What do you want?" Mrs. Radman said.

"Just to ask if you've ever seen this boy around here in the neighborhood."

She accepted the photograph the officer handed her, studied it closely, then sighed. "Yes, I know him. It's Shelley Davis."

"And is he here?"

Mrs. Radman blinked, shook her head. "He's been gone for a while, maybe a week, maybe less. Just took his car and went away. But I guess he'll be back. He's left everything behind."

"What kind of car did he have?" the officer asked.

"A tan car. Small. One of those you see around all the time."

"Small, tan? A VW, maybe?"

"I don't know," she said. "Just tan. Small."

"And how long did you say he's been gone?"

"Around the holiday. Some time around then, I guess."

"And what about this lady?" The officer held out a photograph of Mira. "Have you ever seen her?"

Mrs. Radman gave it a quick close glance. "Yes. I've seen her. Old enough to be his mother, too."

When the officer returned to his station, a correction and an addition was made to the all points bulletin out for Mira Priest. She was traveling, maybe, with a twenty-one-year-old boy, description to follow, possibly named Shelley Davis. She was driving, maybe, a tan VW.

But two days later a small boy chased his collie into a cave near the river, and the body of Shelley Davis was found.

CHAPTER 21.

I T WAS quiet in Myrtle Beach. The Labor Day crowds had gone. Sparse traffic moved slowly through the twilight along Ocean Boulevard. But the neon signs glowed, and the air was warm, and the setting sun glowed like sinking fire on the horizon.

Mira pulled the old tan VW to the curb. She got out and stretched. She was tired, although she'd driven only a hundred miles that day. She was hungry, although she'd had a sandwich just a few hours before.

She walked slowly through the mauve twilight to the place where red and white lights winked off and on, saying "Bar — Restaurant — Welcome, Weary Travelers." It was dim inside. She hesitated on the threshold, listening to the mix of a few male voices, the background of taped music. Then she went to the bar. She took a seat midway. There were empty stools on both sides of her. It reminded her of somewhere else. A place she couldn't quite remember.

She sat up straight, crossed her long slender legs, and took a cigarette from her purse.

The bartender asked what she wanted.

She ordered a martini on the rocks with a twist, and asked if she could have a tuna fish sandwich on one slice of bread. No chips. He told her that she could have whatever she wanted, and smiled at her. He was an older man, partly-bald, with a pockmarked face.

She smiled back, looked around, but with eyes that didn't see.

She wore a locket shaped like a heart and a gold VW charm on a gold chain at her throat. It hung crooked over the neckline of her black long-sleeved shirt. Her red stretch pants had a small stain at the knee, and her sandals were dusty.

It was the end of the first week in September. The time since the previous Friday night was a fading blur. But the embers of a low-banked fury were alive in her.

She remembered running from Shelley through the dark, and getting into his car, and driving away. She stopped in a motel south of Alexandria. She had slept around the clock, awakened to order an enormous meal, and gone back to sleep again.

On Tuesday morning she went to Rockville. When Mary Morgan's bank opened, she was there with her pass book. She withdrew her money, and immediately began a zig-zag ride south, with leisurely stops for clothes and cosmetics.

Driving in the small world of the car, she had time. Time to remember what she didn't really remember. Her mother, John. The bloodied house. Donnie and Seth. She didn't really remember. She thought she was the last one left of all those she had ever loved. She was the only one. There had to be a reason. Otherwise she'd have died. She wouldn't be alone. There was a purpose to it. There was a reason. Soon she'd learn what it was . . .

The bartender brought her the drink, then the

sandwich. She sipped at the martini slowly, waiting for her numbed senses to come alive. There was a reason. Everything that happened had to have a reason. She didn't know that at some time in the past she had crossed into a country where reason didn't exist . . . She clung to a certainty because that was all she knew. And the low-banked fury still was in her.

The door opened, closed softly. She didn't turn to look.

But she was aware when a young man took a place two seats away from her. He had dark curly hair and a narrow sensitive face, and his mouth fell into a faint don't-give-a-damn smile. He ordered a beer in a quiet slow hesitant voice. When he raised the mug to his mouth, she saw a blue eagle tattooed on his left forearm.

He spoke with the bartender about the weather. He said, now the season was over, he guessed he'd be pushing on soon, further south, to Florida maybe, to look for work.

Listening to his deep slow words, she understood why she had been the last one left. She was the instrument. The avenger. The low-banked fury became focused. She didn't know that when she had swung the golf club at John, she had let reality go. That when she had struck Shelley down and fled, she had carried his madness with her.

She listened to the bartender and the twenty-one-year-old he called Mack, but at the same time, she held a long silent conversation in her mind. The boy the bartender called Mack, she called Shelley.

His knife was in her purse, polished and smooth and clean now. He was no more than twenty-one, with calloused hands and the don't-give-a-damn smile that could suddenly turn sweet.

She recrossed her shapely legs, and ordered another drink. When the bartender brought it and had walked away, she murmured, "Thanks, Jimmy," but nobody heard. She sipped slowly, then turned to Mack . . . Shelley . . . and said, "Tell me something. I always wondered. Doesn't it hurt to get tattooed?"

He grinned at her. "Some."

"Then how come you did it?"

"Just one of those stupid things I did when I was a kid," he said.

"I'd never have the courage," she told him.

"It doesn't take much."

Half an hour later, they left the bar together.